White hot fury seared through in its intensity. Rising quickly strike her. As she cowered on the bed before him, ... control and his body trembled with his fury. Turning his back, fists clenched at his side, he continued to fight to control himself. A few minutes passed in silence except for her muffled sobs. Then he turned and walked out of the room and out of the hut.

Outside, he kicked at a bucket that was nearby and angrily paced back and forth in front of the door. After a while he lit his pipe which he angrily puffed as he paced agitatedly.

No wonder he had felt unease. So this is what Uta had in mind for him.

No wonder he could not believe he was that lucky.

Now he knew that it was not luck at all, but deliberate deception.

An African Story

THE
MARRIAGE

L. A. Osakwe

Old King Cole Historical Fiction Books
Old King Cole Publishing Ltd

OLD KING COLE and associated logos are trademarks and/
or registered trademarks of Old King Cole Publishing Ltd

First published by Old King Cole Publishing Ltd 2015
Text © L.A.Osakwe 2015
Cover design by Jessica Barrah

The right of L.A.Osakwe to be identified as the
author of this work has been asserted by her.

ISBN 9780993449604
BXOO117648

A CIP catalogue record for this book is available from the British Library.

Printed in the UK by CPI Group (UK) Ltd, Croydon CR0 4YY

This is a work of fiction. Names, characters, places, incidents and
dialogues are products of the author's imagination or are used fictitiously
as resemblance to actual people, living or dead,
events or locals is entirely coincidental.

www.oldkingcolepublishing.com

CHARACTERS

Akapwon (A-ka-pwon)	Young farmer seeking a bride
Maimuna (My-moon-a)	Akapwon's new bride
Kinefe	Father of Akapwon
Tifi	Mother of Akapwon
Oboto	Maimuna's father
Kaieta (Ka-ee-ta)	Maimuna's mother
Chief Kofo	Chief and Chief Elder of Arana Twee
Chief Comse	Chief and Chief Elder of Arana Monabu
Timpi	Monabu Medicine woman
Boboda	Akapwon's cousin
Muta	Boboda's mother
Tutaba	Akapwon's best friend
Shema	Tutaba's wife
Codou (Ko-doo)	Maimuna's best friend
Sadio	Chief Kofo's son
Shoorai (Shoo-rii)	Chief Kofo's wife
Umar (Oo-mar)	Friend of Akapwon's parent
Ama	Timpi's Assistant
Uta (Oo-ta)	Supreme Deity

To Habibah, Akila and Hossan

1

THE woman sobbed uncontrollably as she stood with bowed head before the Council of Elders. Her body trembled as she tried in vain to control her crying.

Only her family who stood beside her and a farmer from Monabu, a neighbouring village, remained after all other complaints had been heard and dismissed from the hall.

Turning to the farmer, Chief Kofo spoke,

"Sir, I must ask you to wait outside. This is a very delicate matter that I must discuss with the family in private."

The farmer bowed his head, "Yes, Chief Kofo."

When the farmer had left the hall and the doors closed behind him, Chief Kofo called the family to come forward. When they came forward, he asked the young woman to step closer to him. This was a troubling case and privacy was essential. He had fought hard with the other Elders to change the outcome of this case, but he had lost.

Addressing the woman, he told her of the decision the Council had made.

"Do you understand the Council's decision?" He asked her.

When he got no response from her and she just kept on weeping, he repeated what he had just said in case she was too distraught to hear him the first time.

"You have two choices. Stay and be put to death or leave the village and make a life for yourself somewhere else. You have until tomorrow to make a decision. You may leave now and we will expect you tomorrow."

He watched as she walked from the room sobbing,

supported by her parents. He sighed. The sentence had been harsh, but it was the law and he could not ignore it even if he disagreed with it because the Council had made their decision.

This group of decision-makers was made up of five men and five women with him at the head. The Elders had for generations been responsible for making the laws that governed the village. This was true for all the provinces in the Arana Kingdom where each village was governed by a Council of Elders. In each village, the Council was made up of respected men and women of the village who kept the peace and settled disputes that arose between the villagers. The Elders followed the laws as well as making new ones whenever the need arose.

The Elders turned to Chief Kofo and nodded. They were satisfied that he had done his part. But Chief Kofo was not satisfied. He hated to see a woman of such beauty and innocence destroyed.

It was not her fault. She had been raped, and now she was going to lose her life because of it. He wished again that he could help by changing the law but the Elders were stubborn and would not bend. However, he could do one thing: should she choose death, he would be sure to make it a swift one.

It had been a month since she was found unconscious and battered. Her bruised body had caused quite a commotion in the village. But now she was pregnant although no one but the Council, her parents and their closest friends knew and it was too soon to tell by looking at her. Still, those who understood pregnancy would soon begin to notice as her breasts started to enlarge. These women would also be watching to see the almost imperceptible thickening of her waistline. The village would not accept such an affront, especially since she could not name her assailant or put a face to him.

Her assailant had grabbed her from behind, she said, and a hand had been held over her mouth. She was held so tightly that she could not turn her head to get a look at him. But she would never forget his voice.

Chief Kofo had gathered all the men in the village and blindfolding her, had each man repeat the words, "Hold still or I will kill you" which is what she said he told her. But not one voice did she recognize.

2

A KAPWON was getting married. As he sat on a small hill looking out across the valley to the mountains beyond, he sighed. Resting his arms on his knees he bowed his head, wondering again what the woman he was going to marry looked like. She was also from the Arana Kingdom except that she was from the Twee village and he was from Monabu. Arana, one of the oldest kingdoms in Africa, comprised four provinces and the largest village in each province was named after the province.

Trying to convince himself, he asked out loud, "The women of Twee are usually hard working are they not?" He did not care if she was ugly. His hope was that she was a hardworking, nice woman.

"I am not being ungrateful, Uta," he said lifting his eyes to heaven as he spoke. "You know that I have been waiting for a bride for many seasons. It is hard for me to believe that I am now actually getting a bride, and more unbelievable to me, is that she is from Twee. It seems almost impossible for this to be happening."

He wondered again what his new expected bride looked like and why the family had accepted his father's offer. Was she an exception among the women of Twee? Perhaps she was lazy and a miserable person to be around? He did not expect much because of the low bride price they were able to offer. The thought of how she looked had fleetingly crossed his mind, but that was a long time ago and it truly did not matter to him.

Both he and his father had worked very hard for what

4

they finally could offer. But the offer was much lower than what fathers normally made, even when their bids were low.

Most young men in his age group received help from their fathers and could offer a respectable bride price. However, because heavy rains had washed out both his and his father's crops the last two seasons, they were forced to cut back on the number of animals they had originally planned to acquire for the bride price.

It did not matter that Akapwon was a young farmer just striking out on his own. It did not matter that he had worked hard to acquire what his father was now offering on his behalf.

After his offer had been rejected again and again by prospective fathers, Akapwon had resigned himself to the probability that he would have a much longer wait than most men to acquire a bride because of the time it took him to acquire each new animal.

In the Arana Kingdom, negotiation for a bride price was a very serious matter and sometimes the negotiations became very fierce and lasted for weeks because of offers and counter offers. Offers of a bride price could only be negotiated by the father of the potential bride or groom. Akapwon's father, Kinefe, had a difficult task because he was not in a position to even negotiate, he could only make an offer and explain why his offer was low.

After approaching fathers in Monabu, his own village, and also in Bopo, the village next door, without success, his father decided to go to Twee. Knowing the difficulty of acquiring a bride from Twee, he decided to give it a try anyway. Throughout the provinces, any man acquiring a bride from Twee knew that he was extremely lucky. The women of Twee were the most sought after women in all of the Arana Kingdom. They were intelligent, hardworking women, but they were better known for their attractive appearance and pleasant dispositions.

However, it was also common knowledge that they were not eager to marry outside their village. Thus anyone wanting a bride from Twee had to be a skilled negotiator, or a skilled negotiator would be hired to help the father. The negotiations were aggressive and if there were more than one merchant or farmer bidding for the same young woman the bride price would escalate.

Yet here he was, thought Akapwon, a poor farmer who was barely able to put together a respectable offer, getting married to a woman from the Twee village and tomorrow was his wedding day. Could anyone be so lucky? He wondered at such good fortune.

Rising from his sitting position, he shook off his doubts. All would be well. He had to believe that. Walking down the hill, he turned toward the village and as he drew near, he saw his father approaching and he moved forward to greet him.

"You look worried, Son." His father said as he walked up to him. "Are you worried that your bride might be ugly?" And he laughed.

Akapwon looked at him in surprise and his father laughed again as he put his arm around his son's shoulders and turned to walk back toward the village.

"You are surprised that I know what you were thinking, Akapwon? Believe me, probably every man in this village who did not see his future bride before the wedding had these fears. All the men for whom their fathers negotiated a bride price away from home have had the same fears that you have now."

"I understand, Father, but that does not make it any easier. You know that my situation is different from other bridegrooms of the past. I cannot help but wonder what type of person she is."

His father patted his shoulder. "I understand what you are feeling, Son, but as you know, it is not uncommon for a groom to marry without setting eyes on his bride's face until his wedding day. In those instances, only the groom's father knows what his bride looks like."

"But Father, not only have I not seen my future bride, but neither have you."

"Yes. I also have not seen your new bride since it was Chief Kofo who negotiated for us in Twee. She will be okay, Son, trust in Uta." Kinefe smiled "I trust Chief Kofo as much as I trust our own Chief Comse, for I am sure he would have prepared us if she was uncomely." He squeezed his son's shoulder, pride in his indulgent smile.

"I do trust Chief Kofo, Father. It is just that ..." He broke off as he saw his mother walking toward them.

Akapwon's mother, Tifi, walked up and smiled at them both, once more struck by the resemblance between father and son. They were the same height, tall with the same muscular build and they both shared the same attractive smile. Akapwon was just a younger version of his father. In her eyes, they were the most handsome men in the village.

"Greetings, Mother." Akapwon placed his hands on his mother's shoulders and kissed both her cheeks.

"Greetings, Son. Are you ready for tomorrow?"

"He is worried that she might be ugly."

"No, I am not." Akapwon objected. "I just do not want her to be lazy."

"Is there something wrong with a wife who is ugly?" his mother teased him. "At least you would know that no other man would want her." She smiled at her son, humour sparkling in her eyes. "Have faith, Akapwon."

"I am not worried that she might be ugly," he protested again. "Although I hope she is not. I am worried that she might not be a willing worker and I have much planting to do."

"So you want a work ox?" she laughed.

Kinefe laughed too as he looked at his lovely wife. He

gave an affectionate hug to both her and Akapwon before he walked away. "Listen to your mother and have faith, Son. Besides, we all know why the women of Twee are in demand. She might not be a beauty, but she will certainly not be ugly."

After Kinefe walked away, Akapwon's mother patted his shoulders. "Son, you have waited this long to find a bride. Now you have one. Chief Kofo has assured us that she is a good woman. You know Arana Twee women are attractive and hard working. It does not matter even if she turns out to be ugly. I have been to Twee and I have seen their women and therefore I know that it is highly unlikely for her to be ugly. What matters Akapwon is that you now have a bride."

She stood in front of him as she spoke. Then resting her hands on his shoulders, she gave him a little shake, watching him intently to see if he accepted what she said.

"I know Mother; I was not really worried that she would be ugly. I am just very nervous, that is all."

"I am sure your father told you that all men are nervous before they marry. And what he has said is true, not only for men, but for women as well. We all go through this nervousness."

She paused, remembering how nervous she had been at her own wedding. Then she spoke more firmly.

"Even if she turns out to be plain or even ugly, as you work side by side in the fields, be kind, be considerate and try to get to know the person that is inside of her. Get to know the real young woman; the woman you know will win your heart. Forget about the way she looks. You should forget the way she looks even if she turns out to be pretty. For looks are not important, Son; it is what is in her heart that you want to learn about."

"You are right, of course, Mother," He said, knowing that she was right again. His mother, who knew him well, always seemed to know how to change the direction of his thoughts, pointing him to what really mattered in life. Even though he was now a man, he still welcomed her counsel. She patted his arm again and left in a hurry. There was so much to catch up on in her busy day.

3

MAIMUNA was aware that Sadio was watching her but she pretended not to see him. Her friends giggled as they lightly pushed her to make her aware that they knew she saw him but she refused to look at him. He tried very hard to get her attention. He was a handsome man always aware of his good looks and expected women to admire him. But somehow, he could never get Maimuna to look his way. She always walked with her eyes looking straight ahead.

She was his choice for a wife. He had already expressed his wish to marry to his father, and had already told him who his choice was. He was now waiting to speak to Maimuna. However, because she would not look at him, he was uncertain how she felt. To have a wife like her in his home would be an asset indeed. In his mind he already saw how his friends would envy him.

He walked abreast of her but on the opposite side of the unpaved street. It was polite to wait for a woman to acknowledge your presence before speaking to her. So he waited with frustration for her to look in his direction. Finally she did and threw him a glance, grinned and turned her head to look forward again as she hurried past with her friends. His frustration grew because she walked too fast for him to speak. Still, he felt that she was attracted to him.

Once she showed her interest in him, his father, acting on his behalf, would then negotiate with her family to arrange a marriage. He knew her bride price would be high indeed because all the unmarried men in the village also wanted to marry her. She was a beauty. Her father was rich and owned much land and cattle and he had many men working for him. Maimuna was their only child and they would not part with her easily.

Sadio had his chance when the women stopped in the marketplace to buy vegetables. He quickly walked up to her and bid her and her friends, good day. The women nodded and bowed their heads slightly to acknowledge his greeting. Then slowly Maimuna raised her eyes to his. She stared at him for a moment then quickly looked away. So as not to lose that slight invitation, he spoke quickly.

"Do you need help to carry your purchases, Maimuna?"

Instead of answering she shook her head, no.

Sadio would not take 'No' for an answer, however and insisted, "I and my friend will be happy to accompany all of you home and to carry your purchases."

Her friends nudged her and after a moment she nodded her consent. When they had made all their purchases the men walked home with them amidst much laughter and gaiety. Although she joined in the conversations, Maimuna remained shy and reserved. Sadio found that he liked that about her. He felt good about it. It would be easy to mould her into the wife that he wanted. She would be eager to do his every bidding. He knew she would want to please him and he was happy.

Maimuna, on the other hand, was nervous. She was nervous for two reasons. First, she was nervous because she liked Sadio but at the same time, it seemed to her that he expected her to like him. She felt it was a combination of the fact that he was the chief's son and because he was handsome. Secondly, she was nervous because she could not determine his character and wondered what he was really like when one got to know him. As a chief's son, he was somewhat spoiled, she felt, with all the girls flirting with him as they were doing now and the women of the village giving him gifts because they wanted to please the chief or because they wanted the prestige of having their daughter become the wife of a chief's son.

She somehow wished she could be more attracted to him, but she had to admit to herself that she was not. She was quite aware of course, what a great honour it would be to be married to a chief's son. However, for some reason this did not thrill her as it seemed to do her friends. Perhaps it was because she wanted to marry a man who interested her. Sadio did not really interest her because having spoken to him in the past, she found that their conversations had always led back to him choosing a bride or back to him and his likes and dislikes no matter what subject she introduced.

Maimuna was very interested in how Chief Kofo made council and what the Elders talked about among themselves. She knew Sadio had to sit in on most of the meetings because one day he would be chief. But he was never interested in answering her questions and told her at one point that it was nothing of interest to women. She had been very disappointed in him.

At that moment she lifted her eyes to his only to find him staring at her. He smiled and she found herself smiling in return and forgot about her misgivings.

4

WHEN Akapwon decided that he was ready to get married, his father thought it would be easy to find him a bride because his son was well liked and industrious.

However, the fathers of the prospective brides scoffed at his offer of a bride price that they felt was an affront to their daughters. No man who wanted to profit from his daughter's marriage would accept such a low offer regardless of whether Akapwon was worth more than any bride price. He was intelligent and for someone just starting out, his farm was well organized and thriving.

After travelling back and forth without success to Bopo, the closest neighbouring village to Monabu, Kinefe decided to postpone his visits at least for a while and give his attention to harvesting his crops for the winter.

Although their crops had been washed away, Akapwon had been patient about starting over again. He never complained about having to replant almost his entire farm. He set himself to the task and did it with energy and enthusiasm. Seasons of planting and harvesting had passed and they had slowly acquired three cows and five goats.

Now Akapwon did not wish to wait anymore, especially since the negotiations for his bride seemed to take forever. He wanted a wife. But his father was against trying so soon.

"Akapwon, you should wait until you at least have four cows and nine goats, otherwise your offer will be refused. The fathers will ask you if you think their daughters are worth less than the other women in the villages. You should wait, Son."

But Akapwon was impatient.

"Father, I am tired of being alone. I am practically the only man left in this village who is of marriageable age and who does not have a wife. You and mother married at an early age and so you do not remember what it is like to be alone."

Akapwon argued with his father until he finally gave in and agreed to present Akapwon's offer to the fathers of young women who were of marriageable ages.

*

Akapwon chose women whose fathers were not rich or whose financial worth did not allow them to be choosers. In doing so, he hoped the fathers would be willing to accept his offer. In the beginning he had chosen the women he thought already liked him and whom he also liked. He felt that it was important to go into marriage with at least a liking for each other. It would be easier, he felt, to get to know each other and work out any differences in character that might arise. He wanted her to fulfil her dreams as much as he wanted to fulfil his own dreams. It would be pleasing to them both if it turned out that they were good spouses for each other.

It was also his wish to someday fulfil his dreams of having a similar relationship to that of his parents and to that of his best friend, Tutaba. It was wonderful to watch Tutaba and Shema together. His parents also had that relationship and he longed for someone with whom he could share such companionship.

That she should have integrity was more important to him than anything else. However, it would also be nice if she were willing to discuss topics that would be of interest to both of them.

It made no difference that some of the women he had chosen were willing to marry him. Their fathers were looking for a good provider.

"But, Father," the women argued, "He is a nice man and he works hard."

"There are lots of nice men in this village, Daughter, but none as poor as Akapwon. My answer is no."

The rich would not lower themselves to accept such a low price for their daughters and the poor hoped to increase their status through a good marriage and a generous offer. It was not surprising that Akapwon was judged solely on the bride price and not on his character.

Even when Kinefe pointed out, "You have seen Akapwon's farm. It is well organized and thriving and will someday be productive enough to supply his wife and himself with a very comfortable living; although the fathers saw the truth in that, Kinefe's offer was still rejected. Some rejected the offer because of the bride price only. Others, who were concerned for their daughter's welfare, declined with much regret, for Akapwon's parents, Kinefe and Tifi were well liked in Monabu and in Bopo.

"Please understand, Kinefe, it is no disrespect to you, but we want to know that our daughter will be comfortable and will not require our assistance after leaving home. The low bride price you are offering on Akapwon's behalf indicates that that might not be the case."

The fathers surmised that because of the small offering, at some time in the future, they would be called upon for help. None of them was taking the chance that they might be right. Even though they saw the beautiful home Akapwon was building for his future bride, they felt that anyone could do as well if they had his ideas and were willing to work hard. And so they remained firm in their rejection of his offer.

Some of the women genuinely liked Akapwon and argued with their fathers to no avail. Others, however, only professed to like him after they saw what a fine home he was building for his future bride.

The house he was building did not require much trading on his part because almost everything he needed to build it with, he got from the forest nearby or the mountains or the river beds. However, there were still items that he needed to trade for since he wanted to offer his bride something she would enjoy living in. For the outside walls of his house, he used river rocks intermixed with clay to make the walls stronger. Strong saplings supported the roof; the thatch on the roof was layered with clay, which formed a stronger barrier to keep the rain out. It worked much better than layering the roof only with thatch because it prevented leakage from occurring, as some other houses had a tendency to do. His father taught him how to build his home and worked with him in the early stages, encouraging him to add his own ideas and even re-roofing part of his own home using Akapwon's idea of thatch mixed with clay.

As time passed and no family appeared willing to part with their daughters for Akapwon's bride price, he put his energy into his planting. The income from his crops went mainly toward buying another cow or another goat for the bride price. Whatever was left over, he used to bargain to get some item that he needed for the home he was building for his future bride or for yarn for his weaving.

Although it was slow progress, his stockpile grew until he was able to buy a second cow and then a third. Now they had three cows and five goats. There were some in the village who laughed behind their hands at him, but most were sympathetic and even tried to find a bride for him.

Whenever he became discouraged by the slow progress his father was making in finding a wife for him, Akapwon would work on the home for his future bride. Being busy prevented him from brooding.

5

A FTER many seasons of hard work, Akapwon's home was now complete and only a few finishing touches remained, mostly on the inside. He moved into his newly built home and in the evenings, or on rainy days, he worked inside. Therefore, if he was so lucky and his father found him a bride, her home would be ready to receive her.

When the seasons changed and Kinefe could take a break from his farm, he announced to his family that he would go to Arana Twee to try to find a wife for Akapwon. He had waited until after the Big Fair which was held in Dogo once every year so that the excitement would have died down and life would be back to normal in the villages.

Once a year, Arana Dogo, the largest village in the largest province of the Arana Kingdom, held a market fair. It was a great event and was attended by villagers from all four provinces. The annual event attracted many merchants from outside the Arana Kingdom. They brought interesting, beautiful jewellery and exotic fabrics from other lands. These goods were the main reason why the fair was very popular among the women. Exotic and unusual fabrics were sold quickly along with other interesting and unusual items brought from far away. However, the fair was not only for the competitions but more importantly, was to celebrate the seasons of Uta and all the other gods, in whom all of Arana believed and to whom all Arana prayed.

Villagers prayed to Chuku for rain and for help with their crops. They prayed for a blessing from Heitsi before any hunt began and the women always prayed to Yemaja before a birth so that the baby would be brought safely into the world. However, their favourite god was Uta. When the god to whom they prayed for something specific was taking too long to answer their prayers, they would fortify their prayers by turning to Uta for her help as well.

★

Twee, which was larger than Monabu, was a few days journey away. Kinefe looked forward to this journey with hope for Akapwon.

Like Dogo, Twee was a wealthy village but their bride price was even higher than Dogo's. The bride price for a woman of Twee was very near impossible for Akapwon and his father to acquire. They would have to work twice as hard and twice as long than they usually did and for many more seasons than they normally did.

The day before Kinefe left for Twee, he and his wife sat quietly discussing his journey.

"Kinefe, I do not understand why you would go to Twee. It is futile. We do not have the proper number of animals to make an offer for such a bride. You should go to Dogo instead."

"I know, Tifi, but I want to try everything before I make that long journey to Dogo. I feel that there might be a good family to whom negotiating a price is not as important as acquiring a good man for their daughter. Perhaps such a family would welcome a proper match without giving much thought to the offer."

"I do not think you will find such in Twee, Husband. They are already used to receiving wealthy offers from the men in Dogo."

Kinefe agreed but said, "I will try anyway, Wife. I owe it to our son."

Had he been half as wealthy as some Twee farmers, and if he had a daughter instead of a son, Kinefe felt that his acceptance of a bride price would be based on the merits of the suitor and not on the offer. Therefore, the size of the offering would not matter. It would have been more important to him that the man who would become his daughter's husband was someone of good character.

He had seen many young men in Monabu whose families had wealth but whose sons were lazy and had only a poor knowledge of farming. His family, on the other hand, came from a long line of proud farmers. Although they had sometimes been as poor as he and his family were now, at times they had done quite well and had managed to acquire a small fortune. The men in his family were stalwart, dignified and of high integrity and loved their families and their neighbours. The women were cheerful and pleasant and were wonderful wives and mothers.

The next day Kinefe set off for Twee with a light heart and lightness of step. However, after he had made a few trips to Twee in search of a bride, he finally admitted to himself that there was little chance of success. He usually came home depressed and disappointed, because he never returned with some good news. Despite these past disappointing trips, he felt that he owed it to Akapwon to try one more time, regardless of how fruitless his previous visits had been.

He recalled Tifi's words to him. "Kinefe, you would save time if you went to Dogo now instead of Twee, especially since Arana Dogo is such a large village. You will be certain to obtain a wife for Akapwon there much more easily than you would in Twee."

Kinefe knew that Tifi was right. If he did not find a wife for Akapwon in Twee, he would have to make the long journey to Dogo anyway, even though it would take much time away from his planting.

He felt giving up was too easy and he had to be sure that he had exhausted every avenue in his search in Twee before he journeyed to Dogo.

This time, instead of approaching the villagers in the Twee marketplace as he had been doing previously, he approached the chief of the village to ask for his help.

6

IN Twee, Chief Kofo sat with the other Elders of the village in the hearing hall. As soon as they finished resolving the case in front of them and had dismissed the parties concerned, an angry man stood up. Before any Elder could address him and ask what his grievance was, he walked quickly up to table behind which the Elders sat and in a loud voice, proclaimed that he had been robbed.

"My good man, who has robbed you and of what did they rob you?"

Another man stood up and walked quickly toward the Elders. Without turning, the first man pointed behind to the other man, "This man stole my calf. He sold me a calf and then he stole it back!"

"Why do you think he stole your calf?" one of the Elders asked.

"Because Elder, my calf is gone, and he was the only one who knew I had it because I bought it from him." He said angrily, pointing to the man who now stood beside him but with much space between them.

"I did not steal his calf!" The man objected angrily. "Why would I steal something I had just sold and why would I steal it after you paid me for it?"

"Then where is my calf?"

"How should I know? You are careless, that is why you lost your calf. You probably did not tie it up properly. Now because of your negligence you accuse me of being a thief? I ought to teach you a lesson." He said taking a menacing step toward the first man.

Chief Kofo stood up. "Enough!" He said angrily. "You come into this hearing hall and make a spectacle of yourselves while disrespecting the Elders?"

Both men were quick to apologize, bowing repeatedly to the Elders. When they were quiet Chief Kofo spoke.

"If you are so sure that he has stolen your calf, why do you come to the Council? Are we not here for the benefit of making such decisions on your behalf?" Still somewhat annoyed, he looked directly at the first man.

"I am sorry, Chief Elder. But I have waited a full season for that calf to grow enough to be taken from its mother so that I could buy it. And now it is gone."

"Did you look for it?" One of the Elders asked, "Or were you too busy accusing this man of stealing it?"

"I looked for it, Elder, but when I could not find it, I went to ask him if he had seen it but he was very disrespectful to me."

The other man spoke up. "Elder, he did not come to my home to ask me. He accused me and was calling me a thief in front of my neighbours. He had no justification for this because he did not see his calf near my home or in my field."

"Did you call him a thief in front of his neighbours?" Chief Kofo asked.

The man had the grace to look embarrassed and Chief Kofo continued. "It is a serious matter to accuse someone of being a thief. You dirty his name in front of his neighbours and some of them might believe you, yet without proof. Do you understand how dangerous that can be?"

The man looked frightened. "I am sorry, Chief, I was angry."

"But your anger was not justified because you did not first make sure that he did have your calf."

While the man had been speaking to the Elders, Chief Kofo had sent one of his staff to the accuser's home. The man now came forward and whispered in the Chief Elder's ear. The Chief nodded and the man resumed his position at the door of the hall. Sitting back, Chief Kofo watched the two men in silence until they became nervous under his scrutiny. Then the faint sound of a calf was heard outside the door. Everyone turned to watch the member of the Elder's staff walking forward with a man who pulled a calf behind him.

"Is this your calf?" Chief Kofo asked the accuser.

"Yes, Chief, how did you find it?"

"Your handyman here was trying to sell it in the market-place. He heard that you were with the Elders complaining that Mr. Orolo stole your calf from you and he knew that you would be in here long enough to give him time to sell it."

As he spoke the man was forced to walk forward with the calf.

One of the Elders stood up and asked angrily, "Did you steal this calf from your master, Jujube?"

Looking more frightened than embarrassed he answered, "Yes, Elder. My family and I have had a bad planting season and I wanted to trade it for food."

"I am amazed that you found it so easy to sell something that is not yours. Did you think that your master would have just said, okay I do not mind?"

As if realising for the first time that the calf was not his to trade, the man had the grace to look embarrassed.

"If you and your family needed food, all you had to do was come to the Council and ask for help. Instead, you stoop to stealing. However I find it difficult to believe your story since Twee has always been bountiful with food and everyone always willing to help a neighbour. For this offense, Jujube," Chief Kofo said turning to the thief, "You will be publicly flogged in the marketplace."

The Elder pointed to the first man who had brought the complaint to the Council, "And you have caused pain and suffering to Mr Orolo by your hasty accusations. It will be a while before anyone wants to trade with you because they will not be sure if you will also accuse them of stealing. Let this be a lesson to you. However, this will not end here. You will give Mr. Orolo compensation for your insult. Make sure that your compensation is worthy of your accusation. I will be watching."

"Yes, Chief Elder." The first man bowed respectfully, totally ashamed.

*

Kinefe, the farmer from Arana-Monabu waited patiently until at last it came near the end of Chief Kofo's audience hours and he alone remained to be seen.

"Come forward." Chief Kofo said to Kinefe. "How can we be of help?"

He watched as the tall man moved towards him. The man bowed with respect as he came before Chief Kofo and the Council saying, "I am honoured to be in your presence," offering the traditional greeting in a deep, rich voice.

"How may we serve you?" Chief Kofo's response was also a traditional answer.

"Chief Kofo, I have come to ask your assistance in acquiring a bride for my son. We have fallen on hard times, having lost all our crops for two seasons in a row. When we prayed to Chuku for rain, Chuku was over-generous and our crops were washed out. Although it was difficult, we replanted all our crops and now we have managed to have two good seasons with bountiful crops.

"In the past seasons since we lost our crops, we have managed to raise a bride price of three cows and five goats. I know that this might not be acceptable to most fathers. However, I am hoping that the character of my son might give weight to his offer. In spite of our setbacks, my son's farm is once again thriving. This season has given us abundance as well. All the crops that my son and I have planted are producing a bountiful crop and he is ready to reap a very good harvest which will allow him to add more animals to his offer. However, I am hoping that there might be a father here in Twee who would overlook the paucity of my offer and only look at the man my son has become."

After listening to him, Chief Kofo laughed out loud. "You expect to acquire a bride for five goats and three cows? I am sure you know that your offer would be considered an insult to any father, especially in Twee. Thus insulted, you would not stand a chance of acquiring his daughter. Everyone knows that there are always men coming to Twee seeking wives. I can honestly tell you that as far as I am aware, there is not one family in Twee that would accept so little for their daughter. I know it is a harsh thing to say, but I am obliged to tell you the truth."

Observing the dejected look on the farmer's face, he continued.

"However, since it is my duty to make inquiries on your behalf I will do so. I do not hold out much hope for you, though. It would, therefore be wise for you to be ready to accept that. Perhaps you can return at a later date. This will give me time enough to speak to a few parents whose daughters are at a marriageable age and who would be more likely than others, to give consideration to the character of your son."

"Thank you, Chief Kofo. That is all I can ask for." Kinefe bowed. "I will return at a later date." He left the presence of Chief Kofo with a heavy heart. How could he face Akapwon with more bad news?

Chief Kofo watched as the man walked away, tall and proud but nonetheless dejected. The Monabu's were known for their integrity as much as the Twee were known for their attractive, hardworking women. Being a good judge of character, an ability which was required of every chief, Chief Kofo knew instinctively that this was a good man and that any family would be lucky to join their family with his. He knew from experience how devastating it could be to lose one's crops and they had not only lost one crop but all of their crops and for two seasons. With such a setback, it was clear why they had only three cows and five goats to offer.

However, knowing that a bride price of eight cows and twelve goats was considered to be the lowest any father in Twee would accept for his daughter, his chances of acquiring a bride was next to nothing.

Chief Kofo put the farmer out of his mind. There were just too many pressing duties that called him. "I cannot help at this time anyway. I have much more important needs to attend to," he said to himself, almost with a degree of impatience.

When Kinefe returned home and told his son what the chief had said, both parents were distressed but Akapwon, very quickly sensing their distress, assured them that it was okay. He had prepared himself to be ready for good news or bad news.

"Father, I understand completely." He said this as he sat down to dinner with them. He had faith that one day he would get a bride and perhaps Uta had something else in mind for him, he told them. "And Father, I have the feeling that Uta might have in mind just the right woman for me. Maybe she will be the woman of my dreams," he said smiling as he said good night.

Instead of allowing himself to be depressed, Akapwon continued to put all his energy into tending his crops and into making his home beautiful for his bride, should he ever get one. In the evenings, he worked hard in putting the finishing touches to his home and was surprised how quickly time passed.

Then unexpectedly, at a time when he had almost lost all hope of finding a wife, his father received word from Chief Kofo that a bride had been found whose parents would accept their bride price. Now, instead of being brideless, he would soon be married. As far as he was concerned even though it had taken so long, it was the perfect time for him to marry. He was happy.

7

BEFORE going to his fields, Akapwon visited his parents. As he walked through the door, he saw that they had a visitor. He was a man of medium height, ordinary in looks. His hair stuck out as if he had not combed it for days. His clothes had seen much wear. Umar was a person who frequently visited their home. He would come at the most inopportune time and he always stayed to dinner whether invited or not. He was the village's wood seller and he travelled to the different villages collecting and selling firewood. Although he was not native to Monabu, Akapwon had known him for quite a number of years. He was known to all the families in Monabu and each had bought firewood from him at one time or another. Yet, to Akapwon's mind, he seemed to be a square peg in a round hole. There was something about him. He never discussed where he came from and although he spoke to everyone, he kept himself mostly apart. Akapwon's parents were the nearest to what he could claim as friends.

Akapwon watched as Umar peeled an orange. The fruit seller from Bopo had arrived early in the morning and his mother had traded for a nice quantity of fruits. Umar had long fingers that reminded Akapwon of claws as they moved over the orange. Somehow he could never feel truly comfortable in Umar's presence even though he had known him for so long. Umar was friendly enough but Akapwon felt it was a façade, not genuine friendship. He sat and chatted with him for a while but soon left, knowing that he would be unable to get a moment alone with his parents while Umar was around.

Umar was a very private person and he had reason to be. He had travelled from far away, from the ends of the Arana Kingdom, just outside its borders. It had taken him a year of travelling and stopping in villages with the intent of creating a home for himself, then having to leave hastily. He continued his travelling until he finally reached Monabu. Monabu was the only village where he felt somewhat at ease, the only village that accepted him for who he presented himself to be. In order to keep it that way, he indulged his appetites elsewhere.

However, in an obscure village called Himi, his birth village, they knew him for who he was. It was not a small village, not a large one either, but busy enough to be popular. Umar grew up reasonably well and was as happy as it was possible for a child of his nature to be. It was not in his nature to play with other children. When he did play with them, he was often too rough, so they avoided him because they felt he deliberately set out to hurt them as much as he could. He spoke to no one unless spoken to except for his parents, and after growing up, he rarely spoke to them at all.

As he grew older he kept to himself more and more. People respected his desire to be alone until the incident that drove him from his village.

The Elders in Himi came together to discuss the incident and they made a decision to question Umar concerning what happened. On the very day they were going to question him, he disappeared. Umar left Himi under the cover of night and no one saw him go. When the Elders commenced searching for him and could not find him anywhere in the village, they went to his house on the outskirts of Himi. His home, or what he had called a home, was a shack that he had built himself without much care for aesthetics, only some place where he could sleep and keep dry from the rains. When they found his shack empty and he was nowhere to be found, they assumed correctly that he had left the village.

His going was a relief to everyone because they did not want to confront him about the crime of which his victim accused him. Such an accusation would bring a great deal of unwanted grief and discord to the village, which had always been a peaceful place.

As a child, Umar had been fascinated by girls and women. Watching women had become a habit of his. He would stand on the side of a street watching them as they passed. When the women became aware that they were being watched, some found it amusing that a boy was watching them in such a manner. Others became annoyed and offended and complained to his parents.

At a young age he did not understand why it was wrong to watch women. His father explained to him that it was the way he did it that made the women nervous. "For example, it is the way you stare at their breasts or other parts of their body that women find offensive."

After having to leave many villages in a hurry, he understood what his father had explained to him. Once he understood that, he noticed that if he watched the women for a few moments at a time and then moved to a different location, he could continue watching for as long as he desired without the women realising that they were being watched. Then it became a game to him to see how long he could watch unobserved.

Upon arriving in Monabu, he had moved about quietly and in time had made friends with one family, Akapwon's. He needed their friendship, a place he could go when he had been careless in his watching and his other indulgences. Since Monabu did not know the true Umar and since they observed his friendship with Kinefe and

Tifi who were well respected in the village, they accepted him.

*

Leaving his parents' home and continuing on to his fields, Akapwon saw his cousin Boboda who was the son of his mother's cousin. He was older than Akapwon but a little strange. He remained mostly by himself, except for his friendship with Akapwon. Somehow, through the years of their growing up, they had become friends. Akapwon knew that Boboda was not comfortable in the company of others. Sometimes he would act strangely but Akapwon felt that it was because he was shy and embarrassed why he found it hard to relax around people in general.

Akapwon was aware that people had nothing good to say about Boboda and sometimes they laughed at him. Although Boboda seemed oblivious, Akapwon was sure that Boboda heard what was being said about him and he was sure that it must hurt him sometimes. Whenever he could, Akapwon defended Boboda because underneath his strangeness, was a fairly nice person, a kind person. Just a little shy and reclusive, that was all. When he was in Akapwon's company, however, Boboda, being sure of his friendship could relax his guard. They always had interesting discussions and enjoyed each other's company.

Boboda greeted Akapwon with the usual friendly slap on the back.

"I have been looking for you. I am leaving tomorrow for Arana Dogo. Mother wants me to find her some special shade of yellow-dyed straw for her baskets. It is a large order and will bring her much in trade and she is very excited about it. I remembered you said you were looking for a certain coloured twine for your weaving. Do you wish me to look for it for you? I can search for it at the same time that I am finding Mother's colours."

"Oh yes, yes." Akapwon was quite glad about this. "I will bring you something you can trade for it."

"You should let me have one of your tapestries, Akapwon, and I will trade it for the twine."

Akapwon shook his head, "My tapestries are not good, Boboda, and you know that. No one would want to trade for them. You know that I made them when I was just learning how to weave. Do you remember that at that time I was still learning how to undo bumps when they got in the weave? And do you remember how frustrated I got when I dropped a stitch and could not find it again? That is why I have holes in my weaves. Nobody buys a bumpy weave Boboda, especially not one with holes in them. Even though my weaving is much better now, I hardly have anything that I can trade for more yarn, and my weaving has practically come to a standstill since my crops got washed out."

"Oh yes, I understand what you are saying. But except for the bumps and holes, your tapestries are quite good." Boboda said encouragingly. "And someone will want to trade for them because they are very attractive. If I ask a low price for whatever you give me to sell, I am sure someone will buy them. Everyone likes to have something nice in their home. I will come with you to your house and show you which ones I think will be good for trade. I saw one that you made with shades of blue and purple and the way you mixed the colours into your design was very attractive. That particular tapestry looked like early morning just when the sun begins to rise and that beautiful purple stretches across the sky."

Akapwon looked at him in surprise. "You remember that tapestry?"

"Yes, I do. It was very attractive."

"Do you also remember the obvious hole where I dropped a stitch at the bottom and do you also remember the large bump near the middle?" He asked Boboda with a smirk on his face.

Ignoring his playful tone, Boboda replied "I know it has a large bump and a hole in the weave, but it is only a small hole. Some people, like me, would think it is very attractive."

Akapwon was doubtful. "I really do not think anyone will trade for my tapestry Boboda. As I said, I was just learning and I am still learning. There is still a lot for me to learn in weaving you know. You are being kind when you say my tapestries are good because you are my friend and do not wish to hurt my feelings."

Boboda swept that aside, "Of course you are learning, but your tapestries are good. As I said, you have a way of blending your colours that I have not seen anyone else do. Let us take a look."

Boboda threw his arm around Akapwon's shoulder and started walking toward Akapwon's house. Akapwon was forced to go along.

It was tradition that all weaving in Arana was done by men. The patterns and colours of their tapestry, mats and blankets, varied with each province. Akapwon was a fledgling weaver. He taught himself to weave and had been weaving for many seasons. He hoped not only one day to enter the weaving competition in Dogo, but to win it. Once he won first prize in the competition, he would at last be recognized as a master weaver. Although he did not have much time to practice, nevertheless he practised hard at his weaving whenever those moments came along and was encouraged by the fact that Monabu had not only one but two master weavers. He felt certain that one day he would become one too.

★

Many people in the village watched as Boboda and Akapwon passed by. They wondered why Akapwon put up with Boboda. Unlike Umar who was tolerated, Boboda was avoided. Akapwon did not care what they thought. He had always treated Boboda as a friend. Like himself, Boboda was one of the few men in their age group who did not have a wife.

His father died when he was only a boy and therefore he had had no one to intercede for him because women were not accepted as negotiators for a bride. Kinefe stepped forward when he came of age and worked diligently to find him a wife. However, because the women found him strange, it was difficult to get a wife for him even though his bride price was very generous. The women did not care for Boboda because he made them feel uncomfortable. Sometimes he acted very strangely and would laugh at something no one thought was funny. Instead of keeping a respectful distance when he spoke to any of the women, he came too close but was not aware that this made people nervous. Hence none of them wanted to be around him.

Kinefe had finally stopped travelling to the villages but he had not given up. He told Boboda not to give up either. But Boboda felt there was no hope. The women did not like him even though he tried very hard to make them like him. It was also difficult to meet women since he was always off somewhere on errands for his mother. But he loved to watch them and admire them and he dreamed of the time when he would finally get married. There was a lot more to Boboda's character than anyone realised. More or less forced into being a loner, he kept his thoughts to himself but underneath the surface was a mass of conflicting emotions, resentment and anger.

When his father died Boboda's mother turned from a happy woman to one who rarely smiled. She had to work hard to support herself and her son and in doing so, neglected him a great deal. Although he received affection from her while growing up, stern admonitions were more frequent than affection. Thus he grew up craving affection and was drawn to any person who seemed to be happy.

In a lot of ways Boboda had been a strange child. He was fascinated by insects and would examine them and watch them at work. As a young man, he spent a lot of time watching ants, learning how they built their nests and gathered food. When Akapwon first started his farm, Boboda would accompany him until his mother started sending him on errands. He was not of much help because he was always off somewhere digging holes and lifting rocks but Akapwon was happy for the company and did not mind having him around.

Boboda studied the insects that were on Akapwon's farm and found out which insects were harmful to his vegetables. He helped Akapwon save one of his corn crops by telling him which insect was eating his corn and what he should do to get rid of them.

As Boboda watched the insects, he offered them tiny morsels of fruits or vegetables from his lunch. Some of the fruits they ate and some of the vegetables as well but there was one thing in particular they seemed to dislike very much and that was garlic. He told Akapwon this and suggested that he grow garlic next to his corn and his okra, explaining what he had done and how the insects seem to dislike the garlic. Akapwon tried his suggestion and it worked. Thereafter, Akapwon consulted him whenever he had an insect problem. Thus he became a valuable advisor.

Once every month as he grew, Boboda's mother took him with her to the other villages. He was fascinated by the different women in the different villages, especially in Twee because there were more attractive women there than in Monabu. When he became old enough, she started sending him on his own to sell her baskets. She was a good basket weaver and her baskets were popular among the women. The colourful patterns which she used were sought after by the women of both Arana Dogo and Arana Twee. She always did well in those villages.

*

After picking up Akapwon's tapestry, Boboda set off for Twee. The first time he visited Twee, a young lady, just a few years younger than he, had smiled at him when she passed. He had stood perfectly still, too surprised to move. No woman had ever smiled at him before, ever. After that, whenever he visited Twee, he looked for her among the villagers and admired her from afar. He watched her constantly and over the months, looked for a way to meet her alone.

He carried at least fifteen to twenty colourful baskets on his back, all strung together with a sturdy cord. The baskets were light but bulky and so he could carry no more than he had on his back. On this trip, he did so well that he did not leave and continue on to Dogo as he normally would have done. Instead, he lingered in Twee and decided to leave the following morning. As he passed the marketplace, he was surprised to see Umar but then remembered that Umar travelled to all the villages gathering and selling his firewood.

When Boboda finished his evening meal, he went to a place he had scouted earlier among the trees and bushes on the outskirts of the village. It was not far from the well, so that he could get a drink of water without much effort. Once he was settled, he opened up the two tapestries that he had persuaded Akapwon to let him trade. He smiled as his hand caressed the pattern. He knew exactly to whom he would sell them.

He wanted to do something for Akapwon who had

36

always remained his steadfast friend when everyone had abandoned him. Now it was Akapwon's turn to find a bride. Although he no longer cared about getting married himself, he could see that sometimes it hurt Akapwon when he was turned down, although none of the women had made insulting remarks to him as they had to Boboda. Still he understood what Akapwon was going through and wanted to cheer him up. It would be good if he could find the right colour thread for him.

He thought about the women Akapwon's father, Kinefe, had solicited for him and how they had turned away, some with insulting remarks. Their careless remarks had hurt him but he tried not to let it show.

As he prepared to sleep he looked across at the well. It was the perfect place from which he could watch the women as they came to fill their water buckets. The women were not aware of him because he was rendered almost invisible by the trees. As Boboda watched the women as they drew water from the well, laughing and talking all the while, his eyes searched for the woman in whom he was most interested. But she was not among them. After he introduced himself to her, he knew she would be happy to know him.

He watched now, hungrily, as the women gathered, laughing and talking as they waited their turn to draw water. There was a deep longing in him to have one of them as his friend and he wondered what would happen if he finally built up the courage to approach them, especially the one whom he felt was the friendliest of them all.

He knew what women were like because when he came of age, he had gone through the rites of manhood, passing the challenge and proving himself to be a man. It was a challenge which all the young men of all villages had to go through. His reward had been one night with an older woman who taught him the joys of coupling. He wanted that now and very badly. As he watched the women, a hunger grew in him to have again the experience he had had that night.

8

INTENSE eyes focused on the group. It was just a matter of time before she joined her friends and he waited patiently because he knew she would be joining them soon.

Since the first time he saw her in the marketplace and as he watched her whenever he visited Twee, he convinced himself that she would be happy to talk to him. Although in his mind most women were alike, she was kinder than most and so he was sure she would like him.

The children would run up to her as soon as they saw her. She was always talking to children, kneeling in front of them so she could be at eye level. The children loved her and she was always hugging them. Of course this annoyed him. Everything was starting to annoy him and he was becoming impatient. To curb his impatience, he went over his plans for her.

One thing that bothered him was that her friends were always around her. They seemed to enjoy her company and sought her out all the time. The men in the village especially were not immune to her charming ways. She had no need to be afraid. In fact, fear was probably alien to her because she was surrounded by a false sense of security in the village. She was also impulsive and that trait could play in his favour or against it and so he waited.

His greatest challenge was the younger men who were always either in her company or about to join those already in her company. They were strong, healthy looking men. However he had noticed that they rarely accompanied the women to the well.

9

ALTHOUGH her father was a wealthy farmer and her mother could get all the help she needed for the house chores, Maimuna's mother, Kaieta, only hired one cook to help her prepare the meals and to clean and wash up afterward. She did not want to spoil Maimuna, which was easy to do since she was an only child and very sweet-tempered. It was her decision that Maimuna should learn everything about preparing meals and running a house the same as any other young lady in the village. And so Kaieta assigned Maimuna certain chores and taught her everything she should know to prepare her for the time when she would be married and have her own home to take care of.

It was Maimuna's task on certain days to do the washing and to make sure that the water buckets were all filled at the end of the day. On this day she was behind in her chores and had to get to the well and return before the glow of the setting sun disappeared from the sky. After sunset it would be too dark and difficult to see her way properly since it was not going to be a full moon. If it were a full moon, it would be no problem as the moonlight would show her the way more clearly. The well was at the edge of the village, located directly at the end of the main thoroughfare.

Her home was near the middle of the village and so it was not a really long walk to get to the well. Soon there would be a new well nearer the centre of the village and she would not have to walk as far. Digging for this new well had already begun but it was a long process and would take some time before the diggers got to the clear water good enough for drinking.

As Maimuna hurried along to the well holding the bucket on her hip, she was deep in thought about Sadio who seemed more and more to be the man she was destined to marry. When was he going to approach her parents about marrying her, she wondered? He made it obvious that he was going to ask for her but she was not sure she wanted to marry him. He seemed very shallow somehow and as a man, he did not take life seriously enough. To be fair, she wanted to give him a chance to show her a different character than the one she had come to know.

"Would I be happy married to him?" She wondered. It was obvious that any of her friends would be happy to marry someone as prominent in their village, especially someone as handsome as he was. Talking to her best friend Codou, she had discussed Sadio with her and they both agreed that he did not seem very responsible.

All Maimuna's friends had already taken their water from the well and the area was deserted. She hurried forward with her bucket as intent eyes unknowingly watched her from behind the bushes nearby. Her sole concentration now was to get her water and return home. She placed the bucket on the ground in order to lower the dipper which was attached to a sturdy rope. As she straightened, pulling up the dipper now filled with water, a hand was placed over her mouth and a male voice spoke, sending a shock through her. Dropping the bucket, she tried to twist out of his grasp but she was not quick enough. She was dragged backward into the bushes. He kept a tight hold on her mouth.

Then he said, "Hold still or I will kill you."

For a moment she stood stock still and then she was

galvanized into action. Pulling with all her might she tried to escape from his hold. But he held her tightly against his chest and he was very strong. She tried biting his hand where it covered her mouth and that made him angry.

"Fight me, will you?" he said, through clenched teeth as he dragged her further back into the bushes and that caused her to really panic. The grass surrounding the well and covering the ground over which he dragged her made all his movements almost silent. There was no sound loud enough that would alert anyone as to what was happening.

Kicking and fighting for all she was worth, she fought to get away until a blow to the side of her head rendered her unconscious. As she regained consciousness, she realised that the man had dragged her deep into the bushes. A rag was tied tightly over her eyes and over her mouth and her hands were tied behind her back. He had her pinned face down on the ground, in the process of lifting her wrap from around her knees. She was again galvanized into action and fought like a wild woman. He rolled her on to her back and her arms were pinned painfully beneath her. He slapped her hard several times to keep her quiet. All the while he kept her pinned down with his knee in her chest. Even in pain she fought until a second blow stunned her.

The second time she regained consciousness, he was on top of her. When he was satisfied before he left her alone, he kicked and punched her, "For the trouble you caused me," he said in a vicious voice as he aimed one last kick at her head and everything went black.

*

Boboda woke suddenly in the night and immediately a feeling of unease settled on him. He felt an urgency to leave Twee. Trying to push the feelings away, he told himself that no one had seen him in the bushes and that there was no reason to leave. But the urgency was too strong and seemed to be getting stronger by the moment. Finally he gave in and quickly gathered up his baskets and left.

He travelled fast because he wanted to be far away from Twee when morning came. As he planned, he was far away from Twee when the colours of the sunrise lit the sky. A soft, steady breeze made his journey easier and he smiled as he hurried along.

★

When Maimuna regained consciousness again, she was in her own bed and her parents and the village medicine woman were sitting at her bedside watching her anxiously. She felt as if she was waking from a nightmare.

When she became fully awake, her parents told her where they had found her and asked her to explain what she remembered.

"When you did not return from the well at the usual time, we thought that you had probably stopped to speak to Codou. But when it got really late, we went to Codou and she told us you had not come by." Emotion overcame her mother and she had to pause. "We, your father and I, then went to the well and we saw your bucket overturned but you were nowhere in sight. We decided to search the bushes to see if you were anywhere nearby. It was dark so we had to get a torch. We saw a path where the bushes seemed disturbed and followed it and that's when we found you." Tears ran down her mother's face. "Maimuna, we are so sorry we were not there to protect you."

Although she was in pain, Maimuna tried to comfort her mother. When her mother calmed down she told them what happened to her. The medicine woman advised her to be slow in her movement as her ribs had been badly bruised and her left arm had been dislocated and although it was reset, it would still be somewhat painful. Her body was a mass of bruises. Tears rolled silently down her face as she asked one question "Why?"

No one could answer her question but they wanted to know if she recognized the person who did that to her. She said the voice was that of a stranger and he came from behind her as she was drawing the dipper bucket up from the well. She never saw his face.

Her father soothed her brow, his face a mask of anger and pain for what his daughter had suffered. "When we found you, you were blindfolded and your hands tied. I got some men to help me and we searched the area thoroughly but did not find anyone.

Maimuna turned her face away from everyone and sobbed into her pillow. Her parents tried to comfort her. Her father's eyes glistened with unshed tears as he patted her shoulder helplessly, telling her that it was over and she was safe now.

As her father tried to comfort her, the medicine woman gave her mother a packet of herbs with instructions on how to administer the dose. She told them that she had already administered a heavy dose to their daughter to make her sleep and she should sleep through the night.

10

CHIEF Kofo sighed again as he thought back to the discussion he had had with his son. It had been his son's desire to marry Maimuna but now that was out of the question. The Council would not allow it. He had been prepared to encourage his son to marry her anyway, knowing that she would make a good daughter. However, his son had surprised him.

"No, Father," he stated emphatically, "I will not marry Maimuna. She is no longer a virgin and I will not marry soiled goods. Another man has already known her and therefore she is not for me." His arrogance stunned Chief Kofo.

He had stared at Sadio as if he were a stranger. Had he raised such a son? Was his son guided by old customs or was he just conceited enough to think that she was no longer good enough for him? He was greatly disturbed by these thoughts and wondered if he had raised his son the right way.

"Sadio, that is a very shocking, unfair and unkind thing to say. Do you feel you are better than Maimuna because she was raped? She is still the same person. Rape did not change her from a good person to a bad person. Are you so arrogant, Sadio, to consider yourself better than Maimuna, especially at a time when she is in mental anguish and physical pain? Are you telling me that I have raised such a callous son?"

Sadio had the grace to look ashamed but he refused to budge. He would not marry Maimuna.

Chief Kofo and his father before him did not hold too much with tradition if it was being unfair to any citizen of Twee. Now he wondered what kind of chief his son would make. He decided then and there that he would test Sadio and if he found that he only went with tradition while excluding his inner feelings, he would have to begin vigorous training. If that did not work, he would speak out against him becoming chief. If that happened, he knew he would no longer have a son and even perhaps a wife. But he could not allow Sadio to become chief if he was prejudiced in his judgments.

His thoughts returned to the matter before him. He had to admit that the women in his village were good women and to see one so defiled and abused was abominable to him. He regretted his son's decision. However, he was more concerned for Maimuna whom he had watched grow up along with his own daughters.

It was shortly after her rape that the Council debated her sentence. Since she could not name the man who had done it, they doubted her words and decided on their sentence. Chief Kofo had argued long and hard but because they were a united majority, he had to give in to their demands that the law must be upheld. It was with great reluctance that he finally agreed to their sentence.

When the news about Maimuna's rape was first brought to him, he was shocked and angry, especially after visiting her home and seeing how badly beaten she was. Immediately a search was made throughout the village to find someone who was badly scratched or bitten, but no one was found. The Elders wanted to question Maimuna but he prevented them from doing so, stating that she should be allowed to recover and her wounds to heal before she was brought before them. The Elders were angry but he would not budge because he knew that in decisions like these, by law, his was the final say and not the majority vote of the Elders. However, they could overrule him in other areas.

When Maimuna was somewhat recovered and the bruises on her face were not so prominent, he visited her with a view to finding out through her own words, what had happened. It was then that he found out that she was pregnant. After examining her, Sefu the medicine woman, had told her parents and they told him.

His heart contracted for her because that was a death sentence in itself. The shame and degradation that would follow would be devastating not only for her, but for her parents as well. He had always liked Maimuna. She always had a cheerful smile and was always respectful whenever she visited his home to see any of his daughters. Thinking of his own daughters, his mind revolted against this happening to her. It could very well have been his own child as they all went alone to the well for water at one time or another.

It was then and there that he decided to keep her condition a secret. In the matter of her rape, the village was aware of the law and knew that she had to leave the village or be put to death. The fact that they were not demanding he take action immediately was a testament to how well-liked Maimuna was. The Elders had to be told but they would not dare violate the code of secrecy that was the major part of being an Elder. At least he could protect her that much. He told her parents of his decision and advised them to keep it a secret also. They were overwhelmed with gratitude for his kindness.

11

AT last it came near the end of the audience hours of the Council of Elders and Chief Kofo. Again, the last person for him to see was the farmer from Arana Monabu. Anyone seeking counsel who was not of the village had to wait until all the local complaints had been heard. Only then was he permitted to approach the Elders.

"Come forward." Chief Kofo said as he waved the man forward, "Come forward."

He watched as the tall man moved towards him. The man bowed with dignity as he came before Chief Kofo. Again, in his deep voice, he offered the traditional greeting, "I am honoured to be in your presence."

"How may we serve you?" Chief Kofo responded with the traditional answer. Now that the man had come yet again, Chief Kofo's answer had to be the same. No one had yet been found who would accept his bride price. This time was no different from the last, except that this time, the man explained that his son and he had worked very hard and had added another cow to the bride price.

On seeing the pained look of disappointment on the man's face, Chief Kofo had to give him some hope and so he told him, "Rather than making this long journey again, wait until you hear from me. I will send word to you as soon as I have talked to a few more parents. If I can find no one within a month's time, I will let you know and you must look elsewhere. Is that agreed?"

"Thank you. That is agreed. At least I can have a small degree of hope." Kinefe bowed as he left the presence of

Chief Kofo. He did not want to give Akapwon more bad news and decided that he would tell him it might take a month. After a month, if he heard nothing from Chief Kofo, he felt sure that Akapwon would not be too disappointed, for by then he would have come to terms with the situation.

Chief Kofo watched as the man walked away, tall and proud, yet this time his shoulders seemed to droop even more. After the Elders left, since Kinefe was the last to seek Council, Chief Kofo sat thinking a long time, mostly about Maimuna but sometimes also about the man and his bride price. The next day, arriving at the hall before the Elders, he sat thinking. When the Elders arrived, he was still thinking, still despondent, waiting for Maimuna and her decision. He knew that as soon as she left the village she would be open prey for anyone. Maybe she would choose death. Some women in the past had done that. Why could he not find a solution? Maybe she could … suddenly he stood up. "That is it!" He thought, "Why could I not see this before?"

"Is anything wrong, Kofo?" One of the Elders asked as they sat beside him.

He merely shook his head, no.

12

MAIMUNA sat on a stool at the open window of her parent's home staring into the distance with unseeing eyes. Although her body was now healed, her mind would not let go of what she had endured. Her body trembled violently as she remembered the way the man had beaten and raped her. She felt dirty and her skin crawled with revulsion. Why, she asked herself again and again but found no answer. Her hopes had turned to dust and possibly her life would be ended before this day was done.

She had envisioned herself being married amongst happy well-wishers, with all the villagers around attending the happy event. In the past, Sadio, by his actions had made everyone aware that he was interested in her and that it would not have been long before the Chief would approach her parents to offer a bride price for her. Now he would not even look her way. In a way, she was sorry. However, in another way she felt that she probably was lucky to see a side of his character that had not been apparent to her before. He had judged her without first speaking to her about what happened.

"Maimuna," her mother said gently as she came and sat by her side. Her father stood behind her mother.

Continuing to stare out the window, Maimuna replied "Yes, Mother?" Then she turned and looked at them both. "I am sorry to have caused you so much grief. I had hoped to be a good daughter to you and bear you many grand-sons." She looked down at her body. Her pregnancy was not yet visible through her clothing, but when unclothed, she noted an unmistakable curve to her stomach that had not been there before. "But not like this." She said as the tears began to flow. "Not like this."

"You have been the best daughter any parents could possibly ask for, Maimuna." Her mother said.

Her father agreed and he told her:

"We would not ask for any other. But we have come to a decision." He said briskly. "Your mother and I will not stand by and watch you put to death and we will not stand by and have the Elders send you into exile. We have made our decision. We will accompany you."

"Oh no, my Parents! You must not do this!" Maimuna said in earnest as she jumped up from the stool.

"Yes!" Her father said. "We must. There is to be no more discussion about it."

"But, Father, to leave your home; I cannot bear the burden of that. I will find my way. I will go to Dogo and find someone who will take me in, in exchange for my labour."

"But who will protect you while you travel alone to Dogo? Suppose that devil is waiting for just such an opportunity? And he could very well be from Dogo, Maimuna."

The horror of her rape came back in full force and Maimuna said weakly, "I will carry a knife, Father."

At that moment they heard voices and Codou and her parents walked in the door accompanied by Maimuna's parents' closest neighbour. "We have come to accompany you to Chief Kofo. It is time."

Maimuna's father thanked them for their support but they hushed him and hurried them off to the chief. "We know that you would have done the same for any of us."

13

"AKAPWON!"
Akapwon turned as he heard his name called. It was Boboda. As Boboda reached him he handed Akapwon a packet. "I have found the colour thread you were looking for," he said, excitedly. "Open it and see if it is right. It is not exactly gold, but it is very close, a yellow-orange." Boboda rushed on as he watched his younger cousin excitedly opening the package.

"This is wonderful!" Akapwon looked at his cousin with a wide grin on his face. "It is exactly what I wanted and will match perfectly with my other colours." He untied a bit of the balled cotton and tested its strength. "Where did you get it, Boboda? The twine is very strong and probably will not break as easily." He grinned. "My tapestry will not have as many holes as before." As he re-wrapped the twine, he said, "What can I give you in return for such a wonderful find?" He was excited. Now he would be able to continue his weaving and perhaps this time it would be good enough to trade. He also looked forward to the time when he could enter the master-weavers competition in Dogo.

Boboda smiled. Akapwon was always willing to help him. No matter what Boboda asked him to do, if he could do it, he would. He never complained and Boboda liked him for that. He always said what he was thinking but was careful not to hurt any feelings. He could hardly believe that Akapwon was now of marriageable age. He still thought of him as a younger brother. "I got it from Arana

Dogo." He said, "I traded for the tapestry we picked out."

"You sold the tapestry? But who would trade for such bad work? You know the weave was crooked."

"There was a farmer who lived near the hills in Dogo. It gets very cold in winter and your tapestry will keep some of the cold out of his hut and will brighten up the place as well. At least that is what he told me." Boboda said.

"Arana Dogo!" Akapwon was impressed. He paid no attention that his tapestry would be used as a stop gap for the wind. "I know it takes many days to get there and return and I know you've been there before, but was that not a long journey for you?"

"Yes, but remember I told you Mother required a special yellow-dyed straw for some baskets she is making for a special customer. They do not have such in Bopo nor in Twee, so I had to travel to Dogo. I have been away for many days now as you know. But I did not mind the journey. I spent one day in Twee." As he said Twee, Boboda's brows knitted and he paused for a moment but quickly continued. "I stopped in Twee and I sold more of Mother's baskets there than I had expected. However, I did not have much hope of finding any twine or dyes there so I travelled on to Arana Dogo. My journey was a lot easier because I had sold most of her baskets and did not have as much to carry as I had when I arrived in Twee. I expect I will be returning to Dogo soon for Mother. It is a long journey but Dogo is quite a large village with much to see, as you know. Mother was very pleased indeed."

Akapwon's eyes lit with interest. "When you have time, Boboda, perhaps you will tell me more about what is happening in Arana Dogo? I have not been there since the last fair and farmers' competition. However, I expect one day soon to visit when I enter the weavers' competition."

Boboda nodded. "Perhaps we can go together one day after the planting is over."

"Yes." Akapwon said, "When the planting is over. I will remind you."

"Good." Boboda patted him on the shoulder. "But what is this news I hear that you are getting married Akapwon? This is great news. I am sure you will be very happy."

"Thank you, Boboda. Yes, I am very happy to be finally getting a wife." He knew it was not the time to mention about Boboda's search for a wife so he said instead. "But how can I repay you for your troubles Boboda? You found the perfect colour."

Boboda laughed and patted his shoulders. "It is nothing. Do not think about it," he said as he walked away.

14

"Is something wrong, Kofo?" the Elder asked again as they sat in the usual semicircle, five on either side of him, men and women together.

"No, no, to the contrary. Let the audience begin." And he clapped his hands twice, loudly. The door was opened by one of the two assistants and the villagers filed in. The complaints and concerns of the villagers were routine and he dispatched them more quickly than usual. He felt sure his idea would work and was anxious to put it in motion. Soon it was Maimuna's turn to come forward.

Chief Kofo waited until the hall was empty of everyone except the Elders and her family and their friends. Out of respect for the family the doors were closed. He did not want his plan to be known to the rest of the village. The same tradition that bound the Elders to secrecy about Maimuna's pregnancy, bound the family to the code of silence for whatever took place in the Council hall. Finally when the hall was cleared and the assistants stood on the other side of the door to prevent anyone from entering, he bid the family approach.

Keeping his face passive he asked, "Have you made your decision?" He asked Maimuna as she stood, still crying, her parents on either side of her. Chief Kofo wondered if she had been crying all night.

"We have, Chief Elder. We will leave the village." Her father answered.

"But the order was not for you. It was for your daughter."

"Do not think, Chief Elder, that we would leave our only

child to go into exile alone. She would be murdered once she is outside the protection of this village."

"Yes, but it is for the Council of Elders to decide whether you are allowed to accompany your daughter. It is not a decision for you to make."

At his words, both parents looked suddenly afraid. "You would not forbid us, Elder? You know what her fate will be if we do not accompany her."

Kofo knew instinctively that the other Elders were gearing up to deny them exit. But before they could intervene, he spoke and they dared not interrupt him.

"I can understand your predicament, but..." Before he could finish, the mother threw herself at his feet, crying and begging to go with her daughter.

"Woman, be still. I did not say you could not go. I said it was not your decision to make." He waited until she calmed down and then spoke. "However, I have a possible solution for you. I have not discussed my idea with the Council as yet, but I am sure they will forgive me when I present it to you." He turned and bowed to the Council, showing them respect and apology for not first discussing his plan. The Council acknowledged and bowed in return.

The mother stopped crying and looked up at him as she stood up waiting for him to continue. Her daughter's quiet sobs could still be heard. A short silence followed the cessation of the mother's pleas. Only then did Chief Kofo speak. "My suggestion is this. Your daughter can choose death if she feels she must or, she can leave the village or, and this is my solution, you can offer your daughter in marriage."

There was a shocked gasp followed by silence as everyone held their breath. Finally the mother spoke.

"But who would have her when she is with child?"

"A good man, but one who has such a low bride price to offer that it is much too low for any father to accept. However, he is much worried and much concerned on his son's behalf. He does not have to know of your daughter's condition." He noticed that the daughter had stopped crying. "None of the other women in the village, apart from you who are in this room, are aware of her condition. I am sure, however, that it is only a matter of time before they will soon start looking to see whether the rape has resulted in a pregnancy. It is not known to the village and would not be obvious to a stranger, especially to a man who would not be looking for such a thing."

"I feel no guilt about offering him a bride who is with child, because his son will receive a greater gift in your daughter than he would have anywhere in exchange for his bride price offer. She is hard working, amiable and beautiful. No man could ask for more."

He explained about the farmer from Monabu and cautioned them in case they forgot. "Remember that your daughter has only until midday before she will be forcibly removed from the village or be put to death."

Again he reminded them, "Do not forget that it is the right of this man's son to kill her instantly the moment he discovers her duplicity. Either way, her life is in danger. However, as far as I am concerned, an instant death is a much better choice than what awaits her in or outside of our village. There is also the possibility that the farmer's son would accept her as she is. If he does accept her, it would be for one of two reasons, first, because he would want to protect his good name or second, because once he heard her story he would take pity on her. However," he reminded them, "most men would choose to kill her to avenge the insult that her being with child would bring upon them. Will you agree to this proposal? Do you wish to think this over?"

Knowing there was no other way out except exile or a horrible death, both parents spoke in unison, "No we do not need to think it over, Chief Kofo. We accept."

Chief Kofo smiled his approval, "Very good. Please remember however, that everything depends on whether the farmer accepts this proposal. There is a slight possibility and as far as I am concerned, an almost non-existent possibility that he might refuse this offer. However, since we have to pay attention to all possibilities, if by some strange chance he refuses, then we will discuss the other alternative, in the form of your earlier proposal.

I will send a messenger immediately to Monabu. When the messenger returns and if the farmer accepts, you may begin to make wedding preparations and I will give you until the full moon. Because of Maimuna's condition, it is best to act quickly. You will have enough time to prepare and to accompany your daughter to her wedding and her new home. To everybody in this village and in Monabu as well, it will be a normal, joyous occasion for Maimuna and for you as her parents. Her friends will be happy for her as well. Once the wedding ceremony is performed and the festivities are over and praise Uta, if she still lives come morning, we shall look forward to your return."

Both parents thanked him profusely as their friends gathered excitedly around them, happy that Maimuna's life had been spared, even with the possibility that it was only for a short while and happy that she would not be exiled from the village. A messenger was dispatched to Monabu with the proposal and instructions to wait for a reply.

As she walked to the door with her family and friends, Maimuna went over in her mind what had just transpired before Chief Kofo. Her life had been spared, but for how long? She was grateful that Chief Kofo had come up with the idea. Even if it was only another day with her parents, she was grateful. The family headed for the door but she stopped and turned. Walking quickly back to the chief, she bowed deeply and straightening, looked him directly in the eyes. Raising her right hand, she rested it on her heart. "Thank you," she said simply and softly. Bowing deeply again, she walked away and joined her family as they left the hall.

Chief Kofo was surprised by her action. Her eyes had been shimmering with tears as she looked at him and they spoke of her gratitude. However, her action was an almost forgotten custom used only to show someone that they were deeply respected or that they were deeply loved. Although it had been simply done, it somehow impressed him and evoked a heartfelt regret that she would not become his son's wife. By her actions, in the midst of her distress, she had revealed a character that was strong, considerate and which expressed a deeper knowledge of Twee's customs than most other villagers. He glanced at the elders and saw that they were also surprised and pleased.

15

"AKAPWON! Akapwon!"

Akapwon looked up from his planting to see his father running towards him. Alarmed, he dropped his tools and ran to meet him. "What is the matter, Father?"

"Good news, Son. Good news." Kinefe was out of breath. "You have a bride! You have a bride Akapwon!" His father proceeded to tell him about the letter from Chief Kofo. "The messenger waits to return with an answer, so you must make a quick decision, Akapwon. Do you wish to accept this offer?"

"But who is this person, Father? Are her parents poor like us? Who in Twee would accept our lowly bride price when their women are so much in demand and they can get whatever they ask for?" Akapwon voiced some of the questions that came immediately to his mind.

Kinefe brought forward a rolled up piece of material he had been holding. He unrolled the stiff material and read the message to Akapwon. "The letter from Chief Kofo says,"

> *'I am happy this day to inform you that I have found a bride for you. This maiden comes from a very respectable and respected family and she is their only child. She is hard-working and intelligent. Her parents have consented to this marriage because the bride price means very little to them. They are wealthy and were more interested in the character of your son. I have assured them that you are a respectable man, though poor and I explained that your poverty did not hide the fact of your integrity. They did*

not want their daughter married to a man from Arana Twee because they felt that someone outside the village would bring strength to their lineage.

For myself, I must add that your son is a very lucky man. I have had a view for some time now, of marrying her to my own son. However, I must abide by the parents' wishes as much as it hurts for me to loose such a daughter of the village. I must request an immediate reply from you and your son. If you do not reply, the Council will step in and make the decision about her marriage to my son. I know your son's joy will be unbounded in such a wife and I add my wishes to your son for many happy days to come. By this I am assuming that your answer will be yes.'

With respect,

Chief and Chief Council Elder Kofo
Arana Twee

Kinefe smiled quizzically at his son. "Son, a Chief Elder is not permitted to tell a lie. However, he also has no obligation to voice his opinion which Chief Kofo has done. I am certain he is sincere when he says that he wanted her for his son. At the same time, I can understand the parents' desire to bring new blood into their line even through a daughter, because your children will be their children."

"I understand, Father. I will, of course, accept this most generous offer. However, you cannot blame me for having questions about this sudden good fortune of mine, especially since we have seen planting seasons come and go with no luck."

"Yes, well sometimes things happen this way for the best. Perhaps Uta felt you were the best husband for her and she the best wife for you. Have you not been praying to Uta for a good wife?"

Akapwon grinned, "Yes, Father, night and day."

"And if you think of it, it is not so sudden, for I have been to Twee at least three times, have I not?" Kinefe threw his arm around his son. "Come, let us go and tell your mother the good news and then we can send the messenger on his way."

16

MAIMUNA and her parents waited anxiously with their neighbour and Codou's parents. They were all nervous as they awaited the return of the messenger. When he returned there was much cause for rejoicing. The offer had been accepted. The next day, the bride price was sent by Akapwon's family, five goats and four cows.

Word spread in Monabu that Akapwon had acquired a bride. Everyone was happy for the family and many of the young ladies of the village sighed with deep regret and not a few with resentment against their parents. They knew, even though their parents seemed not to know, that Akapwon was quite a catch and any woman would be lucky who married him.

Not long after the bride price was sent an event occurred which caused quite a stir in the village. Gifts started arriving for Akapwon's parents and for himself. Because the bride's family was wealthy they had no need for the bride price but accepted it out of respect for the bridegroom's family. Each day gifts arrived for the bridegroom: a sack of grain, rice, coffee, chickens. Gifts for the parents came as well, a bolt of beautiful cloth for the mother, beautiful pottery, a new hoe for the father.

For the rest of the week gifts arrived. The village was abuzz with the news and this show of wealth. Nothing like this had ever happened before. Everyone said it was a good omen and wondered who this bride of Akapwon was.

Akapwon himself was somewhat confused by the

events. Suddenly he gets a wife after waiting many, many seasons for one, with no hope. Now not only did he get a wife, he got a wife from Twee, which made him the envy of most of the men in Monabu. Then he starts receiving gifts from the bride's people that far outweighed the bride price. Who was this woman, he wondered, that her parents would shower his family with gifts without even meeting them? Maybe their daughter was as ugly as the gifts were beautiful and no one else wanted to marry her? He pondered these things in his mind. Everyone knew how difficult it was to acquire a wife from Twee. Their lowest bride price offer of eight cows and twelve goats, even before negotiations started, was prohibitive for most of the families in Monabu or Bopo. It was well known that some Twee women had received offers of ten cows and fifteen goats before negotiations even began. Dogo, of course, had as many or more wealthy farmers as did Twee.

Having heard of these bride price offers, Akapwon wondered, was something wrong with his future bride? Was he just lucky that his father, in desperation had gone to Twee at the right time? Was he lucky that her parents in that instance were looking for a different type of husband for their daughter, someone not of Twee? In that case, he was certain Dogo would have been their first choice to look for a husband for their daughter. From villagers who had visited Dogo, he heard that there were a great number of eligible men there whose families were wealthy and who would have jumped at the chance to marry their sons to a woman of Twee.

He sighed, well he would know soon enough at the wedding and then he would be stuck with her for good or bad. He prayed to Uta that it was for good. In his mind he envisioned someone quite plain, not quite ugly but far from pretty and somehow that did not bother him. He never dwelled on what a person looked like only on their character. He was happy that at last he would have a companion with whom he could share his thoughts.

17

ALTHOUGH Maimuna was relieved that she would no longer be exiled, she was worried about what would happen to her once her future husband found out her condition. Her closest friend remained steadfast and reminded her that she was lucky to be alive instead of being put to death. Codou, who was more like a sister than a friend, was the only one among her friends who knew she was expecting a child because of the rape.

As they sat on her bed, Codou suggested, "Perhaps it was Uta who sent the man from Monabu to look for a bride in Twee. Perhaps it was Uta who wanted you to marry this farmer, Maimuna, have you thought of that?"

"But what will happen when he finds out I deceived him?" Maimuna asked.

"If it is Uta who wants you to marry him, he will accept you. If it is not Uta who chose him, then you will be dead by morning, Maimuna." Codou said practically. She rushed on when Maimuna was about to speak. "Chief Kofo has made it clear that his father is an honourable man and if he is, so is his son. Do you not see, Maimuna, if his son is honourable, he will understand and forgive you?"

"What do you mean forgive me, Codou? Are you saying I must tell him what happened?"

"Of course, Maimuna." She took both Maimuna's hands in hers. "It is far better to start your marriage with truth. He will either kill you on the spot or he will want an explanation."

"Thank you, Codou. That makes me feel much better,"

she said but Codou looked so upset, she relented. "I am sorry, Codou. It is just that I am very anxious."

"I can only imagine how you must feel, Maimuna. What woman would not be nervous and frightened under the circumstances?"

"In any case, I expect you are right." Maimuna acknowledged. "Perhaps if I plead with him to let me explain, he will listen."

"Yes! That is it!" Codou said excitedly. "You will have to plead for your life."

"I suppose that alone should give me the courage to plead." Maimuna said dejectedly. "Since I know I am pleading for my life it will help me to plead more earnestly and sincerely." She sighed. "I am so afraid, Codou, that my life here is spared only for me to lose it in Monabu."

"Do not think like that!" Codou commanded. "I will be at your wedding to support you. Your parents will be there and all our friends will be there."

"Yes, but no one but the two of us will be there on our wedding night. I can only imagine how angry he will be and it scares me, Codou."

Codou hugged her. "You are strong, Maimuna and more strength will come to you through your fear."

Maimuna looked at Codou and Codou noted with concern that her eyes were shimmering with unshed tears. So far in this ordeal she had been strong and had not given in to defeat. She leaned over to Maimuna. "What is the matter, Maimuna? Apart from being afraid, is there something else?"

Maimuna shook her head slightly. "Have you noticed, Codou, that Sadio is the only one who has not visited me? It makes me sad to think that he would treat me this way."

"Sadio is a jackal and a coward. You are better off knowing what he is like in this time of crisis in your life, Maimuna." Codou patted Maimuna's cheek. "You are better off knowing his character. He has no integrity; otherwise he would have been the first at your side." She looked angrily at Maimuna. "Now look how he has turned out to be. Perhaps this man from Monabu is twice the man Sadio is or would ever be, even though as the son of our chief he is supposed to be a man of good character."

"You are right, Codou." Maimuna wiped angrily at her eyes. "I do not wish to wallow in self-pity, but he makes me so angry. It saddens me to think that he has no backbone after all."

"It is not over yet, Maimuna." Codou looked fiercely at Maimuna. "Believe me. I will give him a piece of my mind whenever I get a chance to see him alone."

Maimuna laughed. "I am sure you will do me justice, Codou. But please make sure you are alone. You do not want anyone to witness you cursing out the son of our chief."

"Yes, I guess I would be punished with a public insult." They both laughed at the thought.

"Do not worry when you go to your bridegroom, Maimuna. You will not be alone. And your parents are so happy that they have this much more time with you."

"Yes, they are so grateful that they are being ridiculous."

"What do you mean by that?" Codou wanted to know.

"They have been sending gifts to the groom's family ever since they accepted me for their son. The farmer must think they are crazy."

"Not crazy, Maimuna. They will think perhaps it is a tradition in your family. But who cares? It is good to have you still here and alive instead of exiled or dead. Just think, Maimuna, Monabu is very near to Twee and I will be able to visit you in your new home."

"Providing I live to enjoy it, Codou. But you would visit me, Codou? Really?"

"Of course! I would not stay away for all the fruits in

Bopo." And they both laughed. "I will want to hear all the details of whatever happens between you and your future husband, Maimuna. You know I will be very anxious about you."

"I will be most happy for you to visit me, Codou. Thank you."

Codou smiled. "Do not thank me yet. You will probably get tired of me visiting you." Then she laughed. "I know that your new husband will not allow you to leave his side once he gets a good look at you. You are so beautiful, Maimuna. How can he resist you?"

"Oh Codou, I am not beautiful. You are just biased because you are my friend. You know you are the beautiful one. How can I compare?"

"Oh shush, Maimuna. Why do you think Sadio was so crazy about you? Of course he has now shown his true colours and that he is nothing but a jackass. But he was very taken by your beauty."

"A lot of good it did for me, did it not, Codou?" Maimuna said. "And it just goes to show how shallow he is."

"Oh, let us not even think of someone as shallow as Sadio. Your bridegroom will see you and he will not be able to help but to fall in love with you, not just because of your beauty but because you are such a kind and generous person." And she hugged Maimuna. "Also, Maimuna, you will have a beautiful wedding after all, with people from two villages. Your parents are sparing no costs with the celebration."

"Yes," Maimuna agreed, slightly embarrassed. "They have hired musicians to accompany us to Monabu and they have sent word to a vendor in Dogo to bring material for my wedding garments. They are being ridiculous because we have men in Twee who could weave fine fabrics just as well."

"Yes, Maimuna," Codou agreed. "But do not forget that

Dogo imports the most exquisite materials from the Timboko Kingdom and other far off lands. I have seen cloth from one of those places and they are truly beautiful. They are said to be made of a material called silk. Apparently this silk is made by worms. Can you believe that?" They both laughed the idea to scorn.

"You are right of course, Codou." Maimuna paused then said, "I have a mind to wear red. What do you think?" She looked at her friend anxiously.

"That is wonderful!" Codou hugged her enthusiastically. "I was going to suggest it myself."

They looked at each other and both said, "Red is for happiness." Then they both laughed.

"Do you think I am going a little too far, Codou, wearing a colour for happiness?"

"No!" Codou said emphatically. "If you had not said it, I would have suggested it. It is the right colour for you. It will lift your spirits and it is better to think that you will be happy than to think anything else." She looked at Maimuna with laughter in her eyes. "Besides, you look absolutely beautiful in red. He will be stunned. You will see." And they both laughed again.

As she was getting ready to leave, Codou said. "Do not forget. I will be there. All of us will be there to support you and I will pray to Uta for your happiness. It will be wonderful. You will see." And Codou hugged her sincerely.

18

A KAPWON continued to dwell on his good fortune. After waiting for so long it seemed so unreal to him. Everyone was happy for him and wherever he went he was congratulated. Everyone was also happy to be involved in his wedding preparations. There had not been a wedding in the village for too long and it was time to celebrate and be merry. The women were excited. They planned with Akapwon's mother as to the different kinds of food and pastries and how much should be made.

They felt that the gifts that had arrived for Akapwon showed that the bride's family was used to the best and so they would rise to the occasion and put on a wedding feast to end all feasts. The village tailor measured Akapwon for his wedding garments and Akapwon attended council with the Elders so that they could inform him what was expected of him during the wedding ceremony and what responses he should make to the few questions that would be asked of him. They advised him how he should conduct himself as a married man; that once he was married, he would share in the responsibility of upholding the morality of his village.

When their discussions were ended Chief Comse asked Akapwon to stay behind after the other Elders left. When they were alone he bid Akapwon to sit next to him.

"Son, I am sure your father has already spoken to you. You have already gone through the rites of manhood and received your reward at the end which makes you one of those young men who have already met your challenges and experienced lying with a woman. However, every man who is to marry has to go through this meeting with me. I myself have had to sit before another Elder and listen to what I am about to tell you."

He drew a deep breath. "It is my duty to advise you that marriage is not all about lying with a woman. It is more about respect, about learning to respect each other. Young women who are about to be married are innocent when it comes to lying with a man and your bride will be no different. That means that she will be very much afraid as to what will happen to her on her wedding night. It is your duty to be patient with her no matter how foolish she may seem. Some women cry when they are afraid. I have even known some women who giggle when they are afraid. Therefore it is up to you to calm her down and help her to see that it will be a good thing. Do you agree?"

"Yes, Chief." Akapwon was slightly embarrassed. He wondered why both the chief and his father felt the need to explain such things to him; after all he was already a man. Chief Comse explained a great deal more to him before he let him go.

At sunset, Akapwon sat quietly talking to Tutaba on the steps of his new home as they enjoyed a mug of beer.

"Tutaba, I am very nervous. I feel that there is something not quite right. How is it that I am acquiring a bride from Twee, the village of the most sought after women in the Arana Kingdom? It seems very unreal to me".

"I can understand your feelings, Akapwon. It is somewhat daunting to think that even in humble Monabu, there are men with much wealth who would never even hope to compete with the men in Twee or in Dogo for that matter. Most of the women in Twee end up as wives for rich merchants or farmers in Dogo. I would like to think that you are very lucky."

"I do not feel lucky."

"Do you wish to back out of this match, Akapwon? If you do, you should speak up before all the arrangements are made. You know that your mother and the women of Monabu are going out of their way to make this one of the biggest and best weddings ever."

"No. I do not wish to back out. It is just that I feel a slight unease. Maybe it is just that I am nervous. Marriage is a big step."

"Yes and like Shema, I am sure this young lady will be very nervous too. Shema was shaking with fright on our wedding night."

"She was?" Akapwon looked at his friend with interest.

Tutaba smiled and his features softened. "Yes. She was terrified."

"What did you do to stop her fright?"

"I held her close and caressed her until she stopped shaking. After our first kiss, she was so surprised how nice it was she forgot to be afraid." Tutaba looked embarrassed.

A muffled chuckle escaped Akapwon's lips and he slapped his friend gently on his back. "I am glad it turned out well." After some thought he said, "You are right. I expect she will be somewhat frightened, especially coming to a village that is not at all familiar to her. And since she knows nothing about me, I expect that would compound her fears."

"So you see," Tutaba continued, "She has even more reason to be frightened."

"You are right, Tutaba. I will remember what you have said."

Tutaba continued, "I just thought of something, Akapwon. We are always so busy thinking about ourselves before a wedding that we never pause to think what these women might be feeling. She could easily be thinking that it is possible you might reject her because you do not think she was the person you were looking for. I never thought of that before. I must ask Shema what she was feeling on her wedding night, if she was afraid that I might reject her if I did not find her pleasing. She is an honest woman and I know she will answer me truthfully. I will let you know what she says."

"Thank you, Tutaba. That would be something worth knowing."

*

In Twee, Maimuna was also being advised by the Council of Elders, except in this case, only the women of the Council. She was instructed on what to do when she was in front of the chief and what her answers to his questions should be. She was advised on everything from how to cook new recipes, how to make sure her house was always clean and how to treat her husband. She received new lessons about planting and preserving food for the times when there was not much rain. She was exhausted by the time they were done with her and wondered if all their instructions were in vain if it turned out that she would not even get beyond the wedding night alive.

The wedding party left Twee in the early morning before sunrise. They made good progress and stopped for a leisurely lunch. Continuing on after lunch, they arrived at mid-point at sunset the next day. Camp was set up and the women proceeded to cook a meal. The villagers sat in a companionable circle, chatting and laughing as they ate.

On the third day, as the men were repacking the supplies, the women took a bath and got dressed for the wedding. A large wrap was held in front of Maimuna by her mother and Codou. No one questioned it. They just assumed that she was being given special treatment because it was her wedding day. She bathed and dressed behind the make-shift curtain and when they lowered it, she was fully dressed. The red complimented her skin and she was absolutely beautiful in her wedding robes. Both the men and the women stared in admiration. Only the veil remained to be put on but it would only be put in place when the village came into view.

★

On his wedding day, Akapwon, already dressed in his wedding garments, sat alone in his usual spot on the hill overlooking the wide valley and on to the distant blue shadow of mountains. He raised his eyes to heaven, "Thank you, Uta, for my bride. Whatever she looks like and even if she is lazy, thank you. Just let us be happy, Uta, that is all I ask." And he laughed at himself. As he lowered his eyes from the sky, he heard the long blast of a horn followed by three short blasts, and then the pattern was repeated. It was a signal that the bridal party was arriving. As Akapwon stood up, a young boy from the village who had been sent to get him came running.

"Akapwon, your bride is coming." He said importantly.

Akapwon laughed, "I know."

"Come on or you will be late for your own wedding." The boy took his hand and pulled him along.

Akapwon arrived in the village circle to find his parents and Chief Comse waiting for him in the centre of the circle. He took his place between his parents. Dressed in white, the traditional custom for all bridegrooms, he stood out among the villagers. No one else but the groom wore white on a wedding day. His short robe, which ended at his knee, was made of soft white cotton, trimmed with a thin band of gold at the neck and the cuff of the sleeves. His loose-fitting pants were trimmed on the sides from top to bottom with the same thin band of gold. As they watched the bridal procession approach, he glanced around him.

The large circular compound was swept clean and around the perimeter of the circle, long tables, heavy with food, were laid out to perfection. The tables were covered with pale green cloth, and the food was interspersed with small arrangements of roses and lavender surrounded by mint leaves. The tables held a satisfying variety of food. There was stewed chicken, fried chicken and chicken cooked in peanut sauce, fresh green corn smothered in butter and seasoned to perfection, plantains mashed and fried into crispy cakes, hot peppered fish stew, mashed yams and meat stew cooked in a beer sauce, mashed bananas with a seasoned nut sauce and many pots of differently seasoned rice. The list went on. For dessert, ground nuts in a tamarind sauce, a pudding made of sweet potatoes, crisp banana fritters and someone had even made sweet things such as small buns brushed with honey and plums stewed with mint leaves and honey for the children. From one end of the table, the smell of freshly baked bread wafted on the breeze. The villagers had done themselves proud.

It was the custom that the villagers contributed to the wedding feast and the groom's or the bride's parents provided the beer. There was not an inch of space left on any table for more food. Timpi, the medicine woman, was the best beer maker in Monabu and Bopo combined. This time she had outdone herself. Both Akapwon and his father agreed that it was the best beer they had ever tasted.

Banners of purple and gold, Monabu's colours and banners of dark blue and pale blue, Twee's colours, snapped in the breeze. They were attached to tall poles placed at intervals around the compound, giving a gay quality to the gathering. The villagers stood in a semicircle on the right side of the compound facing Chief Kofo and the wedding party. Everyone was dressed in their best finery, laughing and chatting happily. It was an occasion in which everyone shared in the happiness of the family.

The bridal procession advanced slowly. They were led by musicians and dancers. As they neared the village the musicians began to play a lively tune and the dancers wove in and out of the procession as it wound along the road leading to Monabu. The villagers in Monabu were impressed that the bride had come not only with musicians, but with dancers as well. A long line of bridal guests all dressed in wedding finery were followed by young men carrying gifts. The bride was carried on a litter by four men. Everyone noted that the bride wore red, which was a good sign, because the village knew that red was the colour for happiness. In front of the bride's litter were her parents and their close friends. Walking beside the litter were the bridesmaids, two on either side. They wore pale green patterned wraps with long ribbons of the same colour trailing from their hair and almost touching the ground. They swayed gracefully to the music as they walked beside the litter.

As they entered the village circle, the party fanned out in a semicircle facing the Monabu villagers and the bridal party was left standing alone at the edge of the circle but inside of it. The litter-bearers rested the litter on the ground and someone helped the bride to step down. She was joined by her parents and followed by her bridesmaids. Slowly they advanced to where the chief and the groom's family stood in the centre of the circle. They stopped in front of the chief and the family.

The bride wore a long, red veil edged with red and gold embroidery over her head and shoulders which reached to her knees in both front and back and rested on her robes. Her face was barely visible through the transparent red cloth because of the many folds which were kept in place by a garland of beautiful red beads. The father of the bride stepped forward bringing his daughter with him. The chief was impressively dressed and next to him, on his right, stood Kinefe, Akapwon's father. To the right of his father stood Akapwon dressed in the traditional white robes of a bridegroom; on his right stood his mother, Tifi.

Oboto, Maimuna's father, stepped forward and taking Akapwon's father's left hand, he placed his daughter's right hand in his.

"Father, I am honoured to present my daughter to you. Behold your new daughter, Maimuna."

Kinefe bowed respectfully to Oboto and to his wife Kaieta. "I am honoured to receive our new daughter. She will be cherished greatly."

He then turned to Akapwon who had stepped forward and repeated the process. Placing Maimuna's right hand in Akapwon's left, he said,

"Son, behold your future bride."

As Akapwon took her hand, following the custom and as she was instructed to do, Maimuna bent from the waist in acknowledgement of him and Akapwon bowed his head in acknowledgement of her. Holding her right hand in his left, they both turned to face the chief who stood before them, and bowed. Maimuna's parents moved to stand to the left of the Chief.

Chief Comse raised his arms, and there followed instant silence. His voice rang out.

"We are here today to witness the marriage of two families. Let us all rejoice in this union of two of our young citizens, Akapwon and Maimuna." Then he turned to Maimuna. "Maimuna, do you consent to marry Akapwon without coercion from anyone, not even your beloved parents or your friends?"

Having been instructed by the Women Elders and her mother as to what the ceremony would be, because it was the same in all four villages, Maimuna knew that she must answer for not only the chief and her parents, but for all the village. Knowing that she must speak, there was absolute silence so that everyone might hear her answer. She lifted her eyes and looked directly into the chief's. Speaking loudly, she said,

"Yes, Elder, I consent of my own free will."

Chief Comse stared at her for a moment, trying to discern her features but being unable, he could still see her eyes clearly enough. Satisfied with her answer he turned to Akapwon and asked the same question. "Akapwon, do you consent to marry Maimuna without coercion from anyone, not even your beloved parents or friends?"

Akapwon's answer rang out, "Yes, Elder, I consent of my own free will."

As he had done with Maimuna, Chief Comse stared Akapwon in the eye for a moment, intent on knowing if either of them was being forced to marry against their will. He knew Akapwon was very happy to be married. However, if Maimuna was not, he would know from some involuntary movement of which neither would be aware. Satisfied that they were both telling the truth, he raised both arms again for silence.

The parents of the bride moved forward and stood on either side of the groom's parents. Stepping forward and further away from the parents so that the ceremony could be seen by all, Chief Comse took Akapwon and Maimuna's joined hands and raised it for everyone to see. Then his wife handed him a long red ribbon, and as he spoke he tied their hands together with a bow, which would remain in place for the duration of the celebration. "We ask Uta to bless these two with many happy years and many children." He raised his arms and rested one on each of their heads.

"Akapwon, behold your new bride. Respect her, keep her safe, protect her and she will make you happy. Maimuna, respect your new husband, care for his needs and he will make you happy." Turning to Akapwon he said, "You may now view the face of your new wife." There was absolute silence as bride and groom turned to face each other. Akapwon lifted the veil from her face with his free hand and tossed it backward.

A gasp went up from the Monabu guests and Akapwon stared for a moment in shock. Before him stood a vision of beauty, a beauty far beyond any girl in his village, far beyond any dream he could possibly have had about how she might look. He had hoped she was not ugly but he never expected the opposite. Her skin was smooth and flawless; her eyes were rich, velvet black and her lips were lush and full. Her hair was braided in an intricate, circular pattern and free of all adornment. He could hardly believe his eyes as they were drawn once more to her lips. He gave thanks to Uta. Then recovering himself, he gave into his desire and resting his free hand on her shoulder, kissed her fully on those beautiful, lush lips.

As Akapwon was staring at her, Maimuna stared at him. She had been taking furtive looks at him through her veil but now she could stare as openly as he was doing. Hope rose in her at what she saw. She saw standing before her, a very pleasant, handsome face with dark, smooth skin, but most importantly, kind eyes that smiled into hers as he bent forward and kissed her lips. No one had told her he would do that. She braced herself as his lips touched hers, but was surprised at how soft his lips were against hers.

"Welcome, my bride," he said in a deep, husky voice as he smiled into her eyes.

"Welcome, my bridegroom," she said in a soft, slightly unsteady voice.

Great cheering went up from the guests, then the music began. The first to congratulate them was Chief Comse and then both sets of parents followed by her friends, his friends and then the guests who began coming forward.

Maimuna's friends crowded around her, inspecting her

bridegroom, laughing and talking and on the whole, very happy for her. When her husband was occupied with his friends, they complemented her on a great match.

"He is so handsome." Codou whispered, so that Akapwon would not hear her. "He is much more handsome than Sadio." Her other friends agreed as they embraced and teased her in turn.

"He looks strong and well-muscled," one of the women said.

"Strong enough to protect you," Codou added and amidst much laughter.

"And those eyes," someone said, "the way he looked at you before he kissed you." And she groaned in a way that had everyone laughing.

The night wore on in revelry and singing, the beer was very strong. Before sitting down to eat, Akapwon and Maimuna stood watching a dance performance. Male dancers were dressed in grass skirts and shells were tied the length of their legs to the ankle. The women dancers wore wrap-dresses in purple and gold and had shells around their ankles.

The second dance was about the mating of animals but done in humour. Gales of laughter rose from the guests. It was all done in such good humour and good taste so as not to be offensive. However, sometimes they got carried away and Maimuna lowered her eyes in embarrassment. Akapwon laughed at her embarrassment and shyness.

Then the music changed and a beautiful melody floated on the air as a man with a rich voice began to sing. It was a serenade to the bride and groom. Nobody had expected it. The circle cleared when everyone realised it was a song for the new couple. The music was soft and soothing. Maimuna, as she stood holding her husband's hand, was not conscious of being stared at by two villages. She was absorbed in the song. As she listened to the beautiful music and lyrics, Maimuna wished she was that girl, wished that she could live to experience the things mentioned in the song, such as him kissing her cheek, his loving arms around her.

At an appointed time, a special table with two chairs only was arranged for them to sit. They were given a bowl of water with slices of lime floating on top, to wash their hands. Akapwon lifted Maimuna's free hand and placing it in the bowl, proceeded to wash it with his free hand. She was surprised and then intrigued. All sorts of sensations assailed her as his fingers slid over hers, rubbing gently. When he was finished, he then looked at her expectantly and she stared at him puzzled until, embarrassed, she realised that she was supposed to reciprocate.

She then proceeded to wash his hands and the same sensations assailed her. There was something very sensuous about that simple task and she wondered if he felt it as well. This was something the elders neglected to tell her about, like the kissing part. She washed his hand the way she had watched him wash hers. But because the experience was so new to her, she used the opportunity to learn about his hand and she explored every inch of it before she was satisfied.

Akapwon was surprised at the strong feelings just her simple touch produced in him. He watched, fascinated as her fingers slid over his. He felt as if she was exploring his hand, getting to know every inch of it and his body responded immediately. He was grateful that he was sitting instead of standing. When she finished washing his hand, he picked up the square of bleached linen which had been brought with the bowl and dried her hand then handed her the cloth for her to dry his.

When they were finished, an attendant came and removed the bowl and cloth. Food was then brought and as was the custom and because their hands were tied, they were given a bowl of hot mashed cassava and a second bowl filled with peppered meat stew, cooked with tomatoes and okra. As did everyone else they would eat with their hands. They sat next to each other, their tied hands resting between them on the table. Her tied hand was the right and his was the left and because he had more control using his right hand, he fed her first.

Although she was embarrassed, she had to accept the food when he scooped it up with his fingers and held it to her lips, because it was the custom and she was hungry. Then she in turn fed him. Eating from the same bowl and being fed by each other brought such a feeling of intimacy to something so simple that Maimuna was very affected by it.

Akapwon was equally as affected. He had never fed a woman before and the touch of her soft lips against his fingers had a strong effect on his body which gave him cause to be glad again that he was seated. Maimuna tried to keep her eyes down and when she finally raised them, they looked directly into his which were intently focused on her with interest and amusement. Embarrassedly she dropped them, only to hear a deep chuckle come from him. It was so effective that it caused an involuntary laugh to slip from her lips as she looked at him again. He grinned and then they both laughed. It was a very personal moment for both of them.

19

As the festivities died down to a happy hum of conversation and laughter, Akapwon and Maimuna moved among the guests, speaking to each one. The people of her village wished her well and congratulated her on a strong, handsome husband. They told her she was lucky that her parents had chosen so well for her. Codou pressed her to have courage. They all liked her new husband and Codou was encouraged that he seemed to be gentle though strong.

The villagers continued steadily to come forward to congratulate them throughout the evening. After a while, as the couple stood quietly on the edge of the festivities, Akapwon was surprised when Umar came to congratulate him on his marriage. Maimuna was turned toward her friends and did not hear him.

"You are a lucky man, Akapwon, to have found such a beautiful wife." He said, his voice very quiet and he smiled a strange smile. Maimuna turned at that moment and he stared at her without saying a word. Then he smiled at her as he bowed over her hand, then walked quickly away. Akapwon was surprised that Umar had not stood there and talked to them all night. He was also relieved because Umar was such a talker and always outstayed his welcome. As he walked away, Boboda walked up and congratulated him. Maimuna had turned back to her friends once more and did not hear him speaking to Akapwon.

"I am very happy for you, Akapwon. Your wife is very beautiful. I am sure you will be happy together." Maimuna turned and smiled directly at him. He became very flustered and bowing to her without a word, he walked away.

"You seemed to take away their voices, Maimuna." Akapwon said and he laughed.

Akapwon held Maimuna's hand at his side as he spoke quietly to Tutaba, whom he had introduced to Maimuna earlier. All the while they were greeting guests and ever since he saw her face, Akapwon's mind was in a daze. Visibly his attention was on Tutaba as they spoke, but his mind was on Maimuna. How could he be so lucky to have acquired such a beautiful wife? Uta had indeed had a plan for him. That is why she had made him wait for so many turns of the planting season. She was looking for someone very special for him and then she had truly blessed him. He would try to be worthy of the gift given him, because a truly wonderful gift it was.

Maimuna watched the villagers with only one part of her mind. The other part was reeling with fear. "What will he do to me once he finds out?" It was his right to end her life on the spot for such an insult. She glanced at the stranger standing so relaxed and confident beside her as he held her hand. His was a kind face and her prayer to Uta was that he was as understanding as he was kind. Still talking to Tutaba, they stood slightly apart from the rest of the guests, holding each other's hands. As she glanced at Akapwon, she felt a slight breeze on her neck and a voice said softly,

"We meet again." Startled she froze for a second, then her head spun around, but there was no one there, only guests milling about. She trembled and tightened her hold on Akapwon's hand as she moved closer to his side. He glanced down at her, pleased that she drew closer but worried because she trembled as well.

"Are you cold, Maimuna?" His low vibrant voice affected her strangely and her name sounded special on his lips. She managed to smile.

"No my husband, I thought I heard a voice and it startled me."

Her smile and her husky voice calling him my husband, drove Akapwon's pulse to a faster pace.

"It is time for us to leave. Are you ready?"

"Yes, my husband." Maimuna dropped her eyes in confusion. Her heart beat so fast she felt out of breath. "Better now." She thought, "Better to get it over with."

Because both she and her parents were apprehensive, their farewells were more poignant. Her parents were guests of his parents for the night. The other guests from Arana Twee were already setting up their camp a little distance from the village centre. They would return to Twee at early sunrise. Her mother knew that she and her father would not sleep, wondering if they would see their daughter alive the next day.

The celebration was in full swing, the beer was still flowing and few people observed the bride and groom's departure from the festivities. But among those that saw them leave were a pair of eyes that gleamed with a feverish light.

They neared Akapwon's compound. He had laboured, bringing clay from the river to build his home and then he had carried red earth from the mountains to colour the clay, which gave it a sort of warm brownish rust hue. The colour gave a peaceful yet welcoming look to the home which was made up of four large individual huts joined to each other. It was built at the edge of the village to the west and in time would become more of the centre when new couples built on the periphery according to custom. It had taken him a long time to build and he had taken his time when he realised that no family wanted to accept his bride price.

After finishing the first hut and finding that neither his planting nor his weaving occupied him enough, he had proceeded to build another hut and attached it to the first and before he realised, he had built four huts. When he explained this to his parents as the reason he had built four huts, they laughed heartily and told him that his bride would be one of the happiest women in Monabu.

On passing through the ungated fence surrounding the home, Maimuna stopped and gasped in surprised delight, forgetting her plight for the moment.

"It is beautiful!" She gave a little delighted laugh as she turned to her husband. "Truly beautiful."

Akapwon's chest swelled with pride. "You like it?"

"Yes!" was the emphatic answer.

The entrance to the house opened on to the kitchen and dining area. To the left of the kitchen was a spare room. To the right of the kitchen/dining area was the bedroom and beyond that was the bathroom. Akapwon had built the bathroom lower than the rest of the house so that no water would flow back into the bedroom. He had also built a wooden platform with slots for the water to pour through so that whoever was bathing did not have to stand on the sand. He had built two tables one on each side of the platform. The first was built low for the bucket of water and the dipper with which to bathe. The other was for the face basin and the water jug. He had attached pegs to the wall to hang a change of clothing after bathing, to keep it dry and away from splashes of water. Although the room had no window, he had left an open space near the roof which ran the circumference of the hut and which brought in lots of sunlight and fresh air, to keep the room free from damp and mustiness.

More exclamations of pleasure came from Maimuna as they entered the hut and she saw how really spacious it was. He showed her her new home, feeling a small degree of pride that she actually thought it was beautiful. That made it worth all the effort he had put into it. As he left each room, he blew out the oil lamp his mother had lit for them earlier when she and her husband had showed Maimuna's parents where their daughter would be living. They noted that the back room was filled with gifts from well-wishers.

Then he led her to the bedroom. The room was large and had a few mats on the earthen floor, one on either side of the bed, another near the door and at the foot of the bed. When he first started to weave Akapwon had worked the loom to relax after a hard day in the fields. At the time he was doing well with his crops so that when a tapestry he was working on got too askew, rather than unravelling it, which always took him a long time, he placed it on the floor and used it as a mat. Later however, after losing his crops, he had to unravel his weaves and start over because he had nothing with which to trade for more twine. Since trading for yarn brought but a fraction of the price of a cow or a goat, he stopped weaving altogether and concentrated on trading his produce to increase his bride price. However, the mats attested to his many seasons of practice. His village was proud of their two Master Weavers and although his weaving was more or less at a standstill, he still hoped to become a Master Weaver by the end of the year. He hoped that his weaving would be good enough to join in the competitions. With the twine Boboda had brought him, he knew he was very close to entering that competition.

The bed, which was raised on a dais slightly above the floor, was covered in a heavy blanket woven by Akapwon in colours of gold, rust and orange. It got very chilly in Monabu in the early mornings. It was not perfect by far, with bumps clearly visible in some parts, but he was proud of it nonetheless. Many pillows in orange and brown were on the bed. The blanket had taken him a long time to weave. He also had done something which none of the other villagers had done. He had placed strips of woven straw on the walls of the bedroom. Covering the clay walls made them very attractive. But they became even more attractive when Akapwon hung a large tapestry on the wall at the head of the bed. Then it became a lovely room. The tapestry, one of his early attempts, was very colourful and attractive. He had endured the time-consuming task of finding dropped stitches and removing bumps. It was the only work he had done which was free of any imperfections.

Maimuna was so nervous she could not fully appreciate the beauty of the room and its welcoming atmosphere. Her apprehension returned a hundredfold as Akapwon sat her on the bed and then knelt before her at her feet. "Do not be afraid of me, Maimuna," he said as untying the ribbon which held their hands together, he saw fear in her eyes. "Did not the Elder mothers explain to you what happens on your wedding night?"

Maimuna nodded her head as her frightened eyes spilled over with tears and visions of her rape replayed itself.

"Then why are you afraid? They did not tell you that it is something of pleasure?" Akapwon was extremely puzzled by her behaviour, especially since she had seemed comfortable in his company throughout the wedding celebration. Then he remembered what Chief Comse and Tutaba had told him, that some women cried when they were afraid. "I will not hurt you, Maimuna," he said as he took her trembling fingers in his. She nodded the affirmative as she looked at him. "Then why are you afraid?" She lowered her eyes as her tears continued to flow. Akapwon sat on the bed next to her and put his arms around her.

"It is all right." He said as he gently ran his hand up and down her back, trying to comfort her. "I will not hurt you. I will take care of you." He held her close as he whispered words of encouragement, believing her to be afraid of what was to happen to her. "I will try to make this as pleasurable for you as I can." Then he kissed her until she stopped crying. "I will remove your robes now," he said, looking into her eyes. She shook her head violently in the negative as her hands clutched her robes closer to her chest. Akapwon slid off the bed and knelt in front of her again. When she raised her eyes she saw anger in his and she realised that he thought she was treating him like a fool. She slowly removed her arms and rested them at her sides. Akapwon nodded and started removing the layers of clothing she wore. The layers were red but of different textured cloth, the top being the finest and most transparent. When he got to the last layer, a white cotton shift, in an attempt to get her to relax, he caressed her abdomen then fell backward in shock.

His eyes flashed anger as he stared at her. Reaching forward, he tore the shift from her body in one vicious sweep then slid back on his knees with a hiss of breath. Before his eyes was a woman with child, not big enough to be detected as yet, but round enough to the touch to be unmistakable. White hot fury seared through him, almost consuming him in its intensity. Rising quickly to his feet he raised his arm to strike her. As she cowered on the bed before him, he fought for control and his body trembled with his fury. Turning his back, fists clenched at his side, he continued to fight to control himself. A few minutes passed in silence except for her muffled sobs. Then he turned and walked out of the room and out of the hut.

Outside, he kicked at a bucket that was nearby and angrily paced back and forth in front of the door. After a while he lit his pipe which he angrily puffed as he paced agitatedly.

No wonder he had felt unease. So this is what Uta had in mind for him.

No wonder he could not believe he was that lucky.

Now he knew that it was not luck at all, but deliberate deception.

A few wedding guests passed on their way home and called laughing encouragement to him.

"Do not give her too much time to think, Akapwon."

"Do not keep her waiting too long." He waved in acknowledgment of their good-natured banter.

As he paced, he exerted tremendous control over his anger. That he was furious was an understatement. He wondered if Uta had played a joke on him, had made him wait so long and then tricked him into marrying a woman who was obviously not a virgin. Then he saw her face again, as it had been when he lifted her veil. He had thanked Uta then, profusely and now this. He stopped pacing and stood thinking. He had always thought Uta had a plan for him. Could it be that there was a plan behind all this?

Then he remembered his mother's words to him. "Be patient with her Akapwon. You will both learn from each other." When he felt he had given her enough time and he had composed himself, he returned to the bedroom. She was sitting upright in the bed, tears still silently flowing down her face. Coming into the room, he stopped just inside the threshold. "Now," he said, "tell me what is the meaning of this!" and he waved his arm in the general direction of her abdomen which she had covered again by replacing one of her robes. "Do you insult me because my bride price was so low, you and your family thought to make a fool and a laughing stock of me in our two villages?"

"No! No, Akapwon. Believe me, please believe me, no!" She sobbed.

"Then how do you explain yourself being with child?" He asked angrily.

"I can explain if you will let me. Please let me explain. Please." She pleaded, not for his understanding, but for her life. As she looked up at him, he raised his arm and she cringed on the bed, covering her head with her arms. For a moment there was silence.

91

"Remove your hands from your face and look at me!"

She did as she was bid and held her breath at the blaze of anger in his eyes.

"Had I been as most other men, you would either have been dead or in need of a medicine woman's attention. Thank my parents for teaching me their beliefs about life which has caused you to still have yours!"

He remained near the door, away from her and removed his wedding garments, remaining only in the loose fitting trousers. He angrily tossed the garments aside as he walked over to the bed, sat down cross-legged but away from her, waiting until she raised her head and looked at him. The fact that her eyes were red and her face blotchy from crying did nothing to diminish her beauty and he felt compassion in spite of himself. Thus his voice was softer than he had intended when he spoke.

"You have my attention. Explain."

She proceeded with a halting voice to explain everything to him. He sat watching her silently and intently in order to catch a slip on her part or an inflection that would tell him she was lying or fabricating her story. However, when she got to the part about the rape and how she was found, he rose from the bed and walked about the room with his hands tightly held behind his back. She halted a moment but proceeded quickly to tell him of her punishment and Chief Kofo's decision.

"I will be a good wife to you, Akapwon, if you let me live. I promise I will work hard to make you happy. Please give me a chance. Please!"

He stared at her for a long time then abruptly said. "I will give you my decision in the morning. Come to bed now." and he raised the covers for her to get under but he remained where he was. She understood that the matter was closed and there was no point in pleading anymore. By instinct she knew that she would only make it worse if she did so. She did not think she could sleep and wondered if in his compassion he would take her life while she slept. For somehow she knew he was compassionate. If he were not, he would have hit her, despite the upbringing to which he attributed his restraint. The emotional see-saw that she had been on since the incident of her rape, and which had intensified since they set out for Monabu, finally took its toll and she fell asleep in spite of herself.

When Akapwon heard her breathing change in sleep, he got up and paced the house, walking from room to room. Going over in his mind what she had told him, he could not believe that anyone in the Arana Kingdom could have committed such an unspeakable crime against an innocent woman. He felt compelled to believe that she was telling the truth, but in his mind he had some grave doubts. Perhaps the father of the child was a powerful, wealthy man and he used his power to get rid of her. Or perhaps a young man who, after finding that she was with child, refused to marry her and denied that he was responsible. There could be a number of different reasons.

He realised that perhaps her plea had been as much for her life as for his understanding and he marvelled at her courage. He was a complete stranger to her, could very easily have been the rapist himself and yet she had faced him and so pleaded, that he had listened.

Finally, when the sun showed itself at the rim of the horizon, he came to a decision and lay next to her on top of the covers.

20

AKAPWON rose much later than he normally did, to the smell of fresh coffee. He sat up abruptly, slightly confused until all events of the night before came back to him in a rush. He went to the bathroom and washed the bitter taste of his humiliation from his mouth. Removing his wedding garment, he dressed for the field in coarse blue trousers and a sleeveless shirt. Noting that the other part of his wedding garment had been neatly folded and placed on a basket by the door, he walked into the kitchen.

On entering, he stopped in surprise and stood watching Maimuna in silence for a moment. Apparently she had found ingredients to make breakfast and was obviously well versed in preparing breakfast and finding her way around a kitchen. It registered in his mind that most women came into a marriage well able to cook and run a household. Apparently her parents' wealth did not exclude her from the lessons all girls had to learn as part of their future duties.

She was a vision in her soft, flowered, yellow wrap-dress. The table was laid for two and the coffee smelled delicious. Turning from the cooking fire with a bowl of millet porridge in each hand, she saw him standing at the door and stopped abruptly. Fear flashed across her face. He watched as she visibly fought for control, strengthening her resolve and strengthening her back. A soft smile appeared and disappeared uncertainly on her lips.

She took a deep breath and said in a quiet voice "Good morning, my husband. Your breakfast is ready."

As he moved to the table, he was amused by her audaciousness. But at the same time he could not help but admire her courage. Any of the other girls in his village would still be on the bed in a sodden heap, but not her. Either she was very conceited or very strong. It was probably the latter, which explained how she survived such a brutal attack as she had described.

As they ate, they talked. He asked for more and more details until he got a completely satisfactory picture for himself. He leaned forward across the table and reached up to almost touch a half-moon scar beneath her left eye that was not fully healed. "Did he do this?" Her hand went up automatically to cover it.

"Yes." was her reply. Then she said something unexpected. "It was his voice that I heard at our wedding celebration when you felt me move closer to you," she said. "He is in this village."

"What!" Akapwon sprang to his feet surprised, shocked, angry and disbelieving after she explained to him what had happened. "By Uta, I will kill him!" As was his habit when he was angry or upset, he paced the room. "For the women in this village and their protection, I will kill that snake!"

"Maybe he does not live here but came for the wedding celebrations. From his voice, I knew he was not of Twee."

"For his sake I hope he does not live here."

When breakfast was over they talked at length until they came to an agreement and made arrangements between them.

He told her, "To everyone else, we will pretend as if we are a happily married couple. You will help me in the field at the time of planting." He warned her to never shame him in public or to his friends or he would surely kill her and tell them why. More specifically, he warned her, should she become unfaithful to him, it was his right to end her life, and he would, without hesitation.

"Make no mistake, Maimuna. I may have spared your life now and I do so only because of what you have told me happened to you. I have let you live because it was not your fault. However," and his eyes were as cold as his expression, "make no mistake that I will end your life if you decide to be unfaithful to me. That would be an added insult I will not tolerate. Do you understand me?"

His coldness frightened her and Maimuna shook her head "Yes, my husband. I understand you although I would not be so ungrateful for this life you have let me keep."

Akapwon nodded. Seeing her fear and that her body shook slightly, he softened his expression. "It is not my intention to make you afraid of me, Maimuna. I only wished to bring home to you what would be your fate should you shame me."

Maimuna on the other hand, had no intention of shaming him. She was grateful for her life and knew beyond a doubt that she was extremely lucky with her new husband. Her heart was full and she thanked Uta because by all rights she would be dead if it had been any other man. Of that she was quite sure and that was but one thing that made her aware of how lucky she was to be married to Akapwon. Not only did he spare her life, but he had actually sat with her and discussed ways to save her from being disgraced because of her pregnancy. She could sense keenly that he was an unusual man.

Had it been Sadio, by the way he treated her after she was raped, she was certain that he would have killed her on the spot, if for nothing else, than for his pride. He would do anything to save face in the eyes of the village. He might even have been puffed up after he killed her, knowing that the village would be behind him.

Akapwon sat across from her deep in thought. Maimuna remained silent as she watched him. He considered for a while whether he should tell his parents about what transpired on his wedding night. Finally he decided against it. He did not want their relationship with Maimuna to be strained and he knew it would be if they knew of her and her parents' duplicity. They would respect his decision and probably be glad of it but nonetheless they would be disappointed in Maimuna. After learning of her deception, a natural relationship could never be, especially for a mother who finds that her son had been tricked into an insulting marriage. He relayed his decision to Maimuna. Before they rose from the table, he told her.

"Maimuna, I have decided not to tell my parents about what happened between us last night. It would upset them and they would never be able to look at you without remembering what you did. It is best that we keep it to ourselves. Do you agree?"

Tears came to her eyes and she jumped from the table and kneeling in front of him, taking his hands in hers, she kissed them over and over, thanking him profusely. Embarrassed, he drew his hands away and patted her shoulder as he got up from the table.

"I am going now to the field but will be back shortly. We will be visiting our parents on my return." He asked, "I expect your parents will be returning home today?"

"Yes, they are." She replied.

"And you wish to see them before they leave do you not?"

"Oh yes, I do, Akapwon."

Maimuna's smile was dazzling as she thanked him. He was aware that she had no idea of its effect on his senses and he turned away quickly lest she saw how much it affected him. It was a while before his pulse returned to normal. His vulnerability to her beauty annoyed him and made him disgusted with himself. Returning from the field shortly after, he entered the house and found that

Maimuna was ready and waiting for him. She had cleared the table and had already washed the breakfast bowls. They set off for his parents' house.

As they walked through the village, he tried to compose himself for meeting her parents. He held her hand as a newly married couple would do. Their walk was constantly interrupted by well-wishers who stared openly and admiringly at Maimuna. She hung her head in embarrassment at their open praises.

Maimuna was extremely nervous. However, knowing that Akapwon would not tell his parents about her betrayal was a heavy load off her mind and made meeting them a lot easier. She did not feel so easy though, as to allay her nervousness, because she would always be aware that things could have been very different between them. She wished it could have been different because she felt they would have been happy together.

As they walked hand in hand, again she marvelled at her good fortune. She could hardly believe what a beautiful home he had built for his bride and the consideration that he had put into the building of it. She wondered at how foolish parents were about bride prices because Akapwon was a man of compassion. She was the proof. He was also kind and considerate. And handsome too, she told herself. The way some of the women in the village stared at her, she knew they were aware of what they lost and were probably angry with their parents for refusing the bride price.

As they entered his parents' compound, her mother and father rushed out to greet her. Her mother hugged her with tears in her eyes and her father kept patting her shoulders, a wide smile on his face. Then they both turned to Akapwon and her mother hugged him too. As she hugged him, Kaieta whispered in his ear, "Thank you. Thank you. Thank you. I cannot thank you enough, Akapwon. You will not be sorry. I promise you."

Akapwon was slightly embarrassed by this show of affection from perfect strangers but then his mother, not to be outdone, rushed up and hugged him too, then she hugged Maimuna. His father grinned and said, "Welcome my son and my new daughter, welcome." They entered the house and before his mother went on to the kitchen, they sat talking for a while. Akapwon was glad to see that both sets of parents got along as if they were old friends. He watched them as they laughed and talked.

He was fully aware of the relief that her parents felt on seeing their daughter alive. Until that moment, he had not thought of what it would have been like for them if he had followed the custom and in anger and vengeance, had taken her life. He guessed that the relief must have been poignant and that her mother's heartfelt thanks were but a shadow of what they really felt.

Finally his father rose and said, "Let us have our celebration dinner." He led the way through his hut to the garden beyond where a table and stools were set up under an arbour covered with bright blue morning glories. Both women had cooked for the private wedding feast and some of Timpi's beer was cooling in an earthen jar in the kitchen.

Before the meal started, Kinefe bid them stay put and be comfortable.

"I will bring the beer to the dining table. No, don't get up." He said to Oboto. "Akapwon will help his mother bring the food from the kitchen. We just want you to relax."

Maimuna's parents took the opportunity of this brief moment alone to speak to her.

"We cannot be more grateful that you are alive, Maimuna," her father said quietly. "But how did you accomplish this miracle?"

"I did not Father, it is just the type of man Akapwon is, that I am here. He left the house and when he returned he was calmer, but not much. When I begged him if I could explain, he reluctantly gave me permission to speak. I knew he did not believe me, Father, but he said he would consider what I had told him." They were interrupted by Akapwon and his mother bringing dishes of food. When they returned to the kitchen she continued.

"In the morning, he questioned me for a long time and then he gave me his rules. He said if I broke any of them he would surely kill me and tell everybody why he had done it. I could see that he did not truly believe what I told him but he was willing to let me live. I know, Father, that I would be dead if it were Sadio or perhaps any other man."

"What rules did he give you, Maimuna?" Her mother asked.

"He told me that if he ever saw that I showed inappropriate interest in another man the way he has seen some wives in the village behave or if I gave him reason to be suspicious or if I shamed him in front of his friends, then he would surely kill me."

"Ah, but he does not know you, Maimuna. That is why he said such things. He will soon discover what a wonderful wife you can be."

"And I, Mother, have already discovered what a wonderful husband he can be. I am very happy that you accepted the offer of Chief Kofo. Sadio cannot be compared to him."

Her parents were satisfied and what she told them was confirmed by their own experience with his parents, that she was in the best of hands and their hearts were eased.

Before leaving his parents' home, Akapwon had a brief opportunity to speak with Maimuna's parents. He warned her parents that if they made the least slip his parents would badger them relentlessly until they got the truth. He suggested that they be careful of what they said when speaking around them, especially since they now felt more relaxed because Maimuna lived.

"We are more aware than you could guess, what would happen to Maimuna should anyone else find out her condition, Son." Oboto said. "Such information will remain only with us. She has suffered so very much and it is enough. And thank you for not telling your parents, Akapwon. It would have been unbearable for her knowing they could not trust her after hearing her story."

Satisfied that they understood, Akapwon left for home with Maimuna.

21

CHIEF Kofo waited somewhat apprehensively for the return of Maimuna's parents. He had said a prayer that Maimuna's life be spared and wondered if his prayers had been answered. It was difficult not knowing whether she still lived or not. It was now seven days since the wedding, enough time for them to visit and to travel back. However, her parents had not returned. Was that a good or bad sign? With all the festivities they must have forgotten to send him word although he had asked that they report to him on their return.

As he sat alone in the hearing room thinking on what might have happened to Maimuna, his son walked in.

"Greetings, Father."

"Greetings, Sadio."

"Have you heard anything, Father, about Maimuna's marriage?"

Chief Kofo was somewhat taken aback. He had not expected such a question from Sadio considering the indifference he had shown of her plight. Except for her family, closest friends and the Council, no one knew of the circumstances of her marriage. "You are interested in her marriage, Sadio? I thought you had forgotten her already."

Sadio looked somewhat ashamed, which surprised Chief Kofo even more. Maybe there was hope for him after all. "I am ashamed of the way I treated her, Father. I have had time to think and I realise that I failed her at a time she most needed my support. I am ashamed that I did not even look at her because I thought only of myself."

"Yes, well, to tell you the truth I was ashamed of you also, Sadio. You showed a disgraceful lack of integrity and character. It saddens a father's heart to see his child behave in the manner in which you behaved toward Maimuna."

"I know, Father, but all I could think of was that everybody would think me stupid if I married her."

In fact he had received a good tongue lashing from Codou after she returned from the wedding. It was only her anger and disgust with him that had caused him to take a good look at himself.

Chief Kofo replied, "It pains me to say it, Sadio, but you show a lack of character that is somewhat disturbing considering you have a responsibility to this village. Since you failed in your responsibility to comfort Maimuna, it makes me wonder if you are capable of any kind of leadership."

Sadio was alarmed by what his father said. Before Codou approached him, he had not thought too deeply about his actions. It had not occurred to him that his actions toward Maimuna would be used to judge whether he would make a good chief or not. Now he understood what his father was telling him. He learned something that he had not known before, that his becoming chief was not a foregone conclusion. He did not want to lose such a position which he had thought up until that moment, was his birth right. He was truly frightened by the implications his father made.

Chief Kofo continued, "Perhaps it is my fault, Sadio, for not being strict enough with you. I felt that you were learning something when you sat with the Council. However, now I see that you were not even listening to the Council's deliberations about any case that came before them. Perhaps you were too busy thinking about how good you would look in the Elder's chair."

Sadio felt himself grow hot with embarrassment because that is precisely what he thought whenever he joined the

Elders in the hall. "Father, I pray that you do not judge me too harshly for I will change. I promise."

Chief Kofo looked at his son sceptically. "Time will tell, Son. At least you have plenty of that right now. However, take note, Son, that time does tend to fly. If you are not serious, you will find that you are out of time more quickly than you had expected. If there are any changes, I will be aware of them as they occur. For the moment, Son, time is all you have in your favour."

Sadio bowed respectfully, "Thank you, Father. That is all I can ask of you."

As Sadio walked from the hall, Chief Kofo did not feel encouraged. However, he would wait and see. He sighed. Well at least he had made Sadio aware that he might not be the one chosen to be chief.

*

Leaving the hearing hall, Sadio's thoughts went back to Codou. She had told him in no uncertain terms what she thought of him. She had gone against custom and sought him out while he was alone. Angrily she reminded him of the brutal beating Maimuna had endured and accused him of being a coward. Apart from being ashamed because he knew she was right, he had seen a new side of Codou he was not aware existed and it intrigued him. However, her calling him a coward had made him angry. But she cared not whether he was angry and proceeded to give him a piece of her mind.

"Maimuna was badly beaten, her ribs badly bruised and she suffered the agonizing humiliation of being raped and all you could think of was that she was no longer pure?" She made a scornful sound. "If she had been raped a hundred times, Maimuna would still be pure. However, as conceited as you are, I do not expect you to understand that."

When he started walking away, she reached out and pulled him back and did not stop her tirade until she herself was satisfied. "You are supposed to be a man. Men are supposed to protect and comfort women."

She wanted him to feel some of the pain and betrayal Maimuna had felt at his treatment of her. "Answer me, Sadio. What would you have done if she had died?"

When he refused to answer her, she walked off in a huff. Sadio had remained where he was, watching her. His body trembled slightly at the anger he felt. "How dare she speak to me like that," he thought as he stood there.

When his anger finally cooled, he began to recall her words. Had it not been for her, he would never have given his actions a second thought. Now, for the first time in his life he felt ashamed. He recalled her face as she accused him scornfully of being a coward. "I always admired you, Sadio. But now I find that you are just a coward."

How that had hurt. Now he faced her words and had to admit to himself that yes, he had been a coward. Recalling his father's words, he acknowledged to himself that he was frightened and it made him even more ashamed.

As Codou walked angrily away from Sadio, she knew that she had overstepped her bounds and being the chief's son, that Sadio could make life difficult for her. Although she was somewhat apprehensive, she did not care. Someone had to let him know how badly he had behaved. She was positive that had she been the injured party, Maimuna would not have hesitated to let Sadio know what she thought of him. In fact, she felt certain that because it was her and not Maimuna, Sadio had got off lightly. It would not have been so with Maimuna. She was very protective of her friends and would fight to defend them. That is why it was so terrible that she had been the one to be injured.

Codou waited apprehensively for Sadio to retaliate. But many weeks passed and nothing happened. However, something had changed. At first she was not aware of it, but then she began to notice that whenever she was gathered with her friends, talking in the marketplace or in the town square, Sadio would walk up and join in the conversation. In the beginning she thought it was a mere coincidence, but as it continued to happen she felt it was deliberate. "If he expects me to apologize he will have a long wait," she said to her herself.

On these occasions Codou refused to look his way. Eventually, after she had done that a number of times when Sadio joined the group, he made it a point to stand next to her. When she continued to ignore him, one day he spoke quietly to her.

"Codou, I need to talk to you, privately."

Codou looked at him defiantly, ready to do battle. "About what?"

He took a step back from the group indicating she should do the same. Somewhat resentfully but also curious, she stepped back too.

Speaking a little above a whisper he said "I wish to thank you, Codou, for pointing out my behaviour towards Maimuna. I apologize for not responding to your words but I was too angry. Had you not taken the time to let me see my behaviour through your eyes, I would still not have seen myself at fault."

Codou bit down hard on her lips to stop her mouth from falling open. Sadio was thanking her and also apologizing? It was something she had not expected in her wildest dreams. It said something for the man after all, that at least he had humility. Seeing the distress in his eyes for her silence, she finally spoke. After all she could be magnanimous too.

"Thank you, Sadio. I also apologize for some of the things I said to you. I was angry and it hurt to see how you behaved toward Maimuna when she had almost lost her life."

Sadio winced slightly at her words.

"I have been very selfish and only thought of myself."

"Your behaviour was more shocking because we expected you to rush to her side and comfort her."

A much-chastised Sadio bowed his head. "I can see that now. It was as though I was looking at everything through a cloud and could not see the real picture."

"Well it is over now and I am sure Maimuna has forgiven you. Shall we put it behind us, Sadio?" She asked, looking at him.

"Yes. But I must tell you that it is a relief to get it off my chest. It was chastening to me when you would not look at me or speak to me, Codou."

"That is because I was very angry, Sadio. But now that you have explained yourself, I am no longer angry."

"Thank you, Codou." And with that they joined the others once more and continued the camaraderie of the group.

But Codou could not get this new image of Sadio out of her mind. It was almost unbelievable that he had apologized. She wondered again if this was a new Sadio or if it was just a ruse.

22

MAIMUNA'S parents returned to Arana Twee. They had bought many large jars of Timpi's beer for their male friends and Muta's baskets for their female friends. The best of both gifts were chosen for Chief Kofo. They had not forgotten their promise to give him a full report of the wedding. As soon as they were settled and refreshed, they hurried over to the hall of Elders and waited their turn to see him.

When Chief Kofo saw them enter the hall, he was pleased that they had not forgotten. Word travelled fast and he knew they had arrived almost as soon as they walked into their home. Trying not to be impatient, he heard complaints from as many people as he thought appropriate and then dismissed the others to return later in the day. Dismissing the Council, he walked over to them.

"Greetings, my friends."

"Greetings, Chief Elder."

From the bright smiles on their faces, he knew that all had gone well and that Maimuna was still alive. He felt relief rush through him.

"I have heard that you arrived but a little while ago. I am sure you have not been here long enough to have eaten and so I wish to invite you to my home for a meal."

They accepted graciously; glad that they would not have to speak to him in the Hall of Elders. One never knew who might be listening. When they arrived at his home, a table had already been prepared in the garden. He had informed his wife by messenger that he was bringing guests for dinner.

"Greetings, my friends. Welcome to our home." Chief Kofo's wife, Shoorai, gave the traditional greeting as they entered. She was a gracious hostess and had long grown used to her husband's unexpected guest or guests coming to her home for dinner. At first she had been angry but soon realised that as the chief of the village, it was a courtesy he had to extend whenever the need arose. In the case of Maimuna's parents, Kofo had told his wife about Maimuna's condition and had kept her apprised of the events that led up to Maimuna's wedding. She had been very sympathetic and concerned for Maimuna. When he sent the messenger to tell her he was bringing them home for dinner, she was happy and waited anxiously to hear what they had to say.

Oboto and Kaieta bowed and returned her greeting. Being the gracious hostess that she was, she would have no talk of anything until they had eaten. They relaxed as her helpers cleared the remains of the meal. Kofo served some of Timpi's beer and Chief Kofo was very impressed with the delicious flavour. Leaning forward in his chair, he asked "Whose beer did you say this was, Oboto?"

"It is made by Timpi. She is the medicine woman in Monabu. Her beer is very popular and very sought after. She made this batch just for us because we wanted to give some as gifts."

"Talla is going to be one jealous man. He thinks his beer is the best in the world."

"Yes, that is why we brought him some as well." Kaieta said and there was a mutual burst of laughter.

"He will be upset for the entire planting season." Everyone agreed.

Chief Kofo was too polite to ask and so he waited for Oboto and Kaieta to begin telling them about the wedding. He did not have long to wait.

"Chief Kofo," Oboto said, "We cannot thank you enough

for what you have done for Maimuna. We ourselves could not have chosen a better husband for her. Akapwon is a very intelligent, kind and extraordinary young man." His wife nodded agreement as he continued. "Maimuna told us what transpired between them on their wedding night." He paused, overcome by emotion. "She said she pleaded with him to let her explain and she said, although it was obvious he wanted to strike her down, he controlled himself and walked away. When he returned he bid her explain and he sat silently until she was finished. Then he told her he would give her an answer in the morning."

"In the morning, she awoke early and prepared breakfast for him but when she saw him at the door to the kitchen, she was almost overcome with fear and needed all her strength to keep her knees from buckling beneath her."

"As they had breakfast, he asked her many more questions until he seemed satisfied enough to let it drop. It was only then that she became sure that he would not take her life. Then she said something that made my heart swell with pride for him and his parents. Before they came to visit us at his mother's house, he told her that he would not tell his parents that she was with child, because he did not want their relationship with her to be anything other than natural."

Kofo was impressed and so was Shoorai. "He sounds like an extraordinary young man indeed. I would like to meet him. Perhaps one day he will bring her to visit then you must bring him to me. From what I have learned of his father, they must be somewhat alike."

"Yes," Kaieta said. "Maimuna said that he told her that were it not for his parents and the way they raised him, she would not have been alive a moment after he found out her deception. She said he was furious and had he hit her at that moment, she was sure that he would have broken her neck."

"Oh, that poor girl. That must have brought everything that happened to her freshly back to her mind," Shoorai said.

"That is exactly what she said," Kaieta replied. "She said she could not stop shaking, expecting him to hit her at any moment."

There was a slight pause as each one was lost in thought for a moment.

"However," Kaieta said "The wedding was beautiful. The whole village was happy for Akapwon. People kept coming up to Oboto and myself and congratulating us on our beautiful daughter and for acquiring a beautiful son through her marriage. They were so gracious." She reached over for her husband's hand. "We could not stop thanking Uta and hoping that that was a sign of Akapwon's good character, which it turned out to be."

Oboto continued, "He had built a beautiful home for her. It is quite large and spacious and he had plastered the outside with brown clay from the mountains, which is something we have not seen before. He also covered the walls inside with straw which he had woven into a mat and stuck to the clay wall while it was still wet. It made the room look very rich. I liked it immediately. His parents showed us around while they were still at the celebration."

Kaieta leaned over to Shoorai. "When they showed us the bedroom, I could not believe what I saw. It was beautiful. He had put colourful mats on the floor and he had hung one of his tapestries on the wall. It is a great idea and it made the room truly beautiful."

Shoorai looked surprised. "He had mats covering the floor? But that must be very expensive."

"He is learning to weave." Kaieta said, secretly proud. "When I asked him why he had put mats on the floor, he told me that when he first started to weave and his tapestry did not turn out right because he had dropped too many

111

stitches and caused too many holes, he put it on the floor. At that time, he said, he could afford to do so because his farm was thriving. Now, however, he could no longer afford to do that because of losing his crops. The mats gave the room a feeling of welcome. I will try it myself I think."

Shoorai nodded. "It sounds like a good idea, especially remembering how cold the floor can be when one gets out of bed first thing in the morning."

23

LIFE settled into a routine for the new couple. Each day after breakfast they would walk to the field. It was planting time and Maimuna worked hard alongside Akapwon, getting the seeds in the ground so that they could grow to be seedlings before the rains came. Maimuna asked many questions and shared information. Conversation flowed naturally between them and Akapwon felt as if he had found a true mate and companion, something he had always dreamed and never stopped hoping to obtain. Her questions were intelligent and showed knowledge of planting that surprised him because although all women in the village grew vegetables for the pot, most were not interested in such a boring subject.

When he mentioned that he was surprised at her understanding of planting and her interest in farming she laughed, a delightful merry laugh that had him smiling.

"Being an only child, Akapwon, and being a daughter, my father decided to teach me as he would have done had I been a son. I accused him of being disappointed that I was not a son but he only laughed and hugged me. Then he said "Who could be disappointed in such a daughter, Maimuna?" he said. "You are..." she stopped abruptly, embarrassed at what she almost told him.

But Akapwon would not let her off so lightly. "You are what, Maimuna?" He asked watching her intently.

She gave an embarrassed little chuckle. "You do not want to know, Akapwon. You will think me conceited if I tell you."

He faced her with a smile, "Maimuna, there is not a conceited bone in your body. Anyone who knows you knows that."

An embarrassed laugh was forced from her although she was surprised at the compliment which was given so casually. "What you said only makes it worse, Akapwon. Do I have to tell you?"

Intrigued, Akapwon nodded, "Yes, Maimuna, you do. You cannot start to say something and then leave me guessing as to what you would have said. Come on, out with it."

She dropped her eyes from his beautiful laughing eyes and said in a muffled voice, so that he had to lean very close to hear. "He said someone as sweet as me would be a blessing to any family." Her cheeks burned with embarrassment and she refused to look at him.

He stared at her for a moment, stunned that she would be embarrassed by such a beautiful compliment. Then he threw back his head and laughed hard and long. And on impulse, he pulled her into his arms and hugged her. "He is right, Maimuna. You are sweet."

When he released her she turned back to her planting, happy that he had hugged her. "In any case," she continued as if the conversation was never interrupted, "although he had many workers, he made sure I helped him in the fields and he taught me everything he knows. He felt guilty about it until he realised that I enjoyed every moment of it and that most of all, I enjoyed the time we were able to spend together. Later he explained that he felt that even though I was a daughter, I should be given the same right to learn as would have been given me had I been his son."

Akapwon was surprised to hear that. Almost all farmers so far as he was aware, felt it was man's work, planting in the fields and tending crops. He was pleased to hear that her father was not one of them. Although he agreed that the heavy work on the farm should be a man's job, he also felt that there was no reason a woman, if she was interested, should not be allowed to learn. Yet in Monabu, there were very few women who were allowed to learn farming. As far as the men were concerned, their garden plots were sufficient for them. He could not help feeling that if Muta, Boboda's mother, had been given the opportunity to learn, life would not have been so hard for them.

Maimuna and Akapwon's friendship grew and slowly Akapwon's generous nature unfolded and Maimuna was very happy. Sometimes Akapwon worried that she worked too hard but he did not stop her. Although they had a great camaraderie and he had forgiven her, he felt it was fitting punishment for her duplicity. But just as he observed her character, Maimuna observed his and as she did so, she grew to admire and respect him even more. In their own way, they were both happy and she worked hard to please him.

Akapwon was aware of how clean Maimuna kept her home. He had been to the homes of many of his friends and not all their wives were clean. Maimuna always had a smile for his friends, no matter how tired she was, and always had a mug of beer for them to drink. He suspected his friends came for the beer and to visit Maimuna more than to visit him. When she first made beer for him, he wanted to know if it was her mother's recipe. Instead she surprised him by telling him that it was an old recipe of his mother's. The beer was not as good as Timpi's but it was good and he was grateful for it after a hard day in the field.

He noticed also that his clothes were always clean. She arranged them neatly in a large basket and asked him to place his soiled clothing outside near the washtub. He also appreciated little things like a flower on the breakfast table, and a clean compound. Sometimes he found a sprig of scented lavender under his pillow after she found out from his mother that he loved the scent of lavender. Their walks in the evenings were his favourite times. At last he had someone with whom he could discuss things other than planting. He told her of his interest in the stars. They compared his and her parents' thoughts on life. And they both agreed that some of their parents' thoughts were incorporated into their own lives. He discussed his own ideas that he had formed for himself over time and was eager to discuss the ideas she herself had formed.

It was always too soon when they reached home and the conversations ended but he was also eager the next day to pick up where they left off. Sometimes they were joined by Tutaba and Shema his wife. At those times, as they sat on his favourite hill overlooking the valley, the conversations became quite lively.

For Maimuna, life had become more interesting and richer than she had ever expected. Wanting to make her surroundings feel more permanent she planted flowers in her compound and the periwinkles she planted were starting to bloom, as well as the wide variety of wildflowers. In all, it gave a cheerful, attractive look to the place.

Often they walked through the village on their way to the market, as playing children ran across their path. On one such occasion a child fell and scraped his knee and Maimuna watched with fascination as Akapwon, without hesitation or embarrassment, scooped the child up in his arms and spoke to him quietly until he stopped crying and started laughing. As Akapwon was comforting the child and her attention was on him, Maimuna felt a hand caress her back. She jumped and turned in fright. Although there were people nearby, all their backs were turned toward her. She looked in every direction but saw no one who looked suspicious enough to have been the person who dared to touch her. This caused her to be more afraid and she drew closer to Akapwon. Unaware of her encounter,

Akapwon put the boy down and they continued walking through the market. Too afraid and not knowing what to do at the moment, Maimuna decided to wait until they got home. However, she stayed very close to Akapwon and held his hand, an action which made Akapwon very pleased.

As they moved around in the marketplace, they stopped to make a purchase and Akapwon surprised her when he angrily raised his voice to a vendor. Knowing he would lose his customers if others heard Akapwon, the man did everything to appease him, including giving him his intended purchase for free. Akapwon later told her that he had taken her to that specific vendor because he had a reputation for cheating and he wanted her to be aware. Maimuna nodded but her mind was on the person who dared to touch her. It made her very nervous and jittery.

When they returned home, she told Akapwon what had happened in the marketplace. He jumped up and for the first time shouted at her. "Why did you not tell me then! I could have solicited the help of some friends in the marketplace to keep an eye out for anyone coming close to you. You should have told me while we were in the marketplace."

"I did not know what to do, Akapwon. I was very frightened that someone would dare touch me in such an open place. That is why I held your hand. I thought it would keep him away and it did. I feel it is the same person from Twee."

Seeing her fear, Akapwon controlled his anger but with some difficulty. When he had quieted down, he went up to her and put his arms around her. "I am sorry. It is just that it makes me feel so helpless to protect you. I can only imagine the fear you feel." He put her a little away from him and studying her face, said "I think it is a good thing that you did not tell me in the market place. I would have reacted in anger and would have made the grave mistake as I said earlier and told all my friends to keep watch. Now that I have had a moment to think, I realise that it is best for no one to know because then the questions would start. Do you agree?"

"Yes, I agree, Akapwon." She said as she lifted her eyes to his. "I would not want to be the subject of pity or gossip. I am grateful to be starting a new life away from my village where everyone talked behind their hands when I passed by. It was a very painful experience for me."

"We will find this person, Maimuna. We will. I promise you."

She had to be content with that but it was sufficient for her. She knew that if it was in his power, Akapwon would protect her. Reluctantly Akapwon let her go. She felt perfect in his arms, as if she belonged there.

After that incident Maimuna was very cautious, always looking around and if anyone would come near her, she would move away, making it harder to be touched. Whenever she had to go to the market alone, eyes watched her. It helped to know that Akapwon's friends were always ready for a conversation with her. They all admired Maimuna's beauty but her quick smile and friendly nature were what really drew people to her; also she was well respected because she was Akapwon's wife. Maimuna knew that Monabu had strict rules of conduct as did all the other villages, except for Dogo, which was so large, anything like that would go unnoticed. So whenever she went to the market alone, she was always glad when someone she knew spoke to her. It made her less of a target.

Akapwon was angry and very frustrated. He did not know where to start looking because he had no clue as to what her assailant looked like, nor could he think of anyone who would be so bold as to do what this person had done. It became difficult for him not to be suspicious of all the people in the marketplace. He hated the feeling of inadequacy that this incident produced. Realising that he was becoming unreasonable when he found himself suspecting some of his childhood friends whom he knew were trustworthy, he did what was his only option. He became very alert and noted the actions of everyone whenever Maimuna was with him.

As they walked through the village talking with Tutaba and Shema, Boboda walked up to them. Because he had not seen him since his marriage, Akapwon greeted him warmly.

"Boboda! I have missed you my friend. You have been away for some time."

"Yes." Boboda's voice was very hoarse as he nursed a terrible cold. He spoke almost in a whisper. "I have been back and forth to Bopo for mother."

"You have a terrible cold, Boboda. How did you come to get sick?"

"I got caught in the rain, walking from Arana Bopo. I am used to walking in the rain but this time I guess I stayed wet too long."

"I am sorry to hear that." Akapwon smiled. "But business must be good then. You met Maimuna at our wedding did you not?"

"I will forgive you for not remembering, Akapwon." He laughed an embarrassed little laugh. "I know your mind was on other things. But yes, you did introduce us." He stared at Maimuna intently as he bowed slightly. "I am happy to meet you again, Maimuna. I hope Akapwon has been treating you kindly?"

"Yes, he has." Maimuna said quietly. "He is a good man."

"Yes, he is." Boboda sincerely agreed. He talked self-consciously for a few moments longer and then hurried away.

Tutaba and Shema were a little upset. "I do not know why you put up with Boboda, Akapwon," Tutaba said.

"Without saying anything he makes me nervous, as if I should be aware of something but can't bring it to mind."

"He makes me nervous as well. I bid him the time of day but that is all I am willing to give him. Did he not strike you as strange, Maimuna?"

Maimuna seemed surprised at the question. "I do not know him enough to say."

Akapwon interrupted. "That is an unfair question and Boboda is my cousin. I am the only friend he has and I will not abandon him because he is strange. He has always been friendly and respectful to me. Admittedly he is a little strange but that is because he has no friends and so is nervous and shy among people. He does not know how to be social because he does not know what to say most of the time."

"Yes." Tutaba agreed, "Because you are the only one in the village who puts up with his strange ways." As it was such a testy subject between them, they dropped the discussion about Boboda and continued speaking of other things.

*

Not having told his friends anything about what happened at the marketplace, Akapwon was truly worried for Maimuna. Obviously whoever had attacked her was not done with her. As always his helplessness to protect her made him angry. It was obvious to him, observing her, how jittery Maimuna remained for quite some time after the incident. The stress she felt was taking its toll on her and it was quite a while before she returned to her normal self. He took the only solution open to him and ordered his dogs to remain at her side while she was at home alone. His dogs were nondescript and of a local mixed breed but they were very intelligent dogs and very sharp.

24

A KAPWON came in from the fields to find his supper ready for him as usual. Often now, as Maimuna was getting larger, even though she was not large enough for her condition to show, Akapwon would escort Maimuna home early and return to the fields. After he had washed up and was sitting at the table, he noticed that Maimuna was more jittery and nervous than was usual for her.

"What is the matter, Maimuna? Is something wrong?"

"It is nothing." she said avoiding his eyes.

He waited because he knew something was wrong and that she would eventually come out with it and she did.

"Your friend came by today."

"Which friend, Tutaba?"

"No. The other one I met at your parents' home. I do not remember his name."

"Umar?"

"Him, yes." she said quietly.

"Did he say what he wanted?"

"Apart from calling your name, he said nothing. He makes me nervous, Akapwon. Why does he stare at me so?"

"Perhaps because you are beautiful?" he said with a quirk to his lips.

"It is not funny, Akapwon. Both he and Boboda stare at me and it makes me nervous."

At her words, Akapwon became serious. "What did Umar want?"

"That is the point, my husband. After calling your name

he just stood there staring at me. As he was coming forward toward me, the dogs came and sat by me at the door and he stopped. Even though I kept asking him what he wanted, he said nothing and just stood in the yard staring at me. I told him that you were not at home and could he come back later. But my husband, he still took a step towards me and that is when the dogs stood up and growled. It was only then that he stopped, nodded his head and quickly walked away." Her hand shook as it rested on the table.

Akapwon reached across the table and covered it with his. "I am sorry he made you nervous. I will speak to him." His brow wrinkled as he looked away, deep in thought, "I have not known him to be shy. Why would he not speak?" Then he smiled at her. "I will speak to him in the morning, Maimuna." After a moment of silence he said, "I am happy that our dogs were smart enough to sit by your side."

Knowing that Umar would be at his parents' home getting a free meal, he went there directly the next morning. As expected, Umar was enjoying a mug of beer and having a conversation with his father. His mother was in the kitchen. After greeting his father and then Umar, Akapwon sat down facing Umar. Without preamble he said,

"Umar, Maimuna told me you came by yesterday and when she asked you what you wanted, you just stood there staring at her. Why did you do that, Umar?"

Umar looked at him with narrowed eyes. "Your wife is very beautiful and she took my breath away, that is all. I feel awkward around her. I did not mean any harm."

Somehow Akapwon did not associate awkwardness with Umar. "Well your actions frightened her. I would thank you, Umar, not to go by my home again, unless you see me there."

His father was surprised at his harsh words. "Akapwon, is that really necessary?"

Akapwon's gaze moved to his father and his father was surprised at the coldness in his son's eyes, a look he had not seen before. "Yes, Father. He frightened her and I do not appreciate that."

Umar nodded and apologized. "I am sorry. I did not mean to frighten her. I will not do that again."

He seemed sincere and Akapwon accepted his apology, but some unease touched his mind fleetingly and then was gone.

Understanding that Umar's actions were totally unacceptable to Akapwon, his father then turned to Umar and asked, "Yes, Umar, why would you do that?"

"Do what?" Umar feigned ignorance.

"Just stand and stare at Maimuna?" Receiving no answer from Umar, he said, in a very annoyed voice. "I certainly hope you mean what you just said about not doing it again, Umar."

"I do mean it, Kinefe. And I am truly sorry." He turned to Akapwon and said again, "I did not mean to upset anyone." At that, Akapwon and his father let the matter drop.

When he returned home, Akapwon spoke to Maimuna. "I have spoken to Umar and he has promised not to come by again unless I am home. I am sorry you were subjected to his ill-mannered behaviour."

She was quick to defend Akapwon. "It is not your fault, my husband. But I am happy to know that you spoke to him. I do not wish to offend your friends."

"Maimuna, his actions were at fault. I am very angry that he subjected you to such treatment. However, the good news is, I believe he will stay away. I made it quite clear that he was not to come by when I am not at home."

With that Maimuna was content and she smiled as she picked up his bowl to serve him his favourite stew of game, sweet potatoes, cabbage, spinach and okra, laced with hot pepper.

25

IT was the festival of the harvest. There was great activity. The village had long settled back to a normal routine since Akapwon's marriage to Maimuna. Now there was excitement in the air and everyone including Maimuna was affected by it and happy to join in the celebration. Everyone participated and donated to the harvest. The farmers gave something from the most abundant of their crops, potters donated some of their wares, tapestry weavers and basket weavers, cloth makers, anyone who had anything to contribute did so. Those who volunteered to cook food for the celebration were given all the help they needed and Timpi's beer as always was preferred above any other beverage. Maimuna made plum pies to donate, getting her plums from a large plum tree on Akapwon's farm that she had discovered as she worked with him. Previously she had made a pie and Akapwon was so impressed he had given half to his parents who loved it. Because of this she felt confident enough to bake pies for her donation. Akapwon donated a sack of corn.

As the time drew nearer, the excitement grew in the village. Visitors always came from Bopo and Twee, since they were Manabu's nearest neighbours and some even participated in the donations. Once the festival was over, the donated goods were divided up among the elderly, the sick and less fortunate families in Monabu and whatever was left, was donated to the elderly in Bopo and Twee. All were grateful to receive and everyone gave thanks that they were able to donate.

Maimuna's parents came to Monabu for the celebration and stayed with Akapwon's parents, who were happy for their company. Her parents donated a cow, which caused quite a stir. No one had ever donated a cow before. After some deliberation, the Council decided not to butcher the cow, but to keep her and give her milk to the children in the village each day. Depending on how much milk she gave, each child would receive a cup or a half a cup a day.

Once more the village circle was well decorated. Some of the tables were set up to receive gift donations and others were set up to receive the food donations. Excited children played at one end of the circle, staying out of the way of the adults. Oboto visited Kinefe's farm with him and they had opportunity to talk and exchange ideas as they got to know each other. Their friendship grew. Both mothers were also getting to know each other, which allowed a warm friendship to develop between them.

The day of the harvest dawned bright and sunny and promised to be cool, as there was a soft but steady breeze blowing from the mountains. Once everything was in place, the circle decorated with flowers and the tables decorated and laid out with food, the visitors and friends gathered and lined up in front of the tables facing the circle. When everyone was in place the music started. Everyone looked to the opening of the circle where the children were lined up. Each child held a gift. At a signal from the chief, the young girls and boys started forward, walking and swaying and singing, holding their gifts in front of them, baskets of bread, baskets of vegetables, bowls of fruits and many other presents, which were gifts from Bopo. The boys carried planting tools with beautiful carved decorations, various utensils and many other gifts, and the families cheered as each child passed.

The children walked with their gifts to Chief Comse who accepted and handed each to other members of the Council.

The gifts were placed carefully on the tables arranged behind him for that purpose. They would be carried into the hall of the Council later, to be sorted. As the last child came forward, the music stopped as Chief Comse raised both arms in the air.

"Today," he said, "We give thanks to Uta for all these gifts and we give thanks to Chuku for the rain and our crops. We give thanks that we have had a good planting season which gives us the ability to share with others." A cheer went up. "We ask a blessing for all the gifts, for those who gave so generously of their crops. We ask a blessing for those who will receive these gifts, that anything they receive will be a blessing to them." A murmur of assent went up from everyone and they began to sing words of praise and thanks.

As everyone disbanded and moved forward into the circle, the musicians started playing again some soft, soothing music. The women began serving food to the children and finally the adults. As everyone ate, some sitting on the ground, others standing in groups, the dancers came forward and the circle was cleared for them to dance. The dance group was made up of young girls who were dressed in pretty wraps. They started singing and swaying to the songs. They danced beautifully and everyone clapped and cheered boisterously when they finished. Children were always praised whether they did badly or not. However, this group had done really well and was given extra praise. The girls went away with smiles on their faces. Then the boys danced and were praised in like manner.

Having eaten, everyone stood around in groups talking and generally having a good time. Maimuna stood by Akapwon, as usual. They were talking to Tutaba and Shema. It was a heated discussion and they were fully occupied. As she argued with Tutaba, supporting his wife's point of view, she felt someone caress her on her bottom. She thought it was Akapwon and glanced at him, surprised that he would do such a thing in public, something that he had never done before in the privacy of their home. However, she saw that he was using both his hands, gesturing as he spoke. Quickly she turned around but it was too late. There was no one near enough to touch either of them. As reaction set in she began to shake. She reached out to Akapwon and he turned to her in concern as he felt the tremors run through her.

Taking one look at her face he excused himself and her.

"Please excuse us, Tutaba, Shema. Maimuna is not feeling well." Before they could respond, he walked Maimuna quickly away from them, heading toward their home.

Shema and Tutaba looked after them in surprise and shock. Akapwon hurried Maimuna along but once their home came into view, before they reached the gate, Maimuna stopped and could not move; sobs wracked her body. Akapwon was greatly alarmed. His alarm grew as she would not or could not be comforted. Finally, in desperation he lifted her up in his arms and hurried with her into the house. A single lamp was burning on the kitchen table but it was enough to light his way as he entered their bedroom and placed her on the bed. She immediately turned aside and buried her head in the pillows sobbing as if her heart was breaking. Lighting the lamp near the bed, he hurried out to the kitchen. Soon he returned with a tray which he placed on the small table by the bed. Maimuna always left some embers burning on the fire hearth so there was always a full kettle of heated water, although the embers were not enough to cause the water to come to a boil.

"Maimuna." He shook her shoulders slightly. "I have brought you some hot bush tea. It will help calm you down so you can tell me what happened. She sat up slowly and accepting the cup that he held out to her and obediently sipped the tea. She drank half the cup and handed it back to him.

Before he could ask what happened, she explained in a husky tear-filled voice. "It was him! I am certain it was him." She looked at Akapwon, tears streaming down her beautiful face. "He caressed my bottom. I thought it was you but when I looked at you, both your hands were in front of you." She buried her face in her hands and sobbed. "I cannot bear this anymore, Akapwon. I feel as if I'm going crazy. I never see who it is."

Akapwon sat on the bed and pulled her into his arms. He rocked her gently back and forth, running his hands up and down her back comfortingly as he repeated over and over, "It is all right, Maimuna. I will find out who it is. It is all right. It will be all right." In the lemongrass tea he had made for her, he had dropped a generous piece of bark that was used to soothe the nerves. It was a fast-acting sedative and he knew it was only a matter of minutes before she fell asleep. Rocking her back and forth he continued to comfort her until the bark took effect and she fell into a deep asleep. After making sure she was comfortable, he went outside to sit on the steps.

He felt helpless, frustrated and furious all at the same time. A feeling of despair was taking hold because he did not know how to begin or where to look to find such a person. Before he had time to sit, he saw Tutaba and Shema hurrying through the gate. He stood where he was and sought to compose himself before they reached him.

As Shema and Tutaba had watched their friends hurry away, Shema had turned to her husband, "Something is not right, Tutaba. It is not like Akapwon to be so rude. Look at the way Maimuna is walking. He is almost carrying her."

Tutaba nodded but said, "We must not interfere, Shema.

I agree that Akapwon did not mean to be rude. He seemed very concerned about Maimuna. Let us go home. We shall find out tomorrow what is wrong."

"No, Tutaba. I cannot just walk away from this. He is your friend and he would not walk away from you either. We must follow them and make sure everything is all right before we go home. Perhaps we can help in some way."

Tutaba was reluctant to interfere but he had to admit that she was right. He could not just walk away from his friend. After considering it, he said, "You are right, Shema. If it were I behaving as differently as he has behaved, he would have followed me and made inquiries. But you know I am reluctant to interfere."

Shema shook his arm. "It is not interference, my husband, but concern that prompts me to follow. Does it seem like interference to you?" She looked at him with a trace of anger in her eyes.

Tutaba looked at her and smiled. "That fierce look in your eyes assures me that you are not interfering." He put his arm around her and said, "Let us go." And they hurried after Akapwon and Maimuna. As they hurried through the gate, Akapwon was standing on the steps.

"What is the matter, Akapwon?" Tutaba asked anxiously. "Why did you and Maimuna leave so quickly? Is she all right?"

"She is well but has gone to sleep, Tutaba. I gave her a tea with the sleep bark. Thank you for asking. Please forgive us for walking away so abruptly."

Shema did not give him a chance to finish speaking. Catching her breath she asked, "Is something wrong with her, Akapwon? Is she hurt?"

She was anxious that something might be wrong with her friend. However, her interruption gave Akapwon time to think. He knew that he could not reveal what had happened to Maimuna. It was something between himself

129

and Maimuna alone. Knowing how the village liked gossip, there would be an endless litany of questions which both he and Maimuna were not prepared to answer. He did not want any speculations on the part of others. As her husband, he was bound to protect her from physical harm and from the harm of gossip. If he was unable to protect her from the former so far, at least he could protect her from the latter. When Shema calmed down he bid her and Tutaba to sit down.

"I have just made some tea." He had made a pot for himself and without asking if they would like to have some, he entered the house and preparing a tray, brought them tea and slices of Maimuna's delicious bun. As they sat sipping the tea he spoke to Tutaba.

"To answer your question, Tutaba, I apologize to you and Shema for leaving so abruptly. Maimuna was feeling ill and I wanted to get her home."

"Ill?" Shema asked. "What is wrong with her? Did she throw up her food?"

He paused for a moment before answering, then plunged in. He knew Maimuna would understand but it was also only fitting that he should tell his friends and ask them to keep their confidence. "We are expecting a baby. Maimuna is pregnant and she wasn't feeling well. But I was concerned for her and so I brought her home. Again, I am sorry we left so abruptly but it is a new experience for me and I just wanted her to be all right." Akapwon was taken by surprise at their reaction.

Throwing her arms around him and hugging him as she laughed with delight, Shema said, "That is wonderful news, Akapwon. You are going to be a father!"

With a little more restraint, Tutaba grabbed his hand and pumped his arm as he grinned, "Congratulations my friend. This is good news indeed. Shema and I had wondered if that was what was wrong with her. At first we decided not to follow you but then we discussed it and we had to come and see if we could help in any way, but we never expected such good news!"

Akapwon could not help but be affected by their mood and he laughed, well-pleased. When they had calmed down and were sitting once more he spoke.

"I must ask you both to keep it to yourselves just until tomorrow evening. We have not told anyone as yet. You are the first to know. We will tell both our parents tomorrow as soon as Maimuna feels well enough to visit them. I know that Maimuna will agree that this is a great opportunity to tell both parents at the same time. I know my mother will be happy to be a grandmother and I am sure Maimuna's mother will be too."

"If that is what you wish, then it is done. We will speak of it to no one until your father informs his friends." Tutaba and Shema had two sons of their own and were eager to advise him on what to expect. "It was the happiest moment of my life when Shema told me we were going to have a baby. It is a good feeling is it not, Akapwon?"

"Yes Tutaba, it is a very good feeling indeed." They chatted for a while longer and when Tutaba and Shema left, he went in to check on Maimuna. Because of the tea he had given her, she seemed so relaxed in sleep, as if she had not a care in the world. "That is how she should always be." He thought. "If only I could give her that peace."

He thought about the baby that was on the way and wondered what he or she would be like. He had never given it much thought until Tutaba's and Shema's reaction. To him, it had merely been a symbol of his ruined wedding night. However, he felt no more anger towards Maimuna. He had managed to overcome what he had felt that night because of Maimuna herself. She was such a willing worker and a good companion and she was so kind and sweet, he could not stay angry with her.

Now however, the baby had become a reality. It was only by chance that he thought of it as an explanation to Tutaba and Shema for his actions, but it was a good enough reason. The news would be all over the village by tomorrow evening and he had to prepare Maimuna for their reaction. He knew that everyone would be happy for them. A first baby was a great event. He or she would be the village's baby, not only his and Maimuna's. As he lay next to Maimuna his mind continually dwelled on the baby until he fell asleep.

At breakfast, he had a long discussion with Maimuna, which was geared toward preventing such an occurrence from ever happening again. Akapwon wished that her parents lived nearby to accompany her whenever she went to the market. Since they already knew everything, it would help to discuss it with them and get their ideas as to the best course of action. However, they did not live in Monabu and informing them of this new problem would only cause them extreme anxiety. He did not want that to happen. As a matter of fact, he felt quite sure that if he told them, they would offer to uproot themselves and move to Monabu to be near her and to try to protect her.

His planting and tending his crops kept him out in the field and sometimes Maimuna had to attend the market by herself. That would have to stop and they agreed that she would only go to the market if he accompanied her. Leaving his dogs with her when he was in the field had proved to be most valuable, especially when they protected against Umar's stupidity or anyone else for that matter. Akapwon told Maimuna he would make a whistle for her to hang around her neck at all times. Now, he told her, he would train his dogs to never leave her side while she was in the field. He also cautioned her to never to be alone in the field or anywhere where anyone could get to her without others seeing.

When they had exhausted all their ideas and finally felt a small degree of satisfaction about how they should handle the situation, he told her about Tutaba and Shema.

"I am relieved that they finally know about the baby." Maimuna said, "Because, as you can see, Akapwon, I am getting to a point where it will soon be difficult to hide my condition even though I am binding my abdomen. Also, I did not like deceiving my new friends."

"I swore them to secrecy until we tell both our parents." Akapwon told her. "It is a good thing your mother and father are here. We can tell both our parents together. If you are up to it, I would like us to go over there and tell them today."

Maimuna nodded. "Yes. It will be nice to be able to discuss it with my mother and your mother. I have been longing to ask questions about the babe."

Akapwon had not thought about that. He only then realised that she must have been worried at times, especially if she felt sick or apprehensive about something else she might be feeling. She must have wanted someone to talk to. It was only then that he remembered that this was something new to her and that she must be worried, never having had a child before.

"Maimuna, why did you not tell me about what you were feeling?"

She looked embarrassed and lowered her eyes. "I was too ashamed, Akapwon, because it is not your child and as a man, I felt you must resent my being pregnant with someone else's child."

"Maimuna, look at me." He waited until she looked up. "I do not blame you for something that was not your fault. And how could I possibly resent an innocent babe? If you want to talk about anything, Maimuna, anything, I will be very willing to talk with you. Do you understand?" He reached over as she was about to lower her eyes and lifted her chin so she was forced to look at him. "Will you promise me you will let me know if anything is bothering you, Maimuna?"

She looked at him for a long moment and then she smiled shyly. "If you are sure you do not mind, I will, my husband." Her smiled widened slightly, "It would be nice to be able finally to talk to you about what I'm feeling. At times, I have wanted to very badly."

"No holding back any more, Maimuna. Do you understand? I will be happy to learn along with you. I too think it will be nice to talk about it."

Later they walked over to his parents' house. Both sets of parents were happy to see them.

"Come in. Come in and have a refreshing drink. It is very hot today, is it not?" Kinefe was all smiles and happy to see them. They had so little time to visit in the harvesting season.

Tifi entered the room with a tray and a clay pitcher filled with a lime and tamarind drink. It was a popular cooling and refreshing drink during the hot seasons and they were glad to receive it. They sat chatting for a while and then Akapwon told them the reason why they had come.

"Maimuna and I have come to tell you something." He forced himself to look very grave as he watched their faces. He saw concern begin to show in Maimuna's parents' eyes and he did not have the heart to prolong their anxiety. Taking Maimuna's hand in his he stood up, bringing her with him. "We are expecting a baby."

But before he was actually finished speaking, Tifi let out a squeal of delight. She rushed over and hugged Maimuna. "A baby! We are going to be grandparents, Kinefe."

Her parents were equally as ecstatic but for a different reason. For a terrible moment, they thought that Akapwon was about to tell them he was divorcing her. Instead, their hearts were full at the way he made it seem to his parents that it was something that just recently occurred. They were also relieved that at last it was out in the open. Both of them had been afraid that someone would see she was pregnant and start calculating. Now that it was out in the open, everyone would be happy for the young couple and would have no reason to question anything.

As her mother hugged Maimuna, she whispered," Everything will be all right now, Maimuna, you will see. As soon as Akapwon sees the babe he will forget everything else."

It was not long before Akapwon's proud father was sharing the news with his neighbours. As the news got out, wherever they were seen, the villagers approached the young couple and congratulated them. Everyone was happy for them and looked forward to the new baby as if it were their own. All except for one, who watched the shared laughter and congratulations resentfully.

"That baby is mine! Everyone should know that I am the father!" And when he realised he could not claim fatherhood, anger blazed in him. Unreasonably, he wanted it to be known that he was the father and because he could not, he seethed with resentment and so he plotted.

*

Accosting Akapwon in the field one day, Boboda said gravely to him, "So, you are going to be a father."

Not sensing his mood, Akapwon smiled. "Yes. Is it not amazing? I never thought about it before this."

"Well you should think about it carefully, Akapwon! A baby is a serious matter and you have to be prepared to give it all the love you can. I will not tolerate you not giving this baby all the love it deserves!"

Akapwon looked at him in surprise. He was even more surprised to see how serious Boboda was. When he realised his seriousness, he answered gravely, "When the child is born, I will give him or her all the love I am capable of giving, Boboda. Does that ease your mind?"

Boboda merely nodded and turning abruptly, he walked away.

Perplexed by his attitude, Akapwon stared after his friend. As his eyes watched Boboda's receding back, his mind dwelled on what had just transpired. Then it dawned on him. He heaved a sigh as he realised that Boboda was concerned that Akapwon should not neglect his child the way his own mother had neglected him. His mind and body relaxed, sure in his assumption that he was correct.

26

A T the appropriate time, Maimuna, who had been binding her stomach so that she would not appear too large, strapped herself less restrictively although she still dressed carefully. She allowed her pregnancy to show, but not too much. Everyone was happy for the young couple and thought they made a handsome pair.

As Maimuna sat on the steps by her door, Timpi came to visit her. "Good day, Maimuna." Timpi smiled.

Maimuna smiled in return as she stood to greet Timpi. "Good day, Mother, it is good to see you."

They chatted for a while and finally Timpi came to the reason for her visit. "Maimuna, I do not know if Akapwon has told you that I am a midwife, that I have delivered most of the babies in this village?"

Maimuna smiled at her, "Yes, Mother, he has told me."

"Would you allow me to deliver your baby when the time comes?" Timpi asked.

"Oh yes, Mother, I was going to visit you to ask you if you would consider delivering our baby. I could not think of having anyone else deliver our baby. I am happy to know that you are willing to help us. Akapwon told me you delivered him also and therefore I will feel safe with you."

Timpi smiled, very pleased. "You have made me very happy. But you know, Maimuna, it is not only about delivering the baby. I will have to examine you a few times before the baby is due to be sure it is doing well and to be sure that you are healthy and not in any discomfort."

Maimuna looked puzzled. "Examine, Mother?"

Timpi reached out to touch her abdomen but Maimuna drew back. Timpi was surprised and looked at her keenly. "I am sorry, Mother, but I do not like to be touched."

Timpi was puzzled, "You do not like to be touched? But does not Akapwon touch you?"

Maimuna was embarrassed "That is different, Mother. He is my husband."

"And I am your medicine woman. I must examine the baby to tell you when it is going to arrive. By examine, I mean feeling the shape of the baby, listening to the heart-beat, seeing the progress it has made in coming nearer to the entrance of the womb; examining things like that so you can be safe and healthy for the delivery."

Maimuna was impressed, "You can tell all of that just by examining me?"

"Yes, I can. I have learned from Momo, the medicine woman before me as she learned from the medicine woman before her. This knowledge passes down, you see."

Maimuna nodded, "I understand."

"So shall we go inside so I can examine you, Maimuna? This way, we can tell how far along in your pregnancy you are and we will know when the baby is due."

Panic blazed through Maimuna. The knowledge that Timpi could tell how far along she was by examining her frightened her. She sought to control her panic. She had thought Timpi would accept it when she told her she did not like to be touched. She did not want Timpi to see how large she really was. If she examined her, with all she had just said, she would know that Maimuna was too far along from the time she and Akapwon got married. Taking a deep breath she said, "I am sorry, Mother, but I do not like to be touched. I cannot let you examine me."

Timpi's mouth fell open, "I have never heard such a thing. Do you not care to be sure that your baby is healthy?"

"Of course I do, Mother. I am being very careful about what I eat and Akapwon and I go for long walks so that I can exercise. I do not wish to be examined, Mother. I am sorry."

Timpi was clearly upset. "This does not make sense to me. However, I will let you think about it. We will talk again tomorrow."

However, when tomorrow came, Maimuna still refused to let Timpi examine her. This caused Timpi to be suspicious and she started to study Maimuna unobserved. Finally, when she was satisfied with what she saw, she approached Akapwon.

"Akapwon," Timpi called, coming up to him. "May I speak with you for a moment?"

"If you do not mind walking with me to the fields, Mother, I have much to do today."

Timpi fell into step with him and they walked in companionable silence for a while. Finally when they were away from prying ears, she said what was on her mind.

"Akapwon, I visited Maimuna a few days ago to talk about the baby."

He smiled at her as they walked, "Yes, I know. She told me. Thank you, Mother, for offering to help Maimuna deliver our baby."

Timpi nodded absentmindedly. She had delivered Akapwon and watched him grow into the fine man he was today. This was a delicate matter and she did not wish to hurt him but it must be said. "Akapwon," she touched his arm as she stopped.

Akapwon also stopped as he turned to face her. "Yes, Mother?"

"Did you notice anything different about Maimuna on your wedding night? Did she act as a bride should?"

Akapwon looked at her in surprise. This was the last thing he expected her to ask. His senses were immediately alerted. "Why do you ask such a question, Mother?"

"Son, I do not wish to hurt your feelings but I think Maimuna has deceived you."

His face was void of expression as he asked, "Why would you say such a thing about Maimuna, Mother. She has been a good wife to me. Why would you suggest this to me? So that I may grow to dislike her?"

Quickly Timpi responded. "No, no, no Akapwon. Please do not think that." She paused. It was difficult to tell a husband that his wife might have slept with another man. She had kept this counsel to herself because she did not want any rumours started about Maimuna. She knew it would ruin their marriage.

"Akapwon, I have reason to believe that Maimuna is further along in her pregnancy than she has told you." She studied his face as she spoke and saw shock in his eyes. She felt compassion for him.

However, Akapwon was shocked for a different reason than she thought. He had heard how accurately midwives could tell when a baby was due. Obviously he and Maimuna had overlooked this fact and he was not prepared for what his response should be. He took refuge in anger and asked somewhat roughly. "What are you saying, Timpi, that Maimuna has been unfaithful to me?'

"Akapwon," she rested her hand on his arm again. "I am not only a midwife, I am a medicine woman and if you do not know, you must have heard that we can tell when a baby is due. I have other skills besides delivering babies. Maimuna is larger than she should be and the shape of her body is that of a more advanced pregnancy."

Regretting his outburst, Akapwon spoke more gently. "Maybe the baby is larger than usual, Mother. That happens sometimes, does it not?"

"Not with Maimuna. She is not a large woman. She also refused to let me examine her, which she has no reason to do. She is hiding something, Akapwon, and I do not wish to see you get hurt."

"Perhaps you are mistaken then."

Timpi lost her patience with him and stood back. "Are you trying to tell me, Akapwon, that I do not know what I am speaking to you about?" She raised her voice. "I am a midwife." She jabbed her chest with a finger as she spoke. "I have been delivering babies before you were born. Do not insult me, Akapwon. I have come to tell you this so that you are aware. I did not want you to be upset should any gossip start."

"What gossip, Mother?" He reached out and held her by her upper arms. "Has anyone been gossiping about us?"

"No, Akapwon." She moved out of his hold. "I believe I am the only one to notice. Ama, whom I am now training, does not know enough to notice. However, as Maimuna grows bigger, she will notice and also other women might begin to notice."

Akapwon sighed and started walking again. He had to trust Timpi for she might approach his parents about it and he did not want that. They walked in silence for a while and then he stopped her and bid her sit on a log nearby.

"Timpi, can I trust you?"

"What do you mean, can you trust me?" She was offended. "You wish to insult me again?"

"No, Mother, but what I tell you must remain with you only. Can I trust you, Mother?" He watched her face alertly for any change of expression or nuance of change.

Her face was expressionless as she spoke. "I am a medicine woman. You would be surprised, Akapwon, at what I know about the people of this village. The first priority in training someone who eventually replaces us, is to find someone with high integrity, who does not gossip. We take a long time to choose this person. I have studied Ama for two years before choosing her, as Momo did when she chose me. Does that answer your question?"

"Yes." Akapwon smiled apologetically. "I do not ask for myself but for Maimuna." He paused for a long while, going over in his mind what he should say. Finally he opted for the truth. "You see, Mother, Maimuna was raped, brutally."

Timpi drew in her breath in shock and her consternation grew as she listened to him. Finally, when he was through, she asked, "Does your mother know?"

"No. No one knows but Maimuna's parents, myself and now you. I would not have told you Mother, except I knew that it would look strange for you not to be visiting Maimuna as you have the other expectant mothers in Monabu."

Timpi wrung her hands, "How terrible for such a young person to endure this. Have they found who did it?"

"No, Mother." He thought for a moment. "It is best that she does not know that you know, Mother. She would be too embarrassed to face you if she knew that you knew."

"It is such a burden to bear, Akapwon, and I have only added to it by pressing her to let me examine her." She thought for a moment. "I will visit her and tell her that I respect her wishes and ask her if I can visit her from time to time. She will not know that I have knowledge of what she has been through, I promise you, nor will anyone else."

Relief to Akapwon was instant and sharp and he said simply. "Thank you, Mother. I cannot help but feel that if the village knew her plight, they would either pity her or gossip about her. In either case, Maimuna would be hurt and people's attitude toward her would change. It is best that no one knows. Can you understand that?"

"Yes. Although I had no intention of telling anyone, Akapwon. Looking at it from your point of view, I have to agree. Villagers being the way they are, would soon start wondering if she was lying and they would start looking at her differently. And you are right, she would suffer for it."

They talked for a while and when finally Timpi rose to leave. She apologized. "I am sorry I was angry with you, Son. It was just my false pride speaking."

Akapwon smiled, "It is nothing, Mother. I apologize for pushing you to that point."

They both laughed. Timpi paused as she stared at him intently. Finally she spoke. "Akapwon, I wish you to know that my opinion of you has risen greatly. By all rights every man in this village would have ended her life that night, but you did not. You are an amazing man, Akapwon. I am truly impressed by your restraint. Maimuna is a truly lucky woman."

"No, Mother, I am the lucky one. She is sweet and strong and amazing herself."

Timpi smiled, leaned over and kissed him on the cheek then turned and walked away. "Do not worry, Son. She will be all right. I will look after her."

27

HOWEVER, Maimuna was not all right. As time went by, she became less and less interested in everything around her. Although Akapwon tried to engage her in the progress of the planting and gossip of the village, she would only smile and look at him while he spoke but he could tell she was not listening. He was worried that she seemed to be losing interest in life. As they worked in the fields he thought about her and kept glancing her way. Being accosted by her assailant had taken its toll. Her strength, the only thing that had kept her going after the rape, was being eroded by each encounter. He realised that being touched so intimately as she had described, had been too much for her to bear. He imagined that it must have felt like another assault on her person.

He felt a trickle of fear when his mother said to him one day, "Akapwon, have you noticed anything different about Maimuna? Have you noticed that she does not take part in our conversations anymore?"

"Yes, Mother, I have noticed and it concerns me. She does not seem to be interested in anything these days. I have tried everything to get her interested but she just smiles. She seems to listen, but I know that she is not really listening at all."

"I have noticed that her mind wanders away from whatever is happening around her. I think it is time you asked Timpi to talk to her, Akapwon."

"If Timpi can help her, I will be very grateful."

Akapwon saw Timpi in the marketplace the following

day and spoke to her about Maimuna's condition. After he explained Maimuna's behaviour to Timpi, she assured him it was normal for some women to behave as she was behaving.

"In treating expectant mothers, I have noticed that some of them become melancholy during their pregnancy. I will speak to Maimuna so that I can know exactly what her symptoms are."

"Thank you, Timpi. I would be very grateful if you do."

Timpi reported back to him the next day. "Maimuna is a little dejected, Akapwon, and she needs to be encouraged to take an interest in what's going on around her, otherwise her melancholy can increase and that would not be a good thing. If you can get her interested in anything, it will help. Once she shows interest in whatever you tell her, then she will be all right."

However, Akapwon's concern grew, because he felt that she was encasing herself in a shell so as not to feel or be afraid. He remembered Timpi's advice and it came home to him that if he did not break her out of her present melancholy, he could lose her all together. Nothing occupied his mind more and he doubled his efforts to interest her in something, anything -- until one day he came up with an idea. He approached her about it. She was sitting on the steps with her back resting against the door jam, staring into space.

"Maimuna, how are you feeling?"

"I am well, my husband." She answered automatically.

"Are you tired?"

"Only a little discomfort, Akapwon," she answered listlessly. She wished he would go away so she could just sit there.

He stooped in front of her so that they were eye to eye. She was then forced to look at him. "Would you like to visit your mother and stay for a while?" He watched as she sat up straighter and a smile spread across her face. As usual, her smile took his breath away. But he had seen those smiles so rarely these days. She actually looked happy.

"Can I?" But quickly her smile faded. "But I do not want you to come home to an empty house and a cold fire with no food."

He took one of her hands and massaged it between his. "It is nothing you need to worry about, Maimuna. I have taken care of myself before. I know how to cook. You do not have to worry about me. You can stay with your parents for the planting season and then I will come for you. You should worry about nothing except to feel well. Do you wish to visit them for a while?"

"You are sure this is all right, Akapwon? You will take care of yourself?"

Seeing the light come back to her eyes was payment enough for how much he would miss her. He would do anything to make her happy. "So it is settled then?" He smiled into her eyes and repeated the question. "You wish to go to visit your parents?"

"Yes! Oh yes. I would very much love to see my mother and father and visit them for a while."

"Then it is settled. It will take me a little while to prepare a cart comfortable enough for you. In the meantime, you can gather together what you want to carry with you." She stood up but slowly and it made him realise how awkward it was becoming for her to move about as her pregnancy grew.

"Let us eat before everything gets cold, my husband." She laughed as she walked slowly into the kitchen where she had already prepared the table for their supper. He could not help but feel happy seeing her change from sadness to happiness.

He informed his parents about their journey and they agreed it might be the best thing for Maimuna. His mother

146

understood that sometimes expectant mothers felt sad for no reason and she felt that seeing her own mother would lift Maimuna's spirits.

Akapwon took the cart that he used to bring his produce from the field and altered it a little to suit his passenger. It was large enough for Maimuna to lie down when she got tired of walking. He made it shallow enough for her to catch the breeze and built a collapsible canopy for shade from the sun. It would take some days of travelling because it would be slow going for her comfort and he knew he would have to take frequent rests so as not to make it a rough journey for her. So he took some of his rugs and padded the cart, putting the softest on top. Finally he was ready to transport her to her parents' home.

Maimuna got ready her clothing and anything else she wanted to carry so that Akapwon could put the basket on the shelf he had built under the cart for that purpose. On the day everything was ready, they left before sunrise. The road outside of Monabu was smooth and flat and it was easy for Maimuna to walk beside him. When he felt she had walked enough, he insisted that she sit in the cart. She was so excited, he had to caution her to take it easy in case she should injure herself. Because of her excitement, she was trying to walk faster than her body was able and had to stand still quite often to ease the pressure of the baby. At these times he hovered over her like a mother hen. Near the middle of the day he realised that she was in pain and discomfort. Stopping under the shade of a large tree, he lifted her out of the cart. While she stood near the cart, he arranged some of the rugs on the grass and helped her to sit with her back against the tree so that she would be comfortable.

While she sat and rested, he proceeded to cook a meal for them both with provisions he had brought. Finding some stones, he arranged them in a circle and placed some twigs and pieces of wood to make a fire. Then he placed a pot half full with water he got from a stream nearby and proceeded to boil some sweet potatoes which he had peeled. He had brought some meat left over from their meal the night before and proceeded to warm it up. The meal was simple but nourishing. After they had eaten, he bid her sleep. She protested and wanted to go on but he could see fatigue in her face. Finally when he could not convince her to rest, pretending that he was tired, he told her that in fact he was the one who needed the rest. Only then did she relent. She was very upset and very contrite, begging his forgiveness for being so selfish.

"Do not worry, Maimuna" he told her. "I will get you home as soon as possible."

"Oh no, Akapwon." She pleaded, "Take as long as you need. I am sorry that I tried to rush you."

He kissed her cheek and after she lay down, he lay next to her. In a short while she was asleep and he was glad he had insisted that she rest. He stretched out beside her and watched her as she slept, marvelling again at her beauty. He had found that her beauty was equal to her courage. His mother was right. He had certainly learned from her and he hoped she had learned from him.

As he watched Maimuna sleep, Akapwon thought about how much courage it must have taken for her to get up and make him breakfast that first morning, not knowing whether she would live or die that day. She had worked tirelessly beside him in the field even when she must have been ready to drop with fatigue. But because she had made him the promise that she would work hard, she would not stop until he made her stop. Then she would let go of whatever it was that had kept her going and sit on the ground abruptly.

She slept for a while and he dozed a little as he lay beside her, relaxed. When she woke the sun was in mid sky and blazing hot. So he told her they would have to wait for the sun to move a little west when it would be less hot. He made them some relaxing lemon grass tea and as they sipped it they talked.

He cautioned her, "You must try to get as much rest as possible, Maimuna. And do not forget, I will be back to pick you up when I am finished planting."

She laughed. "That I will rest is something you have no need to worry about, Akapwon. My mother will treat me as if I were an invalid and probably will not allow me to get out of bed. So you have no need to worry about my not resting."

Akapwon had sent a messenger ahead to let her parents know that he was bringing her home. On their arrival, her friends and neighbour were waiting to greet her. They had not seen her since her marriage and the ones who had not attended her wedding were curious about her new husband. As Akapwon lifted her from the cart, Oboto and Kaieta rushed forward to greet them,

"Welcome, it is good to see you, Son." Oboto said and Kaieta echoed his greeting.

Amid the good-natured cheering of her friends, he carried Maimuna into her parent's home and laid her on a comfortable chair with a foot rest, which had been prepared for her. Once she was settled, Kaieta brought out a large pitcher of a refreshing drink for everyone, but for Akapwon and Maimuna's father, she brought a mug of cool beer.

Although Maimuna's parents had seen Akapwon many times while visiting his parents, they had not had much opportunity to really talk to him privately and properly thank him for Maimuna's life. This visit gave them the opportunity to do so. At first they were apprehensive when they received the message, wondering if indeed he was returning their daughter under the guise of her being depressed. However, when Maimuna and Akapwon arrived and they saw that she had lost weight instead of gaining weight for her pregnancy, they were immediately concerned and grateful that he had brought her home. There was an aura of tiredness about her which was not due to her journey and it gave them reason to be as concerned as he was.

After the neighbours and friends had visited for a while and left, except for Codou and two others, who accompanied Maimuna to her room, Kaieta reached over and grasping Akapwon's hand, thanked him profusely for her daughter's life and Oboto joined her, expressing his thanks as well.

Akapwon saw this as an appropriate time to speak to them about the incidents in Monabu. While Maimuna and her friends were engaged in conversation in the other room, he spoke softly so that he could not be overheard, and told them what had occurred and that he felt it was the cause of her listlessness and lack of interest in anything. They were shocked to hear that her assailant had actually dared to follow her to Monabu.

"But how did he know where to find her?" Kaieta asked, wringing her hands in her anxiety. "How can she be safe anywhere if he is not even concerned that he might be caught?"

"I do not know, Mother." Akapwon said, giving her the honorary title. "But it is my duty to keep her safe and I will do everything that I can."

Kaieta rested her hand on his arm. "We know you will. But that does not stop me from being afraid. I can understand how afraid she must be. You did not see her, Akapwon, how terribly bruised and beaten up she was." Tears came to her eyes and she excused herself and walked out of the room.

Oboto looked at Akapwon with anger burning in his eyes. "That snake! I would like to get my hands on him."

"As would I!" Akapwon agreed heartily.

"It is only right that he should feel what it is like to be beaten so unmercifully." Oboto was silent for a moment and then said, "Perhaps, Akapwon, it would be best if her mother and I moved to Monabu to look after her while you are in the field. The snake would be much less likely to be as bold as he has been."

Akapwon could understand Oboto's anger because he himself was still very angry, and even though it had been many weeks since the incident he was still angry and had to make a conscious effort to calm himself. "I know, Father, but we will catch him and when we do, he will wish that he were dead. But now she is safe with you and he would not dare follow her here. You do not have to move to Monabu. Between my parents and I, we will find a way to keep her safe." He said that not quite believing it. For if the man had touched her in his presence, then he respected no one. And his parents were not aware of the incidents. "Although they are not aware of what she went through or of any danger to her now, Mother will be delighted to visit her while I am in the field and Timpi visits her quite regularly now."

Kaieta returned to the room, more composed than when she left it. She was glad that Maimuna and her friends were in her room, catching up with the latest gossip; otherwise she would have demanded to know what was wrong.

Akapwon told them of the difference in her demeanour after he suggested Maimuna visit them. They could understand now, why she would have been melancholy and why she would slowly lose interest in everything.

Oboto thanked him sincerely again for bringing her home to visit. "We feel certain that she will start to recover quickly."

"I will let her visit you for the duration of the planting season." Akapwon explained, "And then I will return for her."

Kaieta was delighted to hear that. However, like

Maimuna, they were concerned that his wife would not be there to cook for him. "But are you sure you can manage without her being there to care for your needs? Is there any way that we can help?"

He thanked them for their concern but said, "You are already helping by looking after her for me. Because she is here with you and safe, I can work hard and plant my crops without having to worry about how she is doing. I know that she is in the best possible hands and that takes a load off my mind. "Besides," he said, "Mother is already looking forward to my visits. She said she is looking forward to the brief time I will be taking my meals with them."

It was only then that they relaxed and admitted again that they were happy to have her visit them, "Since she is our only child, we have missed her very much."

Akapwon got up to leave but was pressed into staying for supper. He accepted but warned them that he would be leaving immediately after they had eaten. Supper was a pleasant experience with friendship extended to him by Maimuna's closest friends, and by the neighbours who had accompanied the family before Chief Kofo. Very soon it seemed, it was time for him to leave. He wanted to start out before dark and he was sufficiently rested to begin the journey. Taking leave of Maimuna's parents, he then kissed Maimuna's cheek as he bid them all goodbye.

He was given gifts for his mother and vegetables from their garden to take back with him. It was customary that whenever someone visited a home, they never left without a gift. No matter how small a gift, they were never allowed to leave empty handed.

When Akapwon kissed Maimuna's cheek, her friends giggled and her parents were filled with hope that perhaps the couple were beginning to love each other.

He started his journey back as the sun began its descent

but he was not too concerned because he could move faster since his load was light. He returned with the cart because he needed it to transport his produce from the field. Some of his crops, like the corn and the sweet potatoes he planted, would be ready for reaping quite soon. They should be ready shortly after Maimuna's return.

On his arrival in Monabu, he stopped by his parents' home, tired but knowing there would be a hot meal waiting. As usual there was always extra food because one never knew when a visitor would come calling. More accurately, the women of the village always expected a visitor and so they always cooked more than was needed and always had something to offer should a guest arrive unexpectedly.

As he entered his former home, he saw that Umar had arrived, probably "unexpectedly" as he usually did.

"It is good to have you back, Son. How is Maimuna? No doubt she was happy to visit her family?"

"Yes, Mother. She was very happy to see her parents. I feel she will recover more quickly now. Her parents sent these vegetables for you and father. They are always very generous."

"Yes, they are. So Maimuna will remain for the planting season?" His father asked.

"Yes, Father. I thought if she stayed too briefly, healing might not take place."

"You are right, Son. I am sure it also gives you ease of mind for your planting."

"Since Maimuna is not here, Father, I can help you with your planting. Tutaba has helped me a great deal and now I am ahead with my planting. I will also help him with his because I know by helping me he must be somewhat behind. When I am finished helping him, Father, I will help you." His father began to protest but Akapwon held up his hand. "Father, you know that with the two of us working,

Tutaba and I will be finished much more quickly than if we each were working alone. I will help you, Father. I am sure you can use some help. Am I not correct?"

His father smiled, "Of course you are right, Son. It will be nice to receive your help."

Throughout the conversation, Umar remained silent but followed the conversation intently. Then suddenly he asked, "Has Maimuna been ill?"

Everyone turned to look at him in surprise. They had almost forgotten he was there. Akapwon answered, "She has been feeling a little tired lately. We felt it would be good for her health if she visited her parents."

Umar nodded. "Yes, I see. It sounds like a good idea."

*

Akapwon worked very hard. Even though he felt great satisfaction when he looked at the healthy seedlings coming up and even though he tried to bury himself in the planting, he still felt lonely. He missed Maimuna very much and walked through his home at night remembering her at the fire hearth, remembering how she always served him breakfast with a smile. He was amazed at how quickly she had become a part of his life.

Her parents kept him informed of her progress and he was glad to hear that she was actually taking an interest in life once again and that she was even going for short walks with her friends. She had actually started to regain some of the weight she had lost, they told him. Her friends visited her often and they had lively conversations. They were happy to say that she seemed to be on the road to recovery from her melancholy.

28

AFTER what seemed like ages to him, Akapwon was ready to return to Twee to pick up Maimuna. When he arrived, her mother greeted him enthusiastically as she invited him into her home. Her father was in the field.

"Come in, Akapwon." she said happily. "Please have a seat." After they both sat, she told him that Maimuna was not feeling well enough to travel. He stood up, immediately concerned.

"Is she still ill?" He asked her.

"Oh no, no." She hastened to assure him. "Just a slight temperature and she has been sleeping a lot. But we know that sleep is good for her recovery. She is in bed at the moment, sleeping. I was wondering, would it be very inconvenient for you to return in a few days?"

Akapwon was sensitive to her politeness where before she had been effusive. He felt something was not right but agreed he would come back. "I cannot return in the time you asked, but I will be back as early as I can. I hope that she will then feel well enough to travel."

"I am sure she will be." Kaieta breathed a sigh of relief. "Can I offer you some food before your return home?"

He accepted because it would shorten his journey if he did not have to stop to eat. He asked to see Maimuna and Kaieta asked him to wait while she straightened up the room. She returned shortly and he entered the room where Maimuna slept. She seemed more relaxed and rested than she had been at home and so he relaxed somewhat.

Akapwon could not make his return journey to Twee to get Maimuna as quickly as he had anticipated. When he finally arrived, Maimuna's mother rushed forward to greet him. She seemed very nervous and after chatting with him for a while she asked, "Akapwon, could you give us some time to get Maimuna ready?"

Akapwon became suspicious as she was slightly breathless and her speech was rushed. "I have been urging her to get ready but she is slow to move." Without drawing breath she rushed on. "I would like to take you to meet Chief Kofo. He has expressed a great interest in you and asked if you would be kind enough to visit him. Would you mind very much, Akapwon? We have a lot to be grateful to Chief Kofo for and you would do us an honour to meet him." She took a deep breath as she waited for him to reply.

He studied her intently but finally agreed and they walked over to Chief Kofo's house. Chief Kofo's wife greeted them at the door and gave him an enthusiastic hug, something he had kind of expected Maimuna's mother to do but which she had not done. Chief Kofo, who was standing behind his wife as Akapwon entered his home, took his hand in a very strong handshake. "I am very pleased to meet you at last, Akapwon. We have heard a great deal about you."

Akapwon smiled politely as he was shown a seat and was handed a cool mug of beer. "I am very pleased to meet you, Chief Kofo."

"You have come to collect Maimuna?"

"Yes. As soon as she is ready, we will leave."

"It has been a pleasure to have her here. My wife and I visited her shortly after she arrived. We all feel that she is a lucky young lady."

Akapwon was embarrassed and murmured something

indistinct. There was a slight movement at the door and Sadio walked in. He stopped short as Akapwon stood up. "I am sorry, Father, I did not know you had company."

Chief Kofo smiled and said, "Come in. Come in, Sadio. It is a good time for you to arrive. This is Maimuna's new husband." He turned to Akapwon, "Akapwon, this is my son, Sadio. I am glad of this opportunity for you to meet. Perhaps in the future you will meet many times and become friends." He turned to Akapwon, "You met Codou at the wedding did you not?"

Akapwon's smile was genuine. "Yes, I met her. She is very nice."

"Yes, she is. They, meaning Maimuna, Sadio and Codou, all grew up together."

As his father spoke, Sadio studied Akapwon. He liked what he saw and as they all sat talking, he grew to respect him. Finally Akapwon stood up to leave. "I must be starting back. It is a long journey. I am pleased to have met you. Perhaps one day you will all visit Maimuna and I when she is back to excellent health."

"That would be very nice." Chief Kofo shook his hand and he walked away with Kaieta. When they returned to Kaieta's home, both entered the house, but there was no sign of preparation for Maimuna's return to Monabu. Her mother seemed genuinely puzzled and excused herself as she entered Maimuna's bedroom. Codou and another young lady were there. Maimuna still had not gotten dressed. "What is the meaning of this, Maimuna?"

"I am sorry, Mother. I just did not feel up to getting ready. Would you ask Akapwon to visit the market and I will be ready when he returns?"

Kaieta was angry. She looked at her daughter and her face was closed and stern. "Do you think this is proper behaviour to show to your husband?"

"Oh, Mother, he will not mind waiting," she said carelessly. "I would like to talk to Codou and Meta a little longer. I am sure he will not mind." She smiled sweetly at her mother, who did not respond but merely walked out of the room.

In fact Maimuna was shaking inside. She was afraid to return to Monabu, afraid of what could happen if she returned. Her behaviour was out of character and Codou looked at her with a puzzled frown.

As Kaieta re-entered the visiting room, Akapwon stood up. He was surprised that she was not accompanied by Maimuna. "Is she still ill, Mother?"

Kaieta rung her hands in distress. "No, Akapwon. I am truly sorry. She is not ready and asked if you would visit the market for a bit and she will be ready on your return."

His countenance changed and she could see that he was angry. "Can you give Maimuna a message for me?" He asked in a quiet, deadly cold voice, his face void of the usual friendly smile.

"Of course," Kaieta responded quickly.

When he spoke, the anger in his eyes belied the calm in his voice. "Tell her that when I return, if she is not ready, she should be prepared to remain in your household for as long as she wants to, for I will divorce her." Turning, he left the house before she could voice a reply.

Kaieta stood in shock for a moment. Then entering Maimuna's room she relayed Akapwon's message and walked out. Maimuna sat up in shock. She looked at Codou in disbelief. Codou jumped up and started packing Maimuna's basket.

"What did you expect, Maimuna? You have insulted him not once but twice. You are lucky he did not divorce you on the spot. You have behaved very badly towards him, Maimuna. This is how you return all the kindness he has shown? Do you not remember that you are alive because of him? What were you thinking? First he had to go all the way back to Monabu because you did not feel like getting up. He returns and you are still not ready. Now this. If I were him, even I would have divorced you on the spot!"

Maimuna was frightened because she knew Codou was right. Both young ladies had talked to her and prodded her into getting ready but she had refused and said, "Oh he will wait. He will not mind waiting." Not because she did not want to go, but because she was afraid of hearing that voice again. In her parents' house she was protected but when Akapwon went into the field, she would be entirely on her own. She was more afraid than she would admit even to herself. Now she knew that she had pushed Akapwon too far. Not only would he not wait, but he was fully prepared to divorce her, and he had every right to do so.

When Akapwon returned, Maimuna was waiting in the living area. She watched as he walked in the door. She glanced at his cold features briefly and quickly looked down. "I am ready, my husband."

Akapwon saw fear and embarrassment in her eyes and derived a miniscule degree of satisfaction from it. The cart in which he had brought her stood outside the door. He saw that Maimuna's basket was already on the shelf below. He merely nodded in her direction and after also nodding to her mother who waited anxiously beside her, he held his hand out to help Maimuna up from her seat. Nodding slightly in Codou and Meta's direction, he proceeded to help Maimuna into the cart. Kaieta, together with Codou and Meta, watched from the door. When Maimuna saw how much thought and work he had put into the cart to make her comfortable, tears came to her eyes and she felt truly awful.

Akapwon had added extra padding to make it softer for her and had padded the sides of the cart as well. An extra piece of padded wood could be used for a backrest or a pillow if she desired to sleep. Without speaking to her, and after he had seen to her comfort, Akapwon bowed briefly to the other women and picking up the handles of the cart, walked away. He had not uttered a word. Her mother watched them go with great apprehension.

It was a little later than he had expected to be returning and he would have to walk a little faster so he could cover a good deal of the distance before sunset. All the way home he did not speak. He was furious. When they stopped to rest, he offered her drink and something to eat and sat beside her as they ate. Maimuna was too afraid to speak and so their meal remained a silent one. His visit to the market had not been in vain and he had thought about his purchases. He had picked up some really nice tomatoes and onions from the marketplace while he waited for her. His own onions had not yet come in. He had also been fortunate to get some salt. What they had was getting low.

Not for long was he able to keep his mind off Maimuna. He was unable to stop his seething thoughts. How dare she treat him like that! He was angrier because he had not expected something so callous from Maimuna. She had seemed to be always conscious of how she treated others. Apparently she did not think him worthy of such consideration. He should have left her there and felt a strong urge to turn around and return her to her parents' care. The fact that he was not prepared to let her go out of his life, irked him and fuelled his anger.

They travelled in silence until he stopped again for her to rest. He lifted her out of the cart and placed her on the mat he had prepared. Preparing a light snack, he gave it to her. He was too angry to eat himself but realised that because of the baby, she must be hungry. Although Maimuna was not hungry, she did not dare refuse what he had prepared. She was almost in tears because of his silent treatment of her.

She would give anything to return to the companionship they had shared on the way to her parent's house. Why had she let fear rule her? Now he might never speak to her again and he had probably lost all respect for her.

Why should he respect her now after she had shown him so little respect herself? He had warned her not to shame him and she had practically done that. If there had been men present, they would have been disdainful that he could not control his wife.

When she finished eating, she lay down and closed her eyes. She could not bear to look at his rigid jaw line. When he did finally look at her his eyes were cold. She had brought this on herself. Turning on her side she lay with her back toward Akapwon, where he sat next to her on the grass, his back against a tree, eyes closed. Maimuna could not hold back her tears any longer and they ran silently down her cheek. Her body shook with her silent sobs. Finally and mercifully she fell asleep.

Akapwon watched her as she slept. He was aware that she had been crying but he had made no move to comfort her. Covering her with a light wrap, he watched her as she slept. She had dared to insult him in front of her family. He could not understand what had caused her to do so except that she must be having second thoughts about being married to him. Once she got home and was comfortable with her parents and friends, perhaps she wished to end the marriage. He thought again, that he should have divorced her and left her there.

It was good that she suffered for her behaviour. However, as he watched her, he could not help but admire how beautiful she was and against his will, he felt the anger easing from him. Trying to be fair, he wondered how she must feel having that baby growing inside her. Did she hate it or was it a constant reminder of what she described to him had happened to her? Perhaps he would ask her one day. He felt somehow that her heart was big enough not to wish ill on the child, knowing that it was not to blame.

Angrily he shrugged. He did not know her reasons for behaving as she did and he did not want to let go of his anger just yet. Also, he was not prepared to forgive her or forget it. Maybe sometime in the future he would, but not yet, just not yet. Angrily he turned away.

It was dark when they finally arrived home on the third day after leaving Maimuna's mother's house. Indicating to her to remain in the cart, Akapwon went into the house and lit a lamp. Carrying it to the bedroom, he lit the lamp there and turned back the covers on the bed. Going outside, he lifted her from the cart carefully and taking her inside, placed her on the bed.

"Would you like something to drink before going to sleep?" he asked. His voice and his face were expressionless and so she could not gauge his mood. However, she could still feel anger emanating from him. She marvelled that he could still be considerate of her, even in his anger.

"A cup of tea would be nice. Thank you."

Without a word he turned and left the room. More quickly than she expected, he returned with a cup of steaming hot tea. He placed it on the table next to the bed, within easy reach of her hand. "It is hot. Wait until it cools a little before drinking it."

He left the room and she could hear him outside, unloading the cart. After a while his movements stopped and she assumed that he had finished. Then she smelled the pleasant fragrance of his tobacco floating into the room and guessed correctly that he was sitting at the door. The tea made her drowsy and soon she was asleep. He had mixed some sleep bark in with the lemongrass tea because he knew she was hurting from the long journey and both she and the baby needed a rest.

In the beginning Akapwon puffed angrily on his pipe but after a while he calmed down and could think clearly. He examined his feelings carefully, again knowing that he was not prepared to forgive her just yet. Why, he asked himself, was he so angry? Was it because her mother aided her in her behaviour? He did not think so and therefore, he concluded that it must be because of this side of Maimuna's character he had not seen before. In the end he admitted that his male ego was bruised. He had expected her to be as happy to see him as he had been in coming to pick her up. Instead she had avoided him and did not want to return home at all. What a fool he had been, thinking that she was learning to care for him as he had been learning to care for her. It deflated his ego and bruised his pride and that was why he was angry. Not because she had behaved badly toward him, but because she had not looked forward to seeing him as he had anticipated.

29

WHEN she awoke in the morning, memory rushed back to Maimuna and with it great apprehension. Akapwon was not beside her and she assumed he had gone to the field early. She rushed to have breakfast ready for his return and had just finished placing the porridge on the table when he walked in. "Your breakfast is ready, Akapwon." He merely nodded, walked to the basin in the kitchen and washed his hand then returned to the table. Their meal was conducted in silence. Maimuna was very nervous and hardly ate. He noted she barely touched her food but said nothing. He was waiting for an apology and because he was still very angry, he was glad that she did not speak. He knew that he would have vented his anger with some truly cutting remarks that might be unforgivable in the pain that they would cause. Instead, he ate in silence and returned to the field where she followed him later with the dogs, as they had been doing before she had visited her parents.

Their silence continued for days until Maimuna could bear it no longer. Finally she realised that he would not be the first to speak. Because of fear, she had foolishly waited for him to speak to her, even knowing that by right, she should have spoken first and apologized. She knew that he was still angry but also knew she must face his anger and apologize. One day, after he had returned from the field, after he finished his supper, she spoke to him.

"Akapwon," she said nervously.

He merely looked up and waited for her to speak.

"I apologize for keeping you waiting at my parents'

home and for asking you to return home the first day. I have no other excuse except that I was afraid of returning here. Not because of you," she hastened to say, "but because of that person. I do not wish to be approached by him again and when you are in the field, I am truly afraid."

When she finally lifted her head and looked at him, her eyes swam with unshed tears. Grasping a portion of her wrap-dress in her hands, she proceeded to twist it tightly, trying to control the tremor in her voice. "Please forgive me. I am sorry."

Akapwon leaned back in his chair and looked at her. Thoughts were whirling around in his head. Although he was surprised at her words, his expression remained neutral. So it was not because she did not want to be with him. What she said gave him some relief from his anxiety and anger. It had never occurred to him that she would still be afraid after the precautions they had taken. As he watched her, he happened to glance at the tiny scar that remained under her left eye and then he remembered what she told him happened.

If she were telling the truth, any woman would be afraid. But to find that her assailant was nearby and had actually dared to touch her again, would render most women petrified. She had always seemed so brave and because of that, sometimes he forgot after all that a woman's strength lay mostly in her ability to endure physical hardships, not so much mental and emotional assaults. And although they were not as strong physically as men, their endurance helped them to work equally as hard.

But what he also forgot was that women were highly sensitive and their emotions ran deep. When he thought about it, he could fully understand her reaction to being treated as she had and yes, he could now fully appreciate her fear.

Nevertheless he wanted to bring it home to her, that her

behaviour was not acceptable. Leaning forward in his chair, he demanded that she look at him. When he had her full attention, he said in a deadly quiet voice that had more impact than if he had shouted,

"I can understand your fear, Maimuna. However, I want you to understand that, never – *ever* – again, will you get the opportunity to insult me as you did in front of your mother and your friends. That was your first and last chance. Do you understand me?" He saw the fear in her eyes as her tears silently spilled over.

"I understand, my husband, and I am sorry. I am sorry." A sob escaped her as she continued. "I- I was not thinking. I- I was only concerned with my fear." Unexpectedly she jumped up and came to kneel beside his chair. "Please forgive me, Akapwon. I cannot bear your anger and your silence." Her hand grasped his arm as it lay in his lap. "It will not happen again I promise you. I am very sorry."

She tried but could not control her sobs and Akapwon was hard-pressed to control his emotions. Slowly he rose from his chair and lifting her off the floor, he held her in front of him.

"Calm yourself, Maimuna. You will harm yourself and the babe if you continue this way."

When she continued to cry, he sighed heavily and brought her to lie against his chest as he wrapped his arms around her. His actions seemed only to make her cry harder. Leaning back, he brought her head up. "I am no longer angry with you Maimuna, and I forgive you. Now please stop crying." He begged anxiously, afraid that she would make herself sick.

It took Maimuna a little while to control her crying. Finally she lifted her head from his shoulders. "I am trying but it has b- been so hard b- because I've b- been so mi- miserable. I did not mean to insult you or hurt you, Akapwon. I truly did not."

"I realise that now, Maimuna. Let us put it behind us."

"Thank you, Akapwon. I will try." She said in a voice husky from crying.

"Will you stop crying now?"

She nodded and he reluctantly released her. When he let his arms drop, instead of moving away, she leaned forward and kissed him on his lips and quickly rushed into the bedroom before he could react.

Akapwon stood in shock. That was the first time in their marriage that she had kissed him. Yet it was a hollow victory because he knew it was her relief from fear that prompted her to be bold enough to kiss him. Nevertheless it was an experience to feel her soft lips against his once again. Ever since their wedding when he had felt her lips on his, he had longed to repeat that kiss.

Maimuna waited with apprehension for Akapwon to follow her into the bedroom. There was complete silence for a while. When she heard him go out the front door, she breathed a sigh of relief. She did not know what had come over her, only that she wanted to thank him for letting her off so lightly. Her action was so spontaneous that she only realised what she had done when it was over and then she ran. She wondered what he was thinking. If she knew how that kiss had affected him, she would have had real cause to worry.

Akapwon was not surprised at his body's response to Maimuna's kiss. Her smile affected him. Her touch affected him. In fact, everything about her affected him in some way. He found that he was beginning to love her against his better judgment, against his will even. It was against his better judgment because he could not forget her deception on their wedding night. It was still a bitter pill for him to swallow. And it was against his will because he did not want to love her after her treatment of him.

Later on he went over the reason she had given for not

wanting to come home. He had thought about it for a long time, had come to the conclusion that if what she had told him was true, she was somewhat justified in trying to save her own life. However, he had to do something to ease her fear. Whoever this man was, he was bold and had no respect. If it was someone of their village, it must be someone who did not care about him, perhaps, or maybe anyone. Their village was small and therefore respect was very important in order to live peacefully. Since she said the man had touched her inappropriately in his presence, it meant he felt sure of himself and did not expect to be discovered.

After a long discussion, they agreed that she should begin once more to accompany him to the fields. Instead of joining him later in the day as she was presently doing, now she would leave with him each morning.

Akapwon wanted badly to discuss his feelings with someone other than Maimuna but there was no one. He did not wish to discuss her with Timpi even though he knew Timpi was now her strongest ally. He did not want to involve her further in their lives. He valued his privacy too much. And although Tutaba was his best friend, he felt it would be a burden on him if he knew. It was better to keep counsel with himself and so he visited his favourite spot and poured his heart out to Uta.

30

WHEN they returned from the fields, Maimuna hurried into the kitchen to warm up the food she had cooked earlier. She had made her special meat stew with okra and yam and all the vegetables that Akapwon liked. As the food began to warm the delicious aroma wafted through the house, and Akapwon's stomach rumbled in anticipation. Since the food was not completely ready, he decided to take a bath while she finished warming everything up. When he returned to the kitchen, the table was set and a steaming bowl of stew was placed in front of him as he sat down. He smiled as he looked up to thank her and she returned his smile shyly.

It was a pleasant meal and conversation flowed almost as naturally as before between them. It was a good sign and Maimuna was heartened by that little bit of progress, which to her, was a very precious step forward. Afterwards they met Tutaba and Shema for their usual conversation on the hill and sat under the stars. Tutaba was very entertaining that night telling some very funny stories about himself. As they walked home together, Akapwon put his arm around Maimuna as much to hold her close as to protect her. He felt that the man would not dare come close when he held her close like that. The two couples parted company, Tutaba and Shema were left at their gate and Akapwon and Maimuna continuing on to their home.

As they went inside and closed the door, Akapwon breathed a sigh of relief that they had arrived home without incident. However, had he been aware of the man lurking in the shadow of a tree a short distance from his gate, he would have had cause for alarm. An old navy-blue wrap of Maimuna's which he hung over the window, gave them privacy from prying eyes and Akapwon was glad he had thought of covering the window. It had looked strange to him when he first did it because none of the villages covered their windows. However, he felt it was necessary for Maimuna's protection that no one could follow her movements undetected. When they were both in bed, he put his arm around her and she did not object. Instead she turned toward him and the baby rested between them lying partly on his stomach. Maimuna soon fell asleep but Akapwon lay awake for a long time, painfully aware of his desire for her.

31

A KAPWON took on more and more of the work as Maimuna got larger and larger. When she was in her seventh month, they agreed that she would see to the planting of the vegetable garden he had marked in the area next to their home. If she got the seeds in the ground early, the vegetables would be in early then she would be able to preserve them and have vegetables during the winter rains when it was difficult to grow anything. She was glad of this arrangement because her journeys to the field were becoming more and more difficult, although she would not complain. Akapwon saw her difficulty and used the excuse of the garden to help her without acknowledging to himself that he was concerned for her wellbeing. But he was concerned.

He watched her many times rubbing her back and in the evenings after she had prepared their meal, she would lie flat on her back to rest. Sometimes he would massage her back when he saw how uncomfortable she was. His concern for her grew in spite of himself. By her sweet-temperedness and her catering to his needs, she won him over despite his resolution to keep his distance.

Maimuna could not help but be thankful that Akapwon was fair in his sharing of the workload. She also learned a surprising but very pleasant thing about him. One morning she came into the kitchen a bit late. Having felt ill on rising, she had lain down again and had fallen asleep. Waking suddenly and seeing how late it was, she rushed through her toilet and into the kitchen, only to find that Akapwon had made breakfast. This was something so unheard of in her lifetime and she was sure, in her mother's and grandmother's lifetime, that she stood stock still, staring in disbelief as Akapwon turned from the fire with two bowls of millet porridge in his hands. Coffee was already on the table and smelled delicious. A hot cup of lemon tea was placed in front of where she usually sat.

"Have you seen a ghost, wife?" Akapwon grinned at her obvious surprise.

Recovering herself, she rushed forward and attempted to take the bowls from him but he would not let her.

"Sit down, Maimuna, and allow me to serve you today. I have done this many times for my mother."

Her jaw dropped in surprise, "You have?" She felt foolish because it was all she could think to say as she stared at him, amazed at what she was witnessing.

"Oh yes. My father has done it for us both also. We both love my mother very much you see and we both appreciate how hard she works and how she does not complain. You should hear some of the wives in Monabu. Their men must feel as if they are living with hyenas with the constant jabbering that goes on." He looked at her and smiled a funny little smile. "I saw that you were not feeling well, Maimuna, and thought this might help in some small way."

"Oh no, my husband, this indeed is help in a very big way. Thank you." She smiled at him as she sat down.

Akapwon laughed. "Do not get too comfortable with it, Maimuna. It is not something that I will do for you all the time."

"Oh no, Akapwon," she rushed to assure him. "If you never do it again, I am very happy to have this one time." And because she was so happy with what he must have considered a small gift, but which to her was huge indeed, she laughed and talked more openly than she had ever done with him before.

Akapwon stared at her as they talked; enjoying the animated way she spoke, using her hands and her body to better express herself. She had him laughing at her little anecdotes of people in her village or one of her friends. It was a wonderful day for both of them.

32

IN the weeks that Maimuna had spent visiting her parents, Codou and Maimuna had had many opportunities to talk. As Codou relayed what had occurred between Sadio and herself, Maimuna was shocked when she mentioned his apology.

"Sadio apologized to you?" She looked at Codou in disbelief. "I cannot imagine such a thing."

"Nor can I, even though I was the recipient of his apology." Then she said, in a slightly embarrassed tone. "Since that day, we have spoken often and he has changed. Your misfortune accomplished a great deal because he has changed for the better."

"Oh no, Codou, he has changed because you reflected back to him what he was really like and he did not like what he saw of himself. That is what changed him." Then she looked at Codou and her eyes widened slightly. "You like him!"

Codou gave an embarrassed laugh. "I hope you do not mind, Maimuna, but ever since he has changed, we have been able to have some interesting conversations in the group because he no longer dominates the discussions. As a matter of fact, he remains silent unless someone asks him a direct question. But..." and there she stopped.

"But what?"

"Well, he has asked me if we can be friends. When I asked him what he meant by that, he explained that he liked me and would I be willing to speak with him alone sometimes. I said yes, Maimuna. I hope you do not mind?"

"Why should I mind, Codou? I am happy for you."

Codou lowered her eyes and nodded. "He has changed so much, Maimuna. It is almost like speaking to a different person. Unlike the personality he was before, he is willing to discuss anything with me, even when I ask questions about the Council of Elders."

"He discusses that with you?" Maimuna looked at her friend with new respect. Then she smiled. "I am happy for you, Codou. I hope it turns into more than a friendship if that is what you want."

"I do like him very much, Maimuna, the new Sadio, I mean."

"You will let me know how things develop will you not?"

Codou hugged her friend, "Thank you for understanding, Maimuna."

"I do not quite understand yet, Codou. When you meet again in the marketplace, will you ask him if he would be willing to visit me the next time you come to visit me in Monabu?"

Codou laughed as she hugged Maimuna again. "I was hoping you would ask that."

Maimuna smiled at her friend. "Codou, if he makes you half as happy as being married to Akapwon has made me, then I cannot help but like him for that. Do you wish it to develop into something more than friendship, Codou?"

"I do not wish to spoil what friendship we have right now by thinking about it, but yes, I would like it to become something more."

Maimuna hugged her and laughed. "Then I am certain it will, Codou."

"So you are happy with Akapwon?"

"Yes. I love him dearly. He is so kind and considerate; I cannot help but love him."

"Does he love you, Maimuna? And does he know that you love him?"

"No. He does not know and it is not time yet for me to tell him, perhaps after the babe is born." She paused for a moment, considering. "In answer to your other question, I think he loves me but I think so only because he treats me with kindness and respect. However, I could be wrong."

"If he does not love you now, Maimuna, I am sure he will very soon, for you are every bit as kind and as nice as he.

*

True to her word, Codou visited Maimuna in Monabu not too long after their conversation and she brought Sadio with her. They were accompanied by a few other friends who had not visited before. When these friends saw Maimuna's home, they were filled with praise and told her how beautiful it was and that they wanted one just like hers when they got married. They arrived early in the morning just as Maimuna was about to fix breakfast and Akapwon was due to come back from a short errand. When Maimuna saw Codou standing at her door she let out a squeal of delight and rushed forward as fast as she could and threw her arms around her.

"Codou, it is wonderful to see you!" Then she saw Sadio standing in the yard, looking embarrassed. "Sadio!" she cried out with delight and hurrying down the steps she gave him a quick embrace. "It is good to see you, Sadio."

Akapwon walked up at that moment and observing Maimuna with her arms around another man, something she had never done with him, he moved forward quickly and was about to make an angry retort when he saw Codou watching him. He was so surprised to see her, he stared at her for a moment, then with the pleasure of seeing her and knowing she had come all that way to visit, a smile spread across his face and he hugged her happily. He shook hands with Sadio and was introduced to all of Maimuna's other friends.

"Have you all had any breakfast?" He asked, remembering his manners.

They all said no and he told Maimuna to stay where she was with her friends. He would fix breakfast. When he entered the house, they all turned to Maimuna in shock.

"Does he really mean what he said? Is he truly going to fix breakfast, Maimuna?" They asked her in disbelief.

Maimuna smiled happily at her friends, proud of Akapwon for his generous nature. "Yes he means it. He has done the same for me before."

They all crowded around her wanting to hear more about this extraordinary event. It was a lesson for Sadio who had never heard such a thing before either. He also saw that it did not make less of a man of Akapwon, but in fact added to his stature as far as the women were concerned. As Sadio listened with half an ear he saw Akapwon coming through the door with two chairs. He rushed forward and took them from him and arranged them for the women to sit. When all the chairs and stools were brought out, Sadio helped Akapwon bring out the table where they would eat. Everything was arranged under the tree near the stairs. When Akapwon returned to the kitchen, Sadio followed him.

Sadio was surprised to see a fire hearth inside the room. In all the kitchens he had been in, including that of his parents, the fire hearth was outside and everything else was inside. Akapwon had built a fire hearth table wide enough to hold four pots and with enough space left over for other things. A rim was built around it and he had filled the table with river rocks. In the place where each pot would go, he had placed four large rocks and used small pieces of firewood under each pot for cooking. There was a large basket on the side of the fire hearth filled with kindling and firewood cut into small pieces. The rocky surface was covered with ashes from past fires which made it smooth and much easier to work on.

On the wall behind and above the stove he had cut a hole and covered it with a threadbare piece of cloth to keep out insects but to give the smoke an exit so that the kitchen would not be smoky. Above the stove he had also cut a hole through the roof and inserted a fat reed to afford a second exit for the smoke. The table was waist high and seemed a comfortable height for Maimuna to cook on. Silently admiring the convenience of having the stove inside, Sadio asked Akapwon,

"How can I help?"

"It is all right." Akapwon said, "I will have breakfast ready in a short time. I just have to add some more millet to the porridge that Maimuna was about to start cooking."

"No." Sadio said. "I need to do this. I have never in my life seen another man cook. I would like to learn. Please, if you will show me? Please?"

Akapwon watched him silently for a moment, and then he said one word, "Codou?"

Sadio looked embarrassed but he nodded.

A grin spread across Akapwon's face. "All right," he said, "Maimuna has already collected the eggs from the hen house and has already washed them. There are twelve of them. That should be enough for everyone do you think?"

Sadio agreed it would be enough.

Akapwon pointed to where the eggs were sitting in a basket on the work table nearby. "If you could bring them over here... have you cracked an egg before?"

This time Sadio was truly embarrassed as he shook his head, no.

Akapwon laughed outright. "Okay," he said, "let us start." He proceeded to show him how to prepare breakfast. While the onions were simmering he cracked the eggs in a bowl and showed Sadio how he should scramble them. Then he directed him how to make coffee by putting the ground coffee in a small square of cloth and tying it in a knot. He then dropped the little bundle in the water boiling in the kettle. "This," he said, "is the way that Maimuna showed me. It is much better than the way I used to do it because coffee grounds used to get in my mouth. This way, no grounds."

As the delicious smell of coffee spread through the house and outside to the waiting women who sniffed the air, he proceeded to show Sadio how to scramble the eggs with the onions and how much seasoning to put in. Both men were surprised at how well they got along.

Remembering what Maimuna had done when his parents had come to dinner, Akapwon directed Sadio to the bedroom and told him where to find a cloth for the table. On entering their bedroom Sadio stopped short, surprised and pleased at how beautiful the room looked. He realised that Maimuna was indeed loved and cared for. It caused him to wonder about the manner of man that Akapwon was. He knew in his heart, that had it been he on his wedding night, finding Maimuna to be not a virgin -- he knew nothing of her then pregnancy -- he would have killed her. He was glad that Codou had opened his eyes and he was glad that he was no longer the arrogant man he used to be. Finding the cloth for the table, Sadio went back to Akapwon who asked him to give it to the ladies so they could spread it on the table.

The women took it from him and were spreading the table as he walked back to the kitchen. Because they did not have enough plates, Akapwon had found some bowls to make up the amount they needed. Fortunately they had enough mugs. Breakfast was a rowdy and happy affair as they laughed and talked while they ate the food with their hands. When Maimuna wanted to get up to serve the coffee, Akapwon told her to sit and enjoy the company of her friends since they had come such a long way to see her. Sadio followed him once more into the kitchen. On the stove was a large pot with warm water. Akapwon had scattered the coals on the hearth and had placed the coffee pot on them to keep it hot and had also placed a pot of water next to it.

As Sadio watched, Akapwon filled a large wooden bowl with the water and asked Sadio if he would take it to the table for the ladies to wash their hands. But before Sadio moved away, Akapwon squeezed the juice of a lime into the bowl and dropped the two squeezed halves into the bowl as well. A pleasant limey fragrance wafted on the air. Next, he placed a square of linen on Sadio's arm.

"The lime cuts the grease from the eggs," he answered Sadio's unspoken question as he followed him with the pot of coffee and as many cups as he could carry. Sadio returned the bowl to the kitchen after everyone had washed their hands. As he turned from the stove, Akapwon, holding a cup of fragrant tea which smelled of lemon and ginger explained, "Maimuna cannot have coffee while she is with child. It would not be good for the babe." As they walked to the table where the women sat, Sadio was a bit preoccupied. He had just seen another example of Akapwon's concern for Maimuna and he was tremendously happy that she had married him.

The women all slept in the bedroom; some slept on the floor and some shared the bed with Maimuna. They were up quite late and there was much laughing and talking coming from the bedroom. The men slept in the spare room beyond the kitchen. Akapwon had a mat that he was going to unravel at a future date. He spread this for Sadio and he himself slept on the bare floor, overriding any protests that Sadio voiced. Maimuna's friends stayed two days and Akapwon introduced them to his parents. He could see that his mother was pleased to have her house full of young people and she chatted with them as if she were their own mother. All of them liked her immediately.

After Akapwon introduced Sadio to his father, they sat and drank beer. Having had interaction with the Council of Elders in Twee, Kinefe was very interested to discover if there was a difference between the Elders of their two villages. They had a long discussion and each learned from the other. Promising to return for supper, which Tifi insisted on preparing, Akapwon, Maimuna and her friends all walked around the small village chatting and asking questions about everything they saw. When they neared the marketplace, Akapwon put his arm around Maimuna's waist. Not knowing the true reason why he did that, they all assumed he was just being affectionate, especially when she looked up at him with a questioning smile and he answered her with a smile as he touched her cheek with his knuckle. Her friends giggled and teased her when he was talking to Sadio and she laughed good-naturedly.

As they sat on the hills with Tutaba and Shema, Akapwon and Tutaba had many discussions with Sadio and they learned much about Twee and life there and shared much about Monabu.

The visit of Maimuna's friends was a huge success and came at a time when it was most appreciated. As they left for Twee amidst laughter and promises to return, they carried gifts from Maimuna, and Akapwon's mother to the mothers of the women. Maimuna was very happy as she and Akapwon returned home arm in arm after accompanying them a little distance from the village.

33

WHEN Sadio and Codou returned to Twee, their relationship changed. He and Codou had opportunity to talk often. Realising that there was something going on between them, their friends gave them moments of privacy so that they could speak to each other.

Sadio approached his father one day in the hearing hall when the other Elders had left. "Father, may I speak with you?"

"Yes, Son, what is it?" Kofo asked, looking at his son in surprise. He wondered why Sadio would seek him out, which is something he had never done before although their talks had taken a turn for the better. Sadio seemed genuinely interested in the decisions he and the Council made and they often discussed the different cases that came before the Elders. Their discussions usually took place after a meeting.

Sadio came directly to his reasons for seeking his father out. "Father, I wish to marry Codou and would ask for your blessings and also to ask you if you would speak to her parents to present an offer?"

Chief Kofo was startled but nonetheless delighted. "Son, this is wonderful news. I will be most happy to approach Codou's father. However, apart from the bride price, what else do you have to offer? You have yet to start building a home for her and even though your farm is a small one, you have neglected it into weeds. Do you think that her father will be impressed enough with the fact of your being the son of the Chief and Chief Elder to forget that you have nothing else to offer his daughter? I can tell you quite frankly, Sadio, that were I Codou's father, I would refuse any discussions until you show me that you can take care of her."

"I understand, Father, and I have already chosen a spot at the end of the village for our home. I was going to ask your approval to start building." He smiled. "Father, I want to build a home like the one that Akapwon built for Maimuna. He discussed with me how he built it and showed me the different things he did to make it stronger and more comfortable. Although his home is beautiful, it is also very well planned and makes life easier for Maimuna."

"What has he done that makes the house more comfortable?" His father asked.

"Well, Father, he has attached the bathing house to the main house. He made a raised wooden floor so that when you bathe, you do not have to stand on the earth and get your feet dirty. He also built a table for the wash bowl so that Maimuna did not have to bend down to a bucket to wash her face. He has shown me many good ideas, Father."

His father nodded, "I would like to see this house of Akapwon's. He sounds like a very industrious young man."

"Oh he is, Father, and he is very smart. I have also asked him about farming and I have cleaned up my farm and have already started planting."

Chief Kofo was impressed and said so. "It is good news to me to hear you say that, Sadio. It encourages me to believe that everything might turn out to be all right."

"I hope so, Father."

"Tell me, Son, why do you wish to marry Codou?" His father watched him carefully.

Sadio seemed surprised at the question. "I love her Father and she loves me. I want us to share our lives and she says she wants the same thing."

"If I recall correctly, you also said you loved Maimuna."

Sadio looked embarrassed. "I have come to realise that what I felt for Maimuna was not love. I was in love with her beauty. I was a different person then, Father, and I must confess that when I said I loved Maimuna I did not understand what love was about. But now I do."

"Then I am satisfied. Let us go and tell your mother."

34

MAIMUNA watched Akapwon leave for the field. One of the dogs accompanied him because his sweet potatoes were fully matured and were ready to be dug up. Usually the dogs helped him and they were very good at it. They seemed to enjoy themselves digging up the potatoes. He would tell them, "We are going to dig potatoes today." When they heard that, they would prance around and bark happily, circling him, ready to begin. Once he began, they happily proceed along each row, digging up the potatoes so that all he had to do was load his cart and dig up one here or there that they had missed.

Maimuna had stopped accompanying him to the farm, and as usual, both dogs stayed with her. This day, however, one dog would stay with her and the other dog would go with him to the fields. With the dog's help he could work faster and would return home more quickly. He knew she would be safe because the dogs were very loyal to her and whenever they were with her they never left her side. The part of the house where she was working was in full view of anyone passing by and so he felt easy in leaving her with one dog. However, neither Maimuna nor Akapwon had taken into account that if her tormentor was bold enough to touch her in public, he would be bold enough to accost her anywhere.

Other eyes watched Akapwon as he walked away, waving to Maimuna. Those feverish eyes were then turned to Maimuna and they watched her every move as she came out the house and sat quietly for a moment at her doorstep.

He had been watching her more steadily for days. The longer he watched her, the angrier he became. The baby was his and he would not let Akapwon claim it as his own. Knowing the consequences to himself if he revealed that he was the child's father, he was beside himself with anger because he could not claim the child.

The dog sat by Maimuna's side, happy when she caressed his ears. To the man spying on her, the dog was a mere inconvenience. In his conceit he was sure he could get rid of it easily. It was easier than trying to get rid of two. Fate had removed the other dog so that he could accomplish his mission. How accommodating, he smirked to himself.

The village was waking up slowly but there was no one near enough for Maimuna to extend a greeting. Getting up slowly she walked to the side of the house to start work in her garden. She bent to pick up a hoe and as she straightened, from behind a rough arm wrapped around her throat like a vice and a hand was clamped over her mouth.

"Fight me and I will kill you," said the same hated voice she had heard in her ear before she was raped. Her whole body stiffened with shock but only for a second before she was galvanized into action. Without warning or growling in his throat, the dog attacked her assailant, biting his ankle. With a well-aimed, vicious kick at the dog's head with his sandaled foot, her attacker stunned the dog for a moment and it fell. However, it was back on its feet and viciously biting and tearing at his trouser leg.

Pausing for a moment from dragging Maimuna backward, her attacker released her throat and reached with his free hand for a shovel that rested on the trunk of a tree close by. Lifting the shovel with his free hand, he hit the dog on its head with a vicious blow and rendered him unconscious.

Taking advantage of his distraction with the dog,

Maimuna managed to wrench his hand from her mouth and scream at the top of her voice. "Akapwo...!"

Her scream was cut short as he regained control of her mouth. She was in too much of an awkward position of being pulled backward to fight effectively. She tried to slow him down by digging her heels into the soil and holding on to the branches of trees as she was dragged past. Even with her strong efforts, her assailant kept pulling her backward relentlessly and she had to let go of whatever she tried to hold on to.

*

Feeling some unease, Akapwon worked fast to get things done. However, the feeling persisted and he could work no more. Something was not right. Just as he was rising from his kneeling position by the potatoes, his dog took off, barking furiously. Dropping his tools he raced behind him.

The dog headed for home and he followed. As he neared his house the dog's barking became frenzied and then stopped. Arriving at the entrance to the vegetable garden he saw the dog bending over its companion who was lying on the ground. Rushing up Akapwon examined the dog and saw that he was still alive. He ran to the house, calling for Maimuna.

Running back to the garden, it was only then that he saw her tools strewn about. His anxiety escalated as he noticed some of the new shoots had been trampled down. He raced through the bushes, following the trampled trail of broken branches and uprooted shrubs through the thick growth of trees. The dogs came up behind him barking furiously and racing past him they turned left. The other dog seemed fully recovered.

Changing direction Akapwon raced behind them, following the sound of their barking. He crashed through the underbrush, unaware of the branches whipping across his face and scratching his legs as he ran. The dogs finally led him to the wall of the hill where he usually sat and where he and Maimuna frequently sat with Tutaba and Shema; where he had sat waiting for his bride to arrive.

Then in the distance he saw something pink and fear raced through him as he increased his speed. He got close enough to recognize the pink wrap-dress Maimuna was wearing when he left her that morning. When Akapwon saw her body, his knees buckled but he was up in a flash as he raced forward, shouting, "Maimuna! Maimuna!" The dogs were barking in frenzy as they rushed between him and Maimuna.

As he fell on his knees beside her still form, he cried out in shock and pain. Her face was badly bruised and her eyes were swollen shut. Blood oozed from her mouth. A few feet away, Boboda lay unconscious. His face was bloodied and swollen and his arm was in an unnatural position underneath him.

"Maimuna! Maimuna!" He cried as he shook her frantically, trying to rouse her, consumed with almost paralyzing fear that she might be dead. He bent his head and listened to her heart. Relief flooded through him as he realised she was still alive. The dogs whimpered as they fussed around Maimuna.

A terrible sound of anguish escaped Akapwon. Not aware that he had made such a sound, he wrapped her torn clothing around her and picked her up. Holding her securely to his chest he began to run, shouting at the top of his voice as he neared the village. Those who heard him cry out came running.

"Please get Timpi!" He shouted urgently, "please get Timpi!" and he continued running with her toward his home. On seeing Maimuna's face, a woman immediately ran, screaming Timpi's name at the top of her voice.

"Timpi! Timpi! Come quickly!"

Her screams brought out the women of the village and they came running.

Men ran alongside Akapwon wanting to help in any way they could. As he reached his house, he remembered Boboda. Turning to the men, he asked urgently,

"Can someone go and get Boboda? He was lying next to Maimuna and he is badly hurt as well. I do not know if he still lives." Some of the men immediately took off at a run to find Boboda.

Timpi and the women who accompanied her entered the house at a run. Akapwon's mother and father came running behind them. They cried out in shock when they saw Maimuna's face all bruised and swollen. When they saw her clothing splashed with blood, tears filled their eyes. They did not ask what happened, that would come later.

As Akapwon laid her gently and carefully on the bed, they took over immediately and asked that he and his father wait outside. The men of the village crowded around Akapwon as soon as he appeared at the door They wanted to know what had happened; who had done this to Maimuna.

"I do not know. There was no one there but Maimuna and Boboda when I found her."

While Maimuna was being attended by Timpi and the women, Akapwon waited anxiously outside, pacing up and down in front of the house. He finally remembered Boboda and asked the villagers if anyone knew how he was doing.

"He seemed to be as badly hurt as Maimuna, Akapwon." One of the men who had just returned from Boboda's home informed him.

"We took him to his mother's house and Ama and some of the women are with him now."

Akapwon breathed a sigh of relief. He knew that Timpi's

helper would help Boboda. "Thank you." He sat down heavily on the steps next to his father. The men who had returned from taking Boboda home sat on the lower step while other villagers sat on the ground, silently offering comfort by their presence, as they waited for word about Maimuna from Timpi.

When Akapwon looked up, he was surprised to see his compound filled with people. It seemed as if the whole village was there. No one spoke. They sat on the ground wherever they could find a place to sit, and waited with him for word about Maimuna's condition.

Timpi worked with Akapwon's mother and the other women of the village. She had asked for Ama but understood that Boboda was also badly injured and that Ama was attending him. The women helped to clean up Maimuna.

Timpi spoke, "I have to deliver the babe now." She told Akapwon's mother. Turning to her helpers she instructed them how they could help and the women rushed to do her bidding, anxious to help, wanting to be of use in any way. She asked Akapwon's mother for help, knowing that she also needed to be doing something.

When everything was prepared, she began to push gently down on the womb, guiding the baby slowly toward the entrance. When the baby's crown was visible, she proceeded to massage Maimuna's abdomen until she could pull the baby out. The women exclaimed in sadness and cried in sympathy when Timpi could not save the baby. But Timpi had already known that the baby would not survive.

They helped her to gently bind Maimuna's bruised ribs and were shocked again at how badly bruised her body was. Wondering what had happened to her, they were unable to stop themselves crying. Although Timpi had seen worse, it had always been a man, savaged by some animal or the other. She had never seen a woman so badly used. It was worse for her than the other women because she alone was privy to what Maimuna had already endured. Tears were in her eyes as she worked to save Maimuna.

As more people from the village waited outside, those who had first seen Maimuna when Akapwon brought her in described Maimuna's condition to them. They were shocked and distressed that something so terrible had happened in their village. The fact that it happened to a newly-wed couple made it worse. Newly-weds should not have to face such pain so soon after being married.

35

A KAPWON and his father stood quickly as Timpi came to the door. She spoke to Akapwon quietly as she rested a comforting hand on his shoulder. "We cannot say if your wife will live. She is a strong woman but we could do nothing to save the babe. Whoever it was must have kicked her badly in her stomach. Her ribs are badly bruised and she has lost a lot of blood. The baby died from the injuries she herself sustained. It could not survive the rough treatment that she endured. It was a boy child."

It was not Timpi's intention to cause him more anguish, by saying he had a son. She squeezed his shoulders encouragingly. "I am so sorry, Akapwon, but from this point on we must pray to Uta that Maimuna survives. All we can do now is wait. Perhaps your voice and your presence will help her. Come." She led him to the bed. "We have done all we can for her."

A woman was gently bathing Maimuna's face with a damp cloth but moved away as Akapwon approached the bed. He dropped to his knees beside his wife's head. His face reflected the anguish he felt as he looked at her battered face. Watching him silently suffer, brought tears to Timpi, his mother and the women who had attended her. They wished they could take away some of his pain. Knowing he needed some privacy, everyone left the room.

Watching her as he gently soothed her brow, rage ran through Akapwon. He did not realise until this moment that he had never really believed her story. Now he knew she had told him the truth and he felt ashamed because of it. He should have left both of the dogs with her. But they had been so sure she would be safe in the village. The rage was as much toward himself as her assailant.

His thoughts flew back to his wedding night and he realised that she must have been wracked with a double fear, the first that he would end her life and the second, that if he did not he would then rape her himself as revenge. How she must have suffered that night and he had compounded it by leaving her in suspense about whether she lived or died. He watched her struggling to breathe, her breathing laboured as if each breath was an effort.

Drawing a ragged breath he held her right hand and stroked it, speaking softly to her. At first he spoke encouraging words, letting her know he was there and would not leave her, encouraging her to get better. Later on as he watched her struggle to breathe increase, each moment fearing it might be her last breath, his words turned to pleading as he feared she might not live through the night. His voice broke as he struggled to keep his composure. He could not lose her now, not after she had come to mean so much to him, had become an essential part of his life now that he had grown to love her so much.

The villagers remained in the compound to keep vigil and angrily discussed the incident. The young couple had been married for such a short while for something like this to happen to them. They were convinced that no one in Monabu would do such a thing. Nobody in Monabu would be that cruel to newly-weds and especially to a woman so obviously with child. Had they known that she had endured the same treatment once before, they would have been incensed.

Akapwon was informed that there were men out searching the fields and farms and keeping watch on the roads to be sure that no one left and not allowing anyone to enter before questioning them. He was grateful that they were looking, because he would not, could not leave Maimuna's side until he was certain she was out of danger. He felt secure that they would be very thorough in their search.

The men searching wanted to be sure that the person responsible did not have an opportunity to escape. Others headed towards Twee. They felt that there was not enough time for Maimuna's attacker to get as far as Twee but they went anyway with the thought to intercept him if he was headed in that direction. Since they had started looking almost immediately after Akapwon brought Maimuna home, they were certain that the culprit did not have time to leave Monabu.

To get to Bopo, the person would have had to pass through the village. They agreed that someone would have noticed that he was in a great hurry or that he looked frightened, but no one had seen him. There were some who still went to Bopo just in case.

36

STAYING by Maimuna's side, Akapwon watched her closely, but she remained absolutely still, struggling with each breath. He only relinquished his watch when Timpi walked into the room and he explained to her that he was anxious because Maimuna was becoming restless, tossing from side to side. As they stood discussing her restlessness, she suddenly sat up and cried out "No! Umar no!" She screamed as she fought. The women rushed forward to hold her to stop her from struggling, to prevent her from causing injury to herself. Just as suddenly as she sat up, so she fell back on the bed, unconscious once again.

Akapwon's father rushed into the room as she cried out. There was complete silence as everyone stared at her in shock.

"Umar!" Akapwon's eyes blazed with anger as he rushed from the house, pushing past the men who were standing at the door who had also heard.

"Umar!" The name spread and as with one body, the men turned and raced toward where they had first seen Akapwon carrying Maimuna. As they ran, they shouted instructions to each other. Some, with Akapwon, headed for where he had found Maimuna.

*

Umar was furious that for a second time his assault on Maimuna was interrupted but he had heard the dogs and then Akapwon shouting. That is when he took off and ran as fast as he could.

Although Umar had a good head start, the road out of Monabu was a distance away from where he ran. Fear pushed him because of the shouting. He knew that it would act as an alarm and men would come searching. He ran in a roundabout fashion so that he could reach the road without being seen. But when he got near enough to the road, from where he hid behind the bushes, he saw men forming a barrier across it. He had misjudged. In no other village had they come searching so quickly. Days would pass before they even suspected him. Many times he watched with amusement as they searched, not knowing who they searched for.

His arrogance had caused him to misjudge the people of Monabu. Believing Maimuna to be dead when he left her, he had expected the villagers to be more concerned about her than to come looking so soon for whomever they thought might be responsible. The pain in his chest increased as he pushed himself harder.

He ran in a zigzag fashion across the fields and farms until he reached the stream that divided the flatlands from the mountains. Instead of crossing it, he waded in the water, travelling upstream until he reached a point where he left the stream and headed for the mountains to start his ascent. Climbing to a good height he finally found the hiding place he had marked when he first moved to Monabu. Since it was on a high ledge, he felt he could relax as it would be difficult for them to find him there. It would be easy for him to wait them out without fear of being found.

After searching frantically for Umar in the fields and on the farms, Akapwon remembered the dogs. He knew they would find him even when nobody knew where he was. Racing back to his home, he called them to him. They came eagerly and sat in front of him, looking at his face. Kneeling before them, he put his arms on both their heads. "Find Umar for me." He told them. "Come."

He led them to where he found Maimuna and searching the ground, he found a piece of wood the end of which had a slight trace of blood on it where Umar must have hit Boboda. Holding out the opposite end from the trace of blood, he had the dogs sniff it. He dropped the stick and the dogs took off with Akapwon and the men behind them.

Akapwon and the dogs raced ahead, heading to the left and then to the right, following the zigzag pattern that Umar had travelled. The men ran to catch up with them and as they drew near, the dogs stopped under a tree and circled it. Then they were off again, sure of the one whom they tracked. As they neared the mountains, however, there was a wide stream that they had to cross. The dogs stopped at the stream barking frantically. One turned to the left and the other to the right as they ran down the side of the stream, only to come back to where the men stood.

The men realised what Umar had done. He had crossed the stream to hide his tracks. Although he did not know it, he had effectively erased the scent of his trail so that the dogs could no longer find him. When they crossed the creek, there was no scent to pick up so it was obvious to the men that he had walked up stream. It did not matter. They would track him until they found him. It was getting dark but they had brought torches which they now lit. The people of the village could see the torches move up the mountains as the search party spread out.

It was late that night when they found Umar. He had wanted to leave but there were men all over the mountains looking for him and he had forgotten about Akapwon's cursed dogs. Thinking to leave when it got dark, he was forced to change his plans when he saw the torches coming up the mountain. He would remain in hiding until they got tired of looking and then he would slip away without being seen.

Standing and looking over the boulder behind which he hid, Umar watched with amusement as the torches moved away to the other side of the mountain. He sat quietly and reviewed with satisfaction his assault on Maimuna. He had given her the beating she deserved for being unfaithful to him. He had to end her life and that of the baby too. It was the only way he felt justified. Watching the torches move away from where he was, he relaxed, ready for a long wait until the mountain was clear of men. But again, he had forgotten about the dogs. When he heard them barking and coming his way, he was furious. "I should have killed those damned dogs when I had the chance!" he said cursing himself for his negligence. He knew he was smarter than to have made a mistake like that.

When they finally found him, the scratches on Umar's face and arms confirmed in their minds that he was guilty. As they rushed up to him he looked unrepentant and ready to fight.

It was fortunate that an Elder had accompanied the men when they found him, because Akapwon immediately attacked him raining punches on him, and had to be pulled off by order of the Elder. The men were fully prepared to join Akapwon in giving Umar a sound thrashing but the Elder immediately put a stop to that.

"We must seek justice the right way, Akapwon," the Elder told him as he tried to break loose to get to Umar. Breathing heavily, he could hardly draw enough breath due to the anger that blazed through him.

"Did he give Maimuna justice, Elder?" He asked furiously.

Knowing it was better not to answer him in the state of fury he was in, the Elder ordered them to remove Umar.

They escorted him back to the village and placed him in one of the Elders' strong earthen cellars. Two men stood guard to prevent him from escaping.

Although the men were angry, the Elder would not budge and their argument fell on deaf ears. "You appointed us to make sure justice was given to everyone who lives in this village. We will give Umar the justice he deserves." With that the men had to be satisfied.

Realising he would not get another chance to get at Umar, Akapwon returned to Maimuna's side.

37

Maimuna's return to consciousness was slow and painful. At first she was only aware of the blessed, comforting darkness and she wanted to remain in that state. However, the pain was insistent. She whimpered as she tried to move, but as the pain shot through her, she cried out and her eyes flew open. Akapwon jumped up and leaned over her in concern. As her eyelids lifted her vision was filled with Akapwon's face. His eyes were bloodshot and filled with concern and new lines had appeared on his otherwise smooth face. He gently caressed her face. "You are in pain," he stated softly. "I will get you some tea." She raised her hand to touch his face but the effort was too much and her hands fell back as she again slipped into unconsciousness.

Timpi returned to the room just as Maimuna lost consciousness. She rushed over to examine her. After lifting her lids and checking her pulse she said. "It would seem Akapwon, that she has improved a little but we still have to wait and see."

Akapwon stayed by Maimuna's side, watching for any change, talking to her as he gently bathed her face with the cool rag one of the women handed him. He was only vaguely aware of them as they moved about the room, bringing him food, which he did not touch. They spoon-fed Maimuna many cups of weak tea made from the leaves of the Moringa plant. Timpi carefully brewed enough of the tea for her to be fed every few hours. It was as much for pain as it was for sustenance. It would also help her to heal more quickly. All through the next night Akapwon watched and in spite of prodding by Timpi, he would not leave her side. Finally the women went home and only Timpi, Akapwon's parents and another woman remained with him. Once he looked up and was surprised to see his parents sitting on the opposite side of the bed. He had forgotten they were there. They nodded to him and smiled and he nodded in return but was unable to return their smiles. He continued holding Maimuna's hand and stroking it.

The next time Maimuna opened her eyes she saw that Akapwon was still there. However, he was asleep. His face was turned towards her as he held her hand even in sleep. The pain had eased and she was grateful, not knowing that Timpi's herbs were at work. She lost consciousness again but this time her breathing was less laboured and she slept.

After a few days Maimuna regained full consciousness and lucidity. Looking around the room, she was surprised to see her mother and father sleeping on the floor next to her bed while Akapwon's parents slept on the other side. A slight movement caused her to look towards the door as Akapwon entered. He walked towards her with a tray, rested the tray on the small table beside her bed and smiled as he knelt beside her. "How do you feel?"

She swallowed, "Thirsty." Her throat hurt and her voice was hoarse.

Akapwon carefully and slowly lifted her and supported her as he brought a cup containing an amber liquid to her lips. "This should help." She drank a little and then asked anxiously, "How is Boboda? Does he live?" She tried to sit up but pain shot through her and she cried out.

Hastily Akapwon returned the cup to the table and held her shoulders firmly but gently to the pillow. "Please do not move, Maimuna. You will harm yourself. Boboda is alive. He is with his mother and Ama. Please try to rest now." He pressed her gently on to the pillows. "I will be here when you awake and I will bring you word of any new development about Boboda as soon as I can. I promise." He held her hand once more. But before she could form a coherent thought to reply, she was asleep. Akapwon watched her in relief as he noted that her colour was returning to normal instead of the sickly grey pallor she had worn since he found her.

A few days passed without Maimuna losing consciousness, only falling into deep sleep. Only then was Timpi satisfied that she was out of danger. She slept many times during the day and would wake only to drink the herbs. A steady stream of villagers had been coming and going trying to give help and give support any way they could.

When both sets of parents awoke, they took over caring for her and told Akapwon to freshen up and take a walk. They ignored his protests and pushed him out the door. In the beginning they could not move him. He had sat for two days without food and barely taking time to drink water. Now that Maimuna was out of danger, they took control and forced him to eat, forced him to take exercise. They took over his house. They cooked and cleaned and bathed Maimuna, helped with her bandages when Timpi came and were a true blessing to him. Apart from Timpi, they were the only ones he trusted to leave Maimuna with.

When the parents almost literally threw him out of the house, Akapwon took the opportunity to visit Boboda. He was a little ashamed, because he had thought of no one else but Maimuna for the past few days. As he neared Boboda's home, he saw that friends of Boboda's mother had gathered to give her moral support. They immediately inquired about Maimuna's health.

"She is much better and is no longer in danger. My thanks to all of you for your help and your prayers to Uta. I am very grateful."

They brushed his thanks aside, voicing regret that they could do no more for her. He chatted with them for a moment then entered the room where Boboda's mother, Muta, was sitting staring into space. Two women sat with her, quietly chatting. At the back of the room against the wall was Boboda's bed. Akapwon saw that Ama sat beside him, watching him carefully.

"How is he doing, Mother?"

Muta jumped up when she heard his voice and when she realised who it was, cried out. "Akapwon! How is Maimuna? I am sorry I have not been able to visit." Then she burst into tears.

Without a word, Akapwon pulled her into his arms and held her close as she cried. Panic ran through him and he pulled back to look at her. "How is he?" He asked urgently.

Hearing the concern in his voice and realising that she had not answered him, Muta looked up. "He is alive, Akapwon, and doing better. But Ama said that his skull had been cracked. He is still unconscious. She says it will be a while before he comes awake."

Akapwon nodded as relief flowed through him. "Can I see him?"

"Yes." She took his arm and walked him over to Boboda's bedside.

Boboda's entire head was wrapped in a bandage and his face was still slightly swollen with angry bruises. His face was basically in the same state as Maimuna's and his arm was strapped to a wooden splint. Akapwon knelt beside Ama.

"How is he doing, Ama?"

Ama smiled slightly at him. "It seems as if Umar hit him with a heavy object, probably a solid piece of wood or a rock. It will take a while before we know what damage has been done. Timpi and I examined him carefully and it seemed to us that his skull has been fractured by whatever hit him. We were thankful that it was only a fracture but we have to wait and see what the damage really is when he wakes up. In the meantime, it is best that he is unconscious otherwise the pain would be severe indeed, like a bad headache multiplied many times. I helped Timpi to bandage his arm which was broken and to tie it to this piece of wood so he could not move it and cause damage." She sighed. "Umar was vicious, Akapwon. He is not someone we want in our village." Looking at him with concern in her eyes she laid her hand on his arm. "I am sorry that Timpi could not save the babe. However, it is good news that Maimuna is getting better."

Akapwon nodded. "Mostly she sleeps."

"Which is good," Ama said, "Timpi said she had bruised ribs and they must be painful. But it is a blessing that he did not hit her head as hard as he hit Boboda's."

Akapwon was entirely grateful that he had not. He stayed with Ama for a while as they watched Boboda. Boboda's mother came and sat with them and after a while he left, anxious to get back to Maimuna.

38

IT was only a few days, but it seemed like a lifetime to Akapwon. Now that Maimuna was on the road to recovery and both sets of parents were in charge, he felt comfortable enough to visit his farm. When he arrived there, expecting to see weeds taking over, he was surprised to see that someone had been doing his weeding for him. Whoever it was had finished digging up the potatoes he had abandoned to go to Maimuna. They were stacked up in a heap against a tree and the ones for eating were separated from those chosen for replanting. The ones for planting had been stacked on the side away from the others, obviously with the intention of planting them later on. As he walked further on through his fields, he saw someone kneeling near a stack of uprooted weeds. He knew it was not his father because his father was at his home with his mother. As he drew nearer Tutaba stood up and saw him. He was moved that Tutaba had helped him so much.

"Hey, Akapwon. Good to see you. How is Maimuna?"

"She is doing quite well, so well that I felt okay with leaving her with our parents. "Thank you, Tutaba. I am grateful for your help." Akapwon paused then continued, "I know Maimuna has received the best care from Timpi and her women. If it was not for Timpi ..." He broke off and turned away. As he stood with his back to Tutaba, fighting for emotional control, he felt a brotherly pat on his back.

"The important thing, Akapwon, is that Maimuna is alive

and she is getting better each day. Do not think about anything else."

"Yes. But you know, Tutaba," he said as he turned with clenched fist and jaw, "I keep seeing her cut lips and her face all swollen and bruised where he must have punched her."

Tutaba shook his shoulders. "Do not torture yourself, Akapwon."

"But how she must have suffered, Tutaba."

"Yes, but thank Uta, Maimuna is a fighter. She would not be alive if she were not."

"Yes, Tutaba, you are right and I am grateful for that. I have thanked Uta over and over. I cannot thank her enough." It tortured Akapwon that he had not got to Maimuna before Umar did his damage. He also tortured himself that he had not believed Maimuna. How had she endured the first assault and still have the courage to fight a second time?

"As soon as Maimuna is better, Akapwon, you must find out what happened so that we can deal with Umar. Chief Comse said we have to wait to hear from Maimuna before we take action against him. Everyone in the village wants him to be put to death."

Akapwon took a deep breath and nodded. He looked at all Tutaba had accomplished. "You have done so much for me, Tutaba. I am truly thankful."

"It is nothing, Akapwon, you would have done the same for me."

"But you have your own fields to weed and sow."

"I spend some time there in the early morning and later in the day I come here. It has worked out very well. Your crops look healthy this year, Akapwon. You are going to do well at the market."

"Yes. I have been lucky. I changed the planting area and the earth on this side seems to be better for the corn. Last year I planted them over there." He gestured vaguely to the left.

They sat for a while as Tutaba ate his lunch.

"To tell you the truth, Akapwon, if it had been Shema I do not know how I would feel."

It was good for Akapwon to talk to his friend. At last he could voice his anguish and not feel ashamed.

39

A T sunset Akapwon returned home. Both he and Tutaba had worked together and finished the weeding. Now he was anxious to see Maimuna and sit with her. He did not think it was time to discuss her assault as yet. She was still too sensitive and still painful from her bruises. He walked into their bedroom and was struck afresh by her beauty despite the still-present traces of black and blue on her face and her arms. Her head and shoulders were raised slightly by pillows. It was not time yet for her to fully sit up. She smiled when she saw him but he could not return her smile. His heart was not light enough.

"Are you out of pain yet, Maimuna?" He asked, his concerned eyes studying her face carefully.

"No, Akapwon. But it is much less than before."

In spite of his intention not to question her, knowing that he should give her more time, the words were spoken before he could stop them, "Maimuna, I know that this is not the time to ask, but I must. We would like to know what happened and how Umar assaulted you. Can you talk about it?"

Anguish filled her eyes and she turned her head away. "I cannot speak of it now, Akapwon," she said in a tearful voice. "Please do not ask me as yet."

Akapwon felt truly rotten. He realised that any mention of her experience must bring it all back to her. "I am sorry, Maimuna. Please forgive me." He kissed her forehead and knelt beside her. "I was not thinking properly."

She touched his face lightly with the palm of her hand, trying to ease his anguish. "It is all right, Akapwon. I understand that it is your concern which caused you to ask."

He took her hand and kissed it as he looked at her. "I will leave it until you wish to talk about it. Until then, I will put it out of my mind."

"Thank you." She said simply with a slight smile.

He talked with her until she fell asleep and then he himself fell asleep in his usual position at her bedside.

In the morning he woke as both parents walked into the room bearing trays of food, followed by Timpi. Timpi came over and examined Maimuna's face and asked her a few questions. Finally when she was satisfied, she stepped back as she said, "Now you must try to eat something, even if it is only a mouthful. When you are done, I will examine you. And you, Akapwon, I order you to eat a full breakfast. You are beginning to look as if there is a famine in Monabu."

Maimuna's mother set the tray on her lap and handed Maimuna a square of linen. Her breakfast consisted of soft boiled eggs and soft grits. There was no coffee, only a bowl of milk.

Akapwon's mother set her tray before him on the bed. "Eat." she ordered. "I will not have my son looking as if I starve him." His breakfast also consisted of boiled eggs and hot grits but not as soft as Maimuna's. The aroma of strong, hot coffee drifted across his nostrils and he realised how really hungry he was. He picked up the coffee and smiled encouragingly at Maimuna as he took a sip.

She returned his smile, thinking how thin he looked but nonetheless quite handsome. She took a couple of pieces of the eggs and grits but could eat no more and turned away from the food.

Concern shot through Akapwon and he half rose from where he sat. His mother spoke. "Do not be alarmed, Akapwon. She is still very much an invalid and even those few bits will do her a lot of good."

Akapwon relaxed a little and watched as Maimuna's mother removed the tray. He turned to Maimuna and she looked as if she was already asleep. He was amazed at how quickly she fell asleep each time. He watched her as he finished his breakfast talking quietly to Timpi and both sets of parents. Timpi explained that Maimuna was fully out of danger now and although she had to spend a little while longer in bed once her ribs were healed a little more, she would be in less pain. As she regained her health, they would bind her bandages more firmly so that she would be able to sit up.

Maimuna was not fully asleep, however. She was just exhausted but she was also very anxious because she knew that talking about the incident would raise Akapwon's anger. She knew that it would be devastating for him to hear what she went through. She wanted to prolong the telling as much as she could. Apart from the fact that she did not wish to remember what had happened to her, it was also the reason why she had elicited that promise from him. She had come to know him well enough to know that he would never bring it up again unless she herself did. And so she was safe for the time being.

Even though it was obvious that Maimuna was much better, time dragged for Akapwon. The least exertion seemed to tire her and that caused him to be anxious all the time. The days of her recovery seemed like a year to him and he worked in the field to ease his anxiety. He was glad that he was able to do so because he knew Tutaba had to get back to his own field. Also, planting and weeding eased his mind somewhat.

He praised the dogs constantly for helping him find Maimuna and for trying to protect her. He cooked them a special meal of boiled meat with a little seasoning, their favourite food and they were ecstatic, breaking off from eating and coming over several times to lick his hand where he sat on the steps, telling him thanks. He was grateful for their courage and each day he examined the one that Umar had knocked unconscious, making sure that there was no real damage.

Climbing to his favourite hill in the evenings, he often sat talking to Uta, pleading and thanking at the same time. One day he was joined by Chief Comse.

"Akapwon, it is time that you questioned Maimuna about how Umar assaulted her. It has been too long since we found Umar and since she named him. The men are getting restless. They feel that Umar should be brought to justice instead of relaxing in the cellar. She must be feeling strong enough now to face her memories. Boboda has not regained consciousness as yet so we cannot ask him. Both Timpi and Ama agree that it might be some time before he awakes, or it might be tomorrow. They explained that with blows to the head it was hard to say what could happen. He might remember or he might not. Therefore it is left to Maimuna to help us."

Akapwon felt torn, "I have already promised her that I will not bring up the subject until she is sure she can face it. I promised her I would wait until she herself started the conversation about what happened to her."

Chief Comse sat on the ground, facing Akapwon. "I am sure if you explain that the longer it takes, the more difficult it will be for us to keep the men from attacking Umar. Perhaps if you tell her how badly Boboda is hurt, she will comply. I know it will be hard for her to have to face the memory of being beaten as badly as she was, but we must have justice. We cannot let such an abominable thing go unpunished."

"I understand, Chief. Perhaps..." he hesitated. "I will give her until tomorrow and if she does not bring it up, I will." He looked intently at Chief Comse. "It is the best I can do and it will have to do. I cannot risk causing her emotional harm if she cannot face it as yet." He was concerned. "You do understand, do you not, Chief Comse? If it were your wife, you would be concerned for her state of mind, would you not?"

Chief Comse had to admit that he would be concerned. "But at the same time, I would be incensed to put my fingers around the throat of that son of a snake and make him pay!" He said in a raised voice.

"It is also how I feel, Chief. But when I brought up the subject to Maimuna a short while ago, there was such fear and pain in her eyes, I would have promised her anything."

Chief Comse stared at Akapwon silently for a moment. His shoulders drooped a little as he allowed himself to relax. "I am sorry, Akapwon. I could not know, none of us could know, what it has been like for her. You are right. We must respect that she might feel real terror whenever she remembers." He gripped Akapwon's shoulder and gave it a slight shake. "It does not matter how long it takes. The longer it takes the more afraid Umar will be, which is a good thing. In the meantime, I agree with you. We will wait until she brings it up. I will tell the Elder's Council what my decision is. They have all been clamouring for blood." He stood up and Akapwon stood with him. "We will wait. Be at ease. Let her bring it up first. It is best."

After Chief Comse left, Akapwon sat down again, resting his head on his crossed arms. He remained in that position for a long time then he went home.

As she had promised, Timpi and her helpers tightened the bandages around Maimuna's ribs. It caused Maimuna a little pain but she was much more comfortable once they were done. It prevented any strain to her ribs should she make a sudden move. It also enabled her to sit up for a while without tiring. They allowed her to walk supported around her bed and later in the evening she was escorted to the front door and then back to bed.

40

MAIMUNA knew the time had come when she had to speak with Akapwon about what happened. She had been stalling for time. She was aware that she was being unfair since he had promised not to bring the subject up until she wanted to and she knew he was very anxious.

Like any man, she felt he wanted to give Umar what he deserved. When he was not aware, she studied him when he came in from the field for lunch and saw that he was tense and could not relax. She knew the time had come when she must tell him.

The next day, when the time drew near for him to come home from the fields, she sat up as much as she could against the pillows and waited for him. Akapwon came in early as usual, and after he had bathed and eaten he came in to sit with her.

She took his hands in hers, not entirely conscious of what she was doing and far more concerned with what she was about to say. "You asked me what happened, Akapwon, and I said I would talk about it later."

Immediately alert, Akapwon lifted his eyes from looking at her hands holding his. "You can speak of it now?"

"Yes, I can. It was Umar, Akapwon."

"Yes, we know and we have found him and have him locked up."

She looked at him in shock, "But how did you know who it was?"

"You were delirious and called out his name as you tried

to fight him. It must have seemed like it was really happening again."

"Yes." She took a deep breath. "When I saw him, I could not believe my eyes. I tried, Akapwon, I tried to fight him."

"Do not – please do not distress yourself anymore. I only wish to know what happened to you and to Boboda when you were fighting him, Maimuna."

"Perhaps it is best that we let it go, Akapwon. You might not believe it when I tell you."

He lifted her chin and looked into her eyes, "I will believe you, Maimuna. Have no fear of that."

She stared at him, noting his sincerity and he smiled encouragingly. Then she took another deep breath.

"Are you sure you can face telling me what happened, Maimuna?"

She nodded and he sat next to her on the bed and took both of her hands in his warm grasp then he focused on her face and waited. Somehow his holding her hands made her feel more secure and less afraid to speak of her ordeal. Taking a deep breath, she started.

"When you left for the farm I went to work in the garden. I wanted to plant the okra and spinach and some yams we had set aside for planting. As I bent down to pick up the hoe, Umar grabbed me from behind and h-he he..."

Akapwon felt her body shaking and held her hands more tightly. "Take your time, Maimuna. Speak only of the parts that do not cause you distress. I am here with you."

Breathing deeply again, she continued. "H- he grabbed me from behind and he said the same hateful words he had said before! I could not see his face and I did not know who it was but I recognized the voice as that from before. I was so terrified."

Akapwon reached forward and pulled her into his arms. She turned her face to his chest and cried. He held her tightly, letting her cry because he felt she needed to. But when her tears were beginning to torture him he begged her hoarsely, "Please, Maimuna, please do not cry anymore. Please." He held her tighter, careful not to hurt her and rested his cheek on her hair. Finally she got control of herself, leaned back against the pillows and continued.

"He dragged me backward through the garden, out into the bushes. I tried to hold on to the branches of the trees to stop him but he yanked me harder. The more I struggled, the meaner he became. Finally I twisted out of his grasp and saw who it was and I slapped him hard, but he was very quick and he punched me in the face." She paused, reliving the horror.

Akapwon moved his hand caressingly up and down her arm and kissed her forehead in encouragement. He seemed calm but he was in fact, seething with anger.

"He..." She stopped and drew a deep breath. "He was yelling at me and hitting me. He said it was his baby and he would not allow another man to have his child." She rested her face on Akapwon's chest and held on to him tightly. "I scratched him and tried kicking him and that's when he got very angry and slapped me so hard I fell. Then I heard a shout and from the corner of my eye I saw Boboda running toward us. He picked up a stick and swung it at Umar but Umar jerked it from him and hit him across his head. He fell hard and Umar tried to hit him again with the stick but he turned in time to block the blow with his arm. I heard him scream when the stick struck his arm and I heard his bone break, Akapwon. It was awful." Tears ran down her cheeks.

"Umar lost his balance and fell but got up on his knees and started punching Boboda in the face. When he reached for the stick, I jumped on his back b- b- because I knew he was going to kill Boboda if he hit him again. I hit him on his head as he swung to hit Boboda once again and I managed to throw his aim off balance. I saw that Boboda was unconscious and I wondered if he had killed him anyway. Getting up he threw me off him. I fell on the stick which he had dropped. Then he got into a rage and started punching me and I felt as if I would faint."

She paused. "He was furious that I had hit him and he tore at my clothes. I was certain that he intended to rape me again and I could not let that happen. Although I was almost petrified with fear, I fought him hard and managed to get up. I kicked him as hard as I could and scratched his face and his arms. I wanted to hurt him as much as he was hurting me." Not able to continue she buried her face in his chest and sobbed. "I could not fight him anymore and I must have passed out because I do not know what happened after that."

But that was enough for Akapwon. Beads of perspiration stood out on his forehead. He forced himself not to jump up and go after Umar again. He continued to hold Maimuna as she cried. His throat was raw from his own unshed tears. What a memory for someone as young as her to have, and he had been of no help. She had suffered in a few months more than most people had in an entire lifetime. In the midst of his anguish, he could not help but be proud of her. She had fought so bravely.

Then his anger at Umar shot through him like a red hot fire poker. He could contain it no longer. And with a shaking voice he asked Maimuna to rest. "Please try to sleep, Maimuna. I have to go, but our parents will be here with you." She nodded as he laid her gently on to the pillows. Her eyes sparkling with tears, she stared at the anger he could not hide.

"I will kill that snake!"

Maimuna lay against the pillows looking worn and in pain.

Akapwon knelt beside her and put his arm around her. He leaned forward and kissed her forehead again. "I will kill that snake," he repeated in a normal voice which belied the anger in his eyes. "When I think of it I am not at all surprised. There was always something about Umar. But I could not give name to what it was," he said. "Rest easy, Maimuna. You will be avenged. I will see to it. He will rue the day he was born." The coldness in his eyes made her afraid. She had never seen him like this before.

He turned his head toward the door and was surprised to see that both sets of parents stood at the entrance to the bedroom. He had not heard them come in. However, they had heard every word and they saw the fury in his face. He was so angry however, that he did not see the pain in their eyes.

Jumping up, he rushed from the room. He went to the cellar but the guards would not let him in on order of Chief Comse. The Chief did not want anyone killing Umar before he could be brought before the Council.

Fury blazed in Akapwon's eyes as he yelled out. "You are a snake, Umar, and I will give you what you gave Maimuna!" With that he took off again.

Umar sat in a dark corner of the earth cellar listening to Akapwon shout obscenities at him. He had no regrets about what he had done to Maimuna. She was his and no one should have her but him, not even Akapwon. He had made sure that she was dead. It was not his fault that she flaunted and tempted him with her beauty as she walked around the village with Akapwon. He went over in his mind how Akapwon had attacked him when they first found him and how he had tried to kill him in revenge, wanting to spill his blood. He must make Akapwon see that she was his. Just because Akapwon married her did not make her Akapwon's. Her life was his and he took it. The babe was his and he took that life too.

41

THE Council of the Elders met with Akapwon in a private meeting. Afterwards another meeting was held in the large Council hut. The meeting included all the men and women of the village. Something like this had not happened in their village before and they were all angry. It was the law in their village that anyone who had been injured by another had the right to demand a sentence for their offender. However, if the Council of Elders felt that his demand was unjust, they would override it or change it as they thought best.

Since the injured party was Maimuna, indirectly Akapwon was also injured. And since Maimuna was not well enough to be involved in the meeting, the decision for Umar's fate was given to Akapwon. They advised him that he could demand Umar's life and be justified. However, Akapwon should also remember that Maimuna still lived. Her life had been spared and he should consider that.

When it was Akapwon's turn to speak, he stood up in front of the hall and told the Council that he had given much thought to what they had told him and to how Umar should be punished.

"At first I wanted him dead. Then I thought that to kill him was a very easy punishment because once he was dead, he could not feel. I now think that it would be unfair for him to just die while Maimuna continued to suffer as she remembered what he did to her." He drew a deep breath. "I want Umar to have a sentence worse than death, something that would always be in his mind, that would torture him for a very long time, just as his actions are torturing Maimuna now. "He tried to rape her!" he said furiously, "even though she was big with child". Drawing another deep breath, he put forward before the Council what he wanted done to Umar.

Before he could finish talking the room erupted in loud protests and those outside who could not fit in the hut, joined in the fray. Angry voices shouted at Akapwon.

"You do not avenge your wife's honour!"

"Kill the snake!"

Finally after many heated accusations and arguments between the villagers, the Elders and Akapwon, a decision was reached that satisfied everyone because everyone felt that it was not only Maimuna and Akapwon who were injured, but that their wives and daughters were also violated by Umar's heinous act.

On the Elders' orders, scouts were sent out to Dogo and beyond. Weeks passed before they found the person they were looking for; someone who would help them carry out the sentence they had agreed upon. After much searching, at last he was found. When he arrived in the village just before sunset, he was treated with much respect. Chief Comse made sure that he had a hearty meal and a place to sleep.

The next day he was invited to join the Elders who explained what they wanted done. A fee for his services was negotiated and when all was to everyone's satisfaction Umar was taken out of the earthen cellar. He was accompanied by the stranger, Akapwon, Chief Elder Comse who was also the village chief, and seven men from the village.

They marched Umar out from the village towards the hills. The rest of the villagers gathered to watch their departure. Each man in the party, except for the Elder and the guest, held a stout piece of wood, not too heavy but stout enough to cause pain. When they found a suitably secluded place far enough from the village to be private, they formed a circle and put Umar in the centre. As he sat on the ground before them arrogant and defiant, Chief Comse, as Chief and as Chief Elder, spoke on behalf of the group.

He addressed Umar and first listed his crimes against Maimuna and Boboda. He then informed Umar that the sentence he would receive was decided upon by Akapwon, the Council and the villagers who, after much debate, heated arguments and modifications, had finally agreed upon what they felt was fair to everyone.

The reason they had finally agreed to Akapwon's request was because he agreed to the changes they desired and because they in turn agreed that death would be too easy a punishment for Umar. They all wanted Umar to suffer as he had caused Maimuna to suffer. Akapwon wanted him to feel the pain of everything he had done to Maimuna. Thus he would suffer the emotional distress that Maimuna was suffering.

"Before I tell you the punishment that the Council and the villagers and Akapwon have decided for you, Umar, do you wish to say anything in your own defence?" Chief Comse asked him.

A little afraid but not frightened enough for his own good, still defiant and angry nonetheless, Umar looked at all of them with blazing hate in his eyes. "I had every right to take her from you, Akapwon. I saw her before you did," he said facing Akapwon, "and since I saw her first, she was my woman not yours. I had every right to do what I did!" he shouted at them, unrepentant.

Chief Comse addressed him. "Umar, because you have committed an abominable act against an innocent woman, leaving her to die, your punishment will be such: Firstly, because you tried to rape an innocent woman who has never done you any harm, you shall yourself be raped until we feel that what you tried to do to her, has been done to you. Thus you will suffer as she suffers whenever the rape of yourself comes to your mind."

Then they held him down and let the stranger do what he had been hired to do. Chief Comse then addressed Umar again.

"Umar, secondly, for the terrible physical pain and assault that you have inflicted on Maimuna and Boboda, for their pain and suffering we will do the same to you. The injuries that you gave Maimuna will be administered by Akapwon so that he can get some satisfaction of revenge."

The men were first cautioned by Chief Elder that only one blow should be directed at his head and only the bones which he had broken on Boboda and the bruised ribs that he had inflicted on Maimuna were to be injured on him.

Before the men could gather around him, Akapwon rushed in and punched Umar so hard in his face that his head snapped back. He managed another punch before the men drew him back.

The next blow was to his head but it was not as hard or heavy a blow as he administered to Boboda. They did not want him unconscious for days, only for a short time. He received all the blows Timpi described to them that Maimuna and Boboda had received, including her bruised ribs. Umar fainted and they waited for him to regain consciousness. When he finally did, Chief Elder addressed him again.

"Umar, you are hereby banished from this village and you are warned that if you are seen anywhere near the outer area of the Bopo, Monabu or Twee villages, your life will be forfeited. We do not want you around us anymore. You have degraded our village by your vile acts. And every man, woman and child is insulted by you. Just remember, Umar, that by your despicable act, you have not only degraded yourself, but you have brought shame on your family as well. Leave this village now and be thankful that you still live!" Chief Comse said as he pointed.

But before Umar could get moving, Tutaba reached out and punched him in his mouth, splitting his lip, "for Maimuna," he said.

Umar crawled away from the group, broken and in pain, almost losing consciousness again but extremely grateful for his life. A sob escaped as he crawled away. He knew that if Akapwon had wanted it, he would be dead. The law of the village would prevail. He stopped and buried his face in the earth, as shame of his rape washed over him. It was at that point that the enormity of his crime came home to him, through his broken bones and bruised flesh, understanding at last that this was what Maimuna and the other women he had assaulted had suffered. But more than his physical pain was the pain he felt, as he realised at last what he had done to Akapwon, whose family had only ever been kind to him.

Chief Comse and everyone else left the field together and they all returned to the village together. Umar lay in the field where he had crawled, in pain and scared. When he moved again, it was dark.

Akapwon returned to his home and his wife. She was sitting up in bed. As he sat on the bed facing her, she watched him apprehensively but without shrinking from whatever he came to say. Akapwon took her hands in his.

"Be at peace, Maimuna. We have been avenged."

42

KNOWING that it would do Maimuna good to sit out-doors and take advantage of the fresh breezes, Akapwon approached one of the master weavers with an idea he had for a suspended bed to hang outdoors; which he described to the weaver. "If you will accept from me a sack of sweet potatoes as payment," he offered to bargain with the weaver and explained the type of suspended bed that he wanted. "It has to be made so that it does not fold around Maimuna when she gets in it. If you make it this way, she will be very comfortable when she sits or lies in it. It has to be stiff but a little soft so that she can relax in it."

To explain himself more fully, he drew a diagram of what he wanted so that the weaver could more understand what he meant.

When it was time for him to collect the suspended bed, he took a sack of sweet potatoes from his earthen storage and went to the weaver. The weaver was proud of his work and showed Akapwon how he had done it. Akapwon was very pleased indeed. The weaver had inserted a straight, young limb from a tree across the weave at each end of the suspended bed which prevented it from folding. It was perfect and the colours he had chosen were cheerful.

However, the weaver refused to accept the potatoes, telling Akapwon that he would never charge him for something that would be used in Maimuna's recovery. He also told Akapwon that he had just given him a product for his market and perhaps won him the weavers' prize at

Arana Dogo at the next weaver's contest. He was quite pleased with himself and Akapwon was quite pleased with the suspended bed. Before he took the bed home, however, Akapwon persuaded the weaver to at least accept a small quantity of sweet potatoes and they parted, both very satisfied.

When he returned home, Akapwon got two strong logs that could be used as posts and planted them in the ground under the tree near the steps. He placed them there so that when the suspended bed was hung, it would be under the shade of the tree and Maimuna could relax without being uncomfortably hot. He hung the suspended bed between the two posts and tested it himself by lying in it. As he relaxed in the bed, he smiled with satisfaction. It would be good for Maimuna.

When Timpi arrived the following morning she was impressed with the suspended bed and said it would be very beneficial for Maimuna to be outdoors for a while each day. She tested the bed herself and felt so relaxed she did not want to get up. They brought Maimuna outside after she had breakfast and carefully helped her on to the suspended bed. She lay back, breathing heavily because that small amount of exertion tired her but she was very happy. She thanked Akapwon for the bed and smiled as she looked up into the leafy canopy above her.

Thus, Maimuna's health improved and soon she could walk unescorted. She had a stream of well-wishers visit her as she lay in the suspended bed and spent many hours chatting with them.

Codou and her friends from Twee visited her twice and lifted her spirits.

"Maimuna, we came as soon as we could." Codou touched her face gently. "Oh, Maimuna, what a terrible thing to have happened to you again," she whispered. "It was the same son of a snake, was it not?"

When Maimuna nodded, Codou's eyes sparked with anger. She said fiercely, "I heard they did to him everything he did to you!"

Her other friends agreed emphatically. "Yes, they should have buried him. That is the only thing good enough."

Maimuna was happy to listen to all the gossip happening in Twee and was very glad her friends had visited her.

*

Finally Boboda regained consciousness. Ama and Timpi watched as his pain-filled eyes opened and he looked up at his mother. His first question assured Ama and Timpi that he would be okay. "Is Maimuna okay, Mother? Did he kill her?" He asked an anguished look on his face. "She tried to save my life and he hurt her so badly. Does she live, Mother?" He asked again.

"She is alive, Son. She is alive but she lost the babe."

Boboda closed his eyes in pain. "Poor Maimuna. Poor Akapwon. That Umar is a snake! He was hitting her, Mother, even though she was with child. How can anyone do such a thing?"

"I do not know, Son. Perhaps Umar has not been quite himself and nobody noticed. For someone to do such a thing, he has to be ill, Boboda. I am only glad that you were able to help her."

"She helped me, Mother."

"Yes, but you stopped him from beating her and probably killing her. Be comforted, Boboda, that she is alive because of you and you are alive because of her."

"I would like to see her."

Ama and Timpi were very firm on that. "You are not getting out of this bed for a while, young man," Timpi said firmly.

"I will make sure that he does not, Timpi, even if I have to tie him down," his mother assured her.

Before they left Boboda, Ama and Timpi stressed that their instructions must be obeyed.

After they left, Muta looked down at her son and a smile crossed her face but was gone instantly. "I cannot imagine what life would be like without you, Boboda. I do not remember ever being so afraid in my life when they brought you to me."

Boboda took her hands in his. "I am all right now, Mother. I am an old dog and tougher than you think."

His mother laughed softly and then burst into tears. "I was so afraid, Boboda, I thought you were dead." Sobs rocked her body. "I do not wish to live through that again."

"It is okay now, Mother. As you can see, I am very much alive. Do not cry any more, please."

43

A FEW days after Akapwon and the men returned from their dealing with Umar, Akapwon's parents accosted him in the kitchen as soon as he returned from the field. Maimuna was asleep and her parents were in the room with her.

"Akapwon, we wish to speak with you," his father said.

Surprised, Akapwon looked at both of them. They seemed very serious and for a moment his heart stopped, thinking that something was wrong with Maimuna. Seeing his expression they rushed to assure him that she was all right and sleeping peacefully. Her parents were watching over her.

"What we wish to speak to you about," his father said, "is what Maimuna told you when she was explaining who harmed her."

"What did she mean, Akapwon?" his mother asked, "When she said, 'I was afraid he would try to rape me again'?" His mother looked so upset that he knew he had to be very careful with his explanation to both of them.

"Mother, if you and Father would follow me?" Without waiting for a reply, he walked through the kitchen and into the room beyond. "Please sit down." He motioned them to the only two chairs that were in the room and when they were seated, he sat on a low stool facing them. "I did not, could not, tell you before because I did not want you to look at Maimuna differently. However, now that she made that slip and you saw what happened to her, I will tell you everything that she told me on our wedding night."

His mother drew in an audible breath and his father's eyes flashed with anger. He stood up. "Are you saying she came to you, as your bride, defiled?"

"Please do not judge her until you hear what I have to say, Father, and please trust that I am not a simpleton, nor was I duped. Not for long anyway. Please sit, Father."

When his father finally consented to sit, Akapwon told them everything that Maimuna had told him. "I was furious because I had been cheated out of my wedding night but I could not bring myself to end her life after what she explained, especially since she could be telling the truth."

His mother said "Of course not, Son. I would hope that your father and I brought you up to value life more than your pride. I am glad you did not kill her, Son, even though it was your right."

"So am I, Mother, for later I came to love her. She is so sweet and strong and brave." He smiled, "She also has a strong and defiant spirit. I came to admire her."

His father spoke, "We have also come to love her, Son, as our own daughter." He got up again and paced the room. "After we got over the shock of her explanation, Son, we could not help but think how she must have suffered experiencing the same rough treatment all over again."

Akapwon proceeded to tell them of how Umar had insulted her not once but twice by touching her in public, in his presence. However, he jumped up and could not go on as fury raced through him again. "Had I known who it was then, I would have killed the snake," he said viciously.

His father spoke. "I would have joined you had I known the truth."

"And so would I!" His mother said fiercely.

Startled, both he and his father looked at her in puzzlement. Then they both laughed at the fierce look on her face. He walked over and hugged her. "Thank you, Mother. I am sure Maimuna will be grateful to hear that. She was worried that you might hate her when you learned of her deception in marrying me."

His mother smiled slightly. "She was deceptive." She paused and then smiled again. "But I can forgive her now, knowing the reason why."

Akapwon looked at both his parents, "She worries that you might not look on her the same as before because of her rape and losing the babe."

"How could anyone look at her in any way but with sympathy? She has suffered enough."

"Mother, Father," he looked at both his parents. "I must ask you to keep this to yourself. The only other people who know of this first encounter with Umar, are her parents and her best friend, Codou, Timpi and now you. I was forced to tell Timpi because Maimuna refused to let herself be examined by her. As you both know, Timpi always examines every expectant mother in Monabu throughout their pregnancy. Maimuna thought to avoid her finding out how advanced her pregnancy was by refusing to be examined."

"She wanted to keep Timpi from finding out what happened? Then how did Timpi come to find out?" His mother asked.

"Timpi approached me one day and like Maimuna I tried to put her off and she got very angry. I did not want her to go to you and Father, so I was forced to explain everything. She promised not to tell anyone and she kept her promise."

"Yes, Timpi does not discuss any of her patients with anyone, except maybe Ama. But in this case I can see that she would not discuss it even with Ama."

"I explained to her as I am explaining to you, Mother, Father, that the reason I wanted it kept a secret is because you know the village would have gossiped about Maimuna had they known before. And you, Mother, not knowing anything else, would have disliked her for deceiving me and marrying me knowing that she was already with child."

This time his mother jumped up. "She was with child when she married you!"

"Yes, Mother. I told you what her village would have done to her had I not agreed to the marriage offer Chief Kofo sent me. I decided to keep her condition a secret."

"Yes, but you did not say she was with child. You merely stated that that dog Umar had raped her."

Akapwon looked at her, disturbed by her anger. "I thought you understood that, Mother. Did I not just explain why Maimuna did not want Timpi to examine her?"

"No, I did not understand that!" She said emphatically. Then she continued "In that case, I can only thank Uta that she lost the babe. I would not have wanted a grandchild whose father was that dog, Umar!"

This time Akapwon did laugh outright and pulled his mother into his arms. "Mother, you are such a fierce avenging woman."

His father came and hugged them both. "I agree with that, Son."

When his mother disentangled herself from him and his father, Akapwon voiced thoughts that were worrying him.

"Father, Mother, do you think I did right by letting Umar live? I felt sure at the time that death was too good for him. I wanted him to suffer but now I am not so sure it was the right decision."

"It was the right decision, Son." His father said, "Besides, Chief Comse would not have allowed you to kill him, because he did not kill Maimuna. I know you could have taken his life in anger in spite of the Elders, but that would have made you a murderer because Maimuna still lives. Because you are our son, we know you enough to know that you would not have been able to live with that. You have never been unfair to anyone that your mother and I know of. Your decision was right. Now you can rest easy because the mere shame of being raped will keep him away, but he also has the added incentive to keep his life by staying as far away as he can from here."

"I agree, Son." His mother said. "Do you not feel relief that he is alive and suffering?"

Akapwon smiled and a grin spread across his face. "Yes."

Both parents smiled at him, then his mother turned to the door. "Now I have a bone to pick with that Kaieta and Oboto. They have some explaining to do!" then she smiled, belying the anger in her voice. Then she laughed out loud. "I would have done the same thing if it were you, Akapwon. I would have done exactly what they both did." Then she said as an afterthought "You need not worry about the village looking at Maimuna in any way but in sympathy. She now belongs to the village and they will protect her."

His mother was right. The village was very protective of Maimuna. They were ashamed that something so horrible had happened to her in their village and could not do enough for her. In the beginning the villagers watched her carefully and rushed to offer help at the least provocation. When they realised that she was becoming embarrassed and nervous around them because of it, they stopped showing their concern publicly but continued to watch her unobserved for a long time after, until they felt comfortable enough to relax, seeing that things were almost back to normal for her and Akapwon.

44

A T last Boboda was well enough to get up and about. When Ama gave him the okay to leave his house, his first visit was to see Maimuna. She was relaxing in the suspended bed when he arrived. When she saw who it was, she joyously greeted him. Getting out the bed, she hugged him before he realised what she was going to do.

"Thank you, Boboda. Thank you for coming to help me even though you could have been killed."

Boboda did not know where to look when she stood back to look at him, her hands still on his shoulders. He had never been hugged by a woman before, except his mother and that was just a childhood memory.

Maimuna laughed when she saw his embarrassment. "Please get a chair from the house, Boboda, if you do not mind sitting with me a while."

Without answering, Boboda went to get the chair. As soon as he sat down she spoke.

"How are you feeling, Boboda? Are you in any pain?"

He shook his head, no. Then just when she was beginning to think it would all be a one-sided conversation, he spoke. "Are you in pain, Maimuna?"

She smiled, even though he was not looking at her. "Only slightly, my ribs are a little sore and they still hurt but they are healing nicely." His arm was still in a sling. "Is Timpi looking after you, Boboda?"

He looked up only to find her smiling at him and dropped his eyes immediately. She laughed. "Boboda, we both live in the same village. Are you going to avoid looking at me forever?"

After a moment of silence, he lifted his head and looked at her. Then he smiled. She had never seen him smile before and it did pleasant things to his face. "I am not used to speaking to women, except for my mother."

"Well that is going to change, is it not, Boboda? We are going to be friends, are we not?"

When he did not answer, she said. "After all you saved my life. Does that not mean that you are now my friend?"

Keeping his eyes down he said, "Akapwon has been my only friend. I do not know how to be friends."

"Well to begin with Boboda, friends look at each other when they speak."

There was another moment of silence and when he looked up they both laughed. He stayed for a while and had tea with her. She drew him slowly out of his shell and found that Akapwon was right. He was a very nice person and very interesting to talk to. Because he was alone so often, he noticed more than the ordinary person and he studied the workings of nature more than any other person she had met. She hoped that one day a young lady would discover what a pleasant and interesting companion he would make.

*

The villagers now had the opportunity to view Boboda in a different light. Overnight his status had risen from someone shunned, to someone whom everyone greeted as he passed. He was still shy and embarrassed but having learned from Maimuna, he smiled whenever anyone spoke to him and he tried his very best to look them in the eye. He managed to master his strong desire to lower his eyes when talking to men and their wives. However, he still found it difficult to speak to the single women of the village but he treated them with respect and in time they came to view him differently, some even liked his company.

45

MAIMUNA, having fully recovered could walk almost normally. Her ribs were healing well and Timpi stopped binding her abdomen. Instead, she replaced the tight binding with layers of stiffly starched linen to protect her ribs and prevent her from inadvertently hurting them. This bandage, although stiff, was much lighter and less constricting than being wrapped and it gave her more freedom of movement. She could do much more around the house and best of all, it fitted comfortably beneath her wrap. Timpi did the same for Boboda's arm, replacing the wooden splint with starched linen. He was also grateful.

One morning as Maimuna sat at breakfast with Akapwon, she received a note from Codou. The messenger delivered it as they sat at the breakfast table. Akapwon had fallen into the routine of preparing their breakfast, which they ate together before he left for the farm. Although Maimuna did not accompany him to the farm, one of the dogs always remained at her side. Although Umar was gone, Akapwon still wanted to make sure she was protected. Knowing how intelligent his dogs were, Akapwon left it to them to decide between themselves which one would stay with her. It seemed they worked out a system between them and never argued about who would stay and who would go with Akapwon.

After reading the first few lines of the message, Maimuna let out a squeal and jumped up. Concerned Akapwon rushed to her side.

"What is it, Maimuna?" He asked urgently.

Maimuna threw her arms around him. "They're getting married! Codou and Sadio are getting married!" She said laughing and crying at the same time.

Akapwon looked at Maimuna, stunned, his heart slowly returning to normal. Then he realised that one of her arms was still around his neck. He knew she had only hugged him in her excitement but still he enjoyed it.

Maimuna continued, looking at the note and unaware that her arm was still around Akapwon "They want to get married here, Akapwon. They say they do not want me to make the long journey and want us to ask Chief Comse if both he and Chief Kofo could perform the ceremony. Is this not exciting, Akapwon?" Her eyes sparkled with happiness and excitement.

"Very exciting, I am happy for them both. Although I did notice that Sadio had special affection for Codou when they last visited, I did not expect it to be so soon."

"That, my husband, is because you were worried about me and did not notice the many times Sadio's eyes followed Codou around." She removed her arm from around his neck and sat back down. "We must ask your father to speak to Chief Comse. Oh, it will be so exciting."

Akapwon smiled at her happiness. "Yes, it will be good for the whole village."

"However" Maimuna continued excitedly "Since his father is the chief of Twee, it has to be a grand affair indeed. Codou and her friends can stay with us…" They continued discussing the forthcoming wedding. Akapwon was late getting to the field but he did not care. All he could think about was that Maimuna had hugged him of her own volition.

Although they still slept in bed together, he was acutely aware of how much she had suffered and that if he approached her too soon, it would only bring back bad memories. Mindful of her trauma, he set out to gain her trust. Although he kissed her cheek every night and less frequently, her lips, still he slept next to her without touching her except for sometimes when he would hold her hand. Over time, he thought to himself, he would hold her while they slept or touch her arm in passing. However, he felt that he must wait for her to reach out to him. Although her putting her arm around him could not be construed as a step forward, nonetheless, he was grateful for it.

Boboda came to visit Maimuna everyday with the intention of protecting her while Akapwon was out in the fields although he did not voice his intention to anyone. He was always very respectful and they became good friends. Maimuna watched him grow slowly out of his shell and was happy because she came to see what Akapwon had known all along, that up to the time of the attack, he had been a very lonely man and one who was painfully shy around women. Also, she noticed that he was an extremely considerate and kind person. She greeted him happily, genuinely glad to see him. Soon Boboda realised that her friendship was genuine and he was grateful.

When word spread about the forthcoming wedding, the village was as excited as they had been about Akapwon's and Maimuna's wedding. Both villages began to plan and messages were carried back and forth between them.

When Codou arrived with her friends, Akapwon was prepared for their visit. He fixed up the back room to accommodate them and built two large beds that could sleep three women each. He covered the wooden slots with dried grass, mixed with the sweet fragrant clover and lavender. Then he covered the grass with material Maimuna had brought for her own bed, part of her belongings that she brought for her new home. Maimuna's parents stayed with his parents and Chief Kofo and his wife stayed with Chief Comse and his wife. Sadio stayed with Boboda and his mother because with their three children, Tutaba and Shema had very little room. Muta was so honoured to be included in the wedding family that she could not do enough for Sadio and pampered him profusely. The old Sadio would have expected nothing less but the new enlightened Sadio was somewhat embarrassed and told her not to worry so much about him. Boboda, not used to having anyone in his home besides himself and his mother, was very nervous around Sadio until Sadio put him at his ease by being natural and friendly.

Before arriving in Monabu, Codou had sent a message to Maimuna asking her if she could borrow her wedding garments. Although her parents could afford to buy whatever she desired, she liked Maimuna's and thought they were beautiful and would be perfect for her. Also, she wanted to honour Maimuna by wearing it. Maimuna was delighted that Codou actually wanted to wear her garments and asked her several times after she arrived if she was serious.

After they arrived, Codou and their friends sat on Maimuna's bed as Maimuna sat on the floor beside a small beautifully made basket that Muta had given her in gratitude for saving her son's life. She lifted the lid and lifted out the topmost layer of her wedding gown. The beautiful shade of the red transparent cloth seemed to glow and shimmer as the silk flowed over her hands. She passed it to Codou. Next she lifted out another red silk garment, not transparent, equally as beautiful with a soft glow to it. Then she pulled out the two white shifts, one of silk and the other of soft cotton. Their friends were surprised that she had worn so many layers and wanted to know why.

Codou answered for her as she saw Maimuna's embarrassment. "We thought since the silks were so soft, anyone would be able to see through them and it would be embarrassing for Maimuna to stand in front of a whole village with a wedding garment that revealed everything underneath."

Having felt the material and seeing the transparency of the top layer and to a lesser degree, the second layer, they were satisfied and agreed that it had been a good idea. Codou removed her garment and put on the first two white shifts and then the red silk, the top layer of transparent silk and finally the veil. The red lit up her skin just as it had Maimuna's and caused it to glow. Her friends fussed over her and exclaimed how beautiful she was and Maimuna agreed wholeheartedly. After Maimuna refolded the garments and returned them to the basket, she handed the basket to Codou. Then they sat talking and planning how Codou should arrive at the village centre for the ceremony.

"Have the Elder mothers spoken to you yet, Codou?" Maimuna asked. Codou made a face and she laughed. The other women wanted to know what the joke was but instead of telling them about the meeting with the Elder mothers, Maimuna merely said "When you get married you will go through it as well. Until then, you will have to wait just as we had to wait to find out what they talk about." She and Codou both laughed heartily and the girls joined in in good humour.

Chief Kofo and his wife visited Maimuna and she felt much honoured that they should have taken the time to do so. She was happy to see them and treated them to a wonderful tea accompanied by some small sweet buns she had made. They stayed a while and as they chatted, Akapwon came in from the field. As he went to take a bath she invited them to dinner which they regretfully refused, reminding her that Chief Comse's wife was already preparing something for them. They stayed a little longer and chatted with Akapwon when he returned to the kitchen. Again, they were impressed by his quiet manner and the attention he gave to Maimuna fascinated them.

Akapwon and Maimuna offered their home to Codou and Sadio for their wedding night. The newlyweds were going to remain in the village for two days after the wedding and they happily accepted the offer. Maimuna and Akapwon would stay with his parents.

The wedding day for Codou and Sadio dawned bright and sunny. Everyone was happy and there was much laughter and conversation as guests and family from Twee began to arrive. The market circle had been broadened to accommodate more guests since they expected at least half of Twee to attend their chief's son's wedding. Monabu had not seen so many people since Akapwon and Maimuna's wedding. The ceremony was basically the same as Akapwon's and Maimuna's, except for the fact that there were two chiefs conducting the ceremony. It was very interesting how they divided the ceremony between them and caused it to flow so effortlessly that it seemed natural and something that was an everyday occurrence instead of the rare occurrence that it really was.

As father of the groom, it was Chief Kofo who tied the red ribbon around Codou and Sadio's wrists. After the ceremony and after Sadio lifted the veil from Codou's face, he kissed her on her lips. Codou was surprised but smiled happily. She realised that he did it because he had heard that Akapwon had done it. From the moment Codou had told him that Akapwon had kissed Maimuna when he lifted her veil, he knew he would too because, like Akapwon with Maimuna, he wanted to kiss Codou very badly.

As their relationship had grown closer, Sadio had asked Codou to tell him a little about Akapwon and Maimuna's wedding. She had told him how impressed she had been when Akapwon had kissed Maimuna on the lips. She had never seen anyone do that before and felt that it brought a beautiful finishing touch to the ceremony. Other young women were also impressed by what Akapwon had done and decided that they wanted that to happen at their wedding also. When Sadio kissed Codou in the same manner, the young men and ladies who had not attended Maimuna and Akapwon's wedding were positive that it had to happen at their own wedding and thus a tradition was born and it became part of all future wedding ceremonies.

The happy couple mingled with the guests as was the custom, receiving well wishes from each guest in turn for a long and happy life together.

Standing by Akapwon's side and observing how happy Codou and Sadio were, Maimuna sighed wistfully. If only she had been half as happy as they seemed to be. Akapwon, hearing her sigh looked at her. He too had been thinking how happy this part of his wedding day had been. "Are you sad, Maimuna?" He asked her puzzled, squeezing her hand a little.

"Not really, my husband. I was foolishly wishing that our wedding day had been as happy as theirs."

"But it was, for me at least."

"But not for me. I was so afraid of what would happen to me afterward. It was hard to relax, much less to really enjoy myself."

"I am sorry to hear that, Maimuna. However, not being aware of what you were thinking, I thought I was the luckiest man in Monabu."

"But not for long. I will never forget the anger in your eyes when you found out my deception and I fully believed I was about to die that night."

Releasing her hand, he put his arm around her and drew her closer, kissing her forehead. "Do not think about it, Maimuna. However," he gave her a broad smile "I would gladly go through the ceremony again, just to remove your veil. You were the most beautiful woman I had ever seen. I was so happy and so taken by your beauty that I gave in to my desire and kissed you on your lips. I could see your surprise but now I thank you for not objecting."

"How could I object, my husband? I thought it was a tradition in Monabu that we did not know of in Twee. Also I did not object because your lips were so soft and it was a new experience for me."

Akapwon laughed "Had I known that, I would have made excuses to kiss you throughout the reception." And they both laughed. Then he smiled into her eyes. "One day, Maimuna, it will be our wedding night as well. I look forward to that." He continued smiling at her as he watched her fight her fear, knowing that the mere mention of any intimacy between them made her nervous.

"I am grateful for your kind understanding, my husband," She said at last, shy and embarrassed at the same time.

Akapwon said nothing and merely hugged her closer to his side, happy when he felt her arm circle his waist. Because they were so engrossed in each other, they were not aware of how many people had glanced their way, during the ceremony, and now as they stood talking. There were only good wishes for the young couple and admiration and good thoughts for Maimuna for her steady recovery.

"I wonder how they will feel about feeding each other" Maimuna speculated. She smiled up at Akapwon. "I had never fed anyone in my life, let alone a grown man."

"Nor I." Akapwon agreed and then he grinned "But it was very enticing, feeling your lips against my hand. I wanted to forget about the food and just kiss them."

Maimuna looked at him in surprised embarrassment. "You did?"

"Absolutely." And then he laughed out loud at her embarrassment.

46

MANY seasons passed before Maimuna's mind was completely healed, because it was much slower to heal than her body. Akapwon was patient with her and as time went by, he kissed her or caressed her more and more often so that she could get used to the feel of his touch. He held her hand when they walked, kissed her good morning and touched her face as often as he declared his love for her. In bed, he would ask her permission to hold her before he reached out. Sometimes she would allow it and sometimes he would see the fear in her eyes and would keep his distance.

He discussed things and events that he was sure would keep her mind away from her memories of the assault on her body. Many evenings they would meet with Tutaba and Shema and their discussions were as lively as they used to be. After a while, Maimuna relaxed enough to laugh. At those times, Akapwon would hold his breath at the beauty of her smile and the melodic sound of her laughter.

Her parents visited often and they would gather with Tutaba and Shema for a wonderful dinner and conversation. When Maimuna's parents talked about building a home in Monabu so that they could visit her without imposing on Kinefe and Tifi, Akapwon's parents would not hear of it. They insisted that it was not an imposition and that they liked having them there. To settle the matter, Kinefe built another, spacious room on to their home and added a bathroom in the style of Akapwon's. This gave them a degree of privacy and they were more comfortable whenever they came.

★

It was planting time and Akapwon and Maimuna started out early in the morning. It turned out to be a particularly good planting day. The sun was not too hot and they made great progress and finished planting all the onion shoots. As they stood admiring their handiwork, Akapwon put his arm around Maimuna's waist and kissed her forehead.

"Because we did so well Maimuna, tonight I will cook and you will relax."

She leaned back to look at his face. "Are you sure, my husband? You were working just as hard as I was."

"Aah, but I am stronger." He grinned and leaning over, kissed her gently but thoroughly. And before she could voice a protest, he spun them around and headed for home. "Come." He said as if it was the most natural thing between them, his kissing her. "I will make you your favourite supper." He threw back his head and laughed with joy.

"Why are you so happy, Akapwon?" Maimuna looked up at him with suspicion, noting his smile.

"Because I have a wonderful wife, whom I love. What more could I ask, except for your happiness as well." He smiled into her eyes. "Are you happy, Maimuna?"

She always thrilled at the way he said her name in that deep voice of his. Looking up at him she laughed "Very happy, my husband."

When they arrived home, he suggested she take her bath while he prepared the food. She had already seasoned the chicken before they left and she watched as he quickly peeled the potatoes and put them to boil. It always surprised her how efficient and at ease he was in the kitchen and how well he cooked. She had once mentioned it to Tifi and asked if she had taught him to cook at an early age since he was so good at it. Tifi laughed.

"No, Maimuna, he learned it on his own. After he finished building your home, he moved in and practiced cooking until he got it right. He told me that he wanted to be able to cook for you sometimes as his father did for me. When he needed help, he would ask me. Later on, when he had learned enough, he invited his father and me to dinner. The meal was delicious and I felt so proud of him. I still do."

As she moved toward the bedroom, Maimuna heard Akapwon singing softly to himself as he prepared the meal. She smiled. When her bath was finished, she took the bucket, preparing to go to the well and fill it for his bath. As she entered the kitchen on her way outside, he stopped her.

"No, Maimuna. I will do that. Did I not ask you to relax?"

"Yes Akapwon, but since you are cooking, I thought I would help you by having your water already in the bathhouse."

At any other time, he would have consented, but Akapwon was thinking ahead. He wanted nothing of her rape to be in her mind and going to the well could easily trigger such a memory. He was not taking any chances. Tonight was going to be special for both of them.

"What you can do to help, Maimuna, is set the table and dish up the food while I fetch the water. I do not want you to be lifting anything heavy after working all day in the field."

Seeing that he was determined, Maimuna agreed and gave him the bucket. He soon returned and went to bathe. As he was taking his bath, Maimuna proceeded to fill their bowls with mashed potatoes and stewed chicken cooked in crushed tomatoes and onions with a little added spice of pepper and thyme.

Akapwon returned to the kitchen refreshed and they had a lively but very intimate meal. Maimuna felt a warm glow of happiness. Every time she looked across at Akapwon, she found his admiring gaze fixed on her face. He made her feel beautiful and relaxed. He bid her not to move as he cleared the table and brought them both a mug of honey sweetened coffee. He wanted to be sure she would not be sleepy this night. Since they had had a long day working in the field, from experience, they would both be sleepy quite early. He wanted this night to last.

Taking the cups he bid her follow and they sat on the steps talking companionably. When they had finished drinking the coffee, he suggested to her that they lie in the suspended bed for a while, which she was quite happy to do.

Looking up at the stars through the leaves of the tree, Akapwon said "Look Maimuna, there are those stars that look like a pot with a handle." He pointed to an open spot between the leaves where the sky could be seen clearly. "Do you see it?"

Following the path of his pointing finger, Maimuna answered "Yes, I see it. I used to look at the stars a lot when I was growing up and I used to wonder if anybody lives on them."

Akapwon looked at her in surprise, "You did? So did I."

Turning carefully toward him so as not to tip the bed she stared at him. "You did think that too? Do you think people live up there?"

Lying on her side she rested her hand on his chest, not conscious of doing so.

Akapwon felt a warm tingle where her hand rested and he turned to face her, putting his arm around her waist to steady their bodies in the suspended bed. "What do you think they look like?"

Their conversation continued until clouds covered the

stars and he suggested that they go inside. As she prepared for bed, he washed the dishes. When he entered the bedroom, she was already in bed and he smiled. Going to the bathroom, he cleaned his teeth and when he was done he reached into his breast pocket for a couple of rose petals he had placed there and he proceeded to chew them as he removed his clothing and put on the soft pants he usually slept in.

Getting into bed, he reached over and kissed her.

Leaning back, she looked at him in surprise. "You smell of roses Akapwon. How is that?"

He smiled, "I chewed some rose petals because I wanted to kiss you and I wanted you to remember."

"To remember what? I always remember when you kiss me, Akapwon."

He looked at her in surprise "You do?"

"Yes."

"Well this will be a better memory." Holding her face between his hands, he kissed both cheeks, then soft little kisses on her eyes, her nose and her lips. "Maimuna," she heard him say just before he captured her lips and kissed her in a way he had not done before. It felt so good she forgot to be afraid. From her lips his kiss moved down her throat. When he kissed her breast, she was startled but then he said her name again in a voice she had never heard before.

"Maimuna."

Sensations stormed through her but she did not want him to stop. When he finally joined their bodies, he did it so slowly and so gently that no memory of her assault entered her mind or even came near it. She was transported to a different world and finally learned the pleasure she had only wondered at before. Now she knew how Codou felt on her wedding night and if things had been different, how she would have felt.

She was very happy that she could bring Akapwon the pleasure that he said she gave to him. She just wanted to make him as happy as he made her.

He had once told her that Uta had sent her to him. Now she felt that instead, Uta had given him to her. Just when she thought her life would end, he had given her hope and now he had given her unbelievable happiness. She thanked Uta again.

Akapwon held Maimuna in his arms, a smile on his lips and a prayer in his heart. He thanked all the gods for letting the night he planned go as beautifully and as smoothly as it had gone. He knew somehow that this night would be a turning point for Maimuna and that she would never again be afraid for him to touch her. However, being realistic, he also knew that there would be times when her memories would haunt her. At those times in her life, he wanted to be her support, a solid conviction in her mind that he would always be there for her, sustaining her and understanding her needs at those times.

*

Akapwon proudly held his beautiful son in his arms and laughed as his friends slapped him on his back and bowed respectfully to Maimuna. They were strolling around the village circle. When her friends in Twee heard that they were planning to perform the naming ceremony, everyone wanted to attend. Maimuna was moved and delighted to know that her friends cared enough and wanted to be there for her.

Together she and Akapwon chose the name Jumoke for their son, because it meant "loved by everyone," and they wanted that for him. Then Maimuna asked Akapwon if she could name him also after Akapwon's father and her father. Akapwon was touched that she would do that and readily agreed. Thus Jumoke had three names, more than most boys in the villages, Jumoke Kinefe Oboto. He also had four mothers, more than any boy in both villages, his birth mother Maimuna, Akapwon's mother, her own mother and Codou. Codou had wanted to be his second mother but was happy to move to fourth place.

The villagers from Monabu and Twee were gathered and ready to celebrate the birth of Akapwon and Maimuna's first child. The village was again happy to have another reason to celebrate. They gathered in the village circle, which was decorated with flowers and the tables around the circle were once more loaded with food. It was time to participate in the naming ceremony which would soon begin after everyone quieted down and took their proper place before the chief and holy man of the village, Chief Comse.

The End

ACKNOWLEDGEMENTS

To my sisters: Jean for her unfailing encouragement and her belief in my work; to Ruth, Flora and Helen for their valuable critiques and to Gloria for any help she gave me.
Thank you all!

Thanks also to Joyce, Sandra, Karen and Lola for their emotional support.